RISE OF THE DARK REALM

CHRONICLES OF THE SUPERNATURAL:
BOOK SIX

JM HART

ALSO BY JM HART

CHRONICLES OF THE SUPERNATURAL SERIES

Book One

The Emerald Tablet Omnibus

Book Two

Realm of Lost Souls

Book Three

The Devil's Harvest

Book Four

Separated by Evil

Book Five

The False Prophet

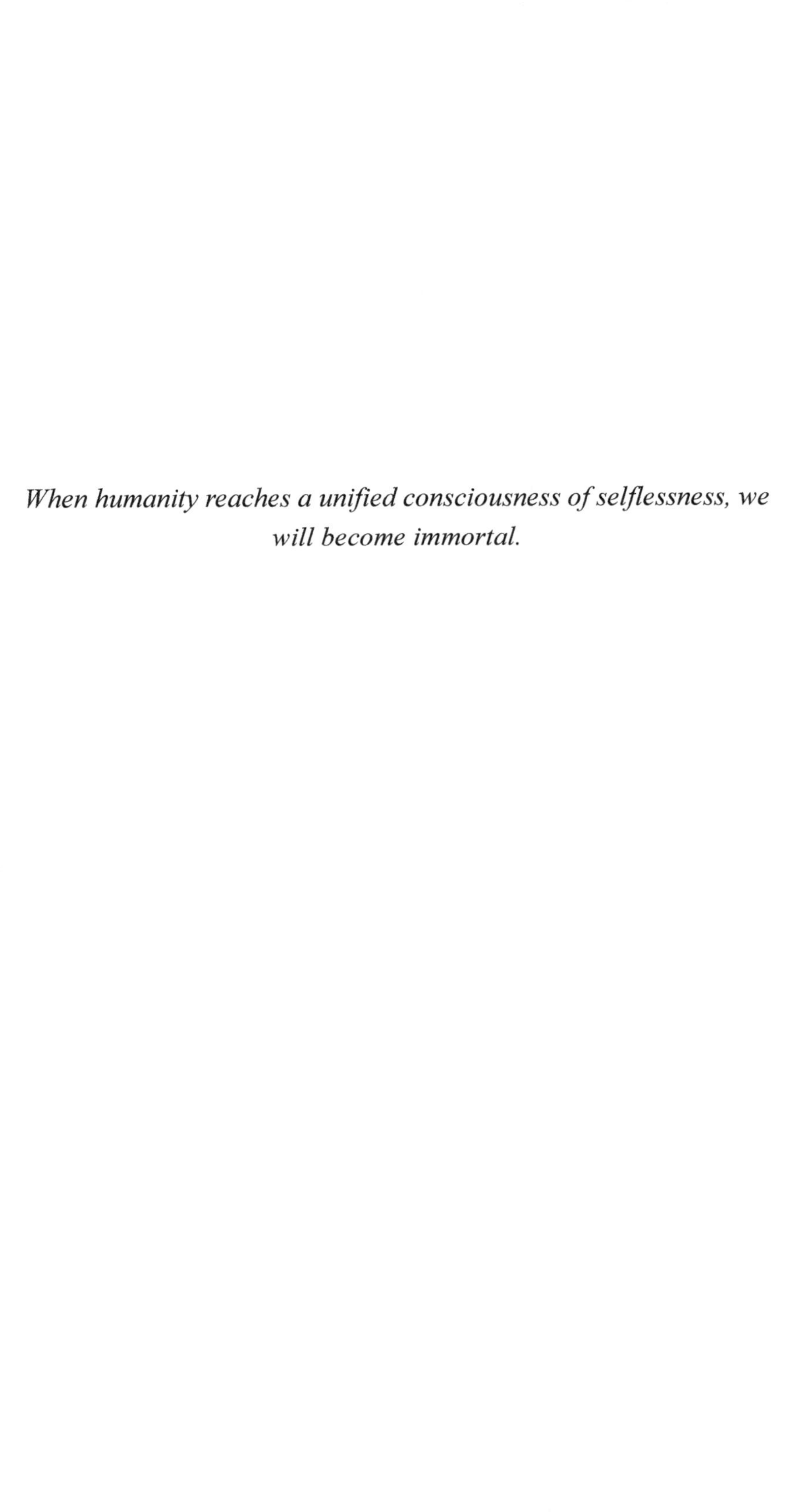

When humanity reaches a unified consciousness of selflessness, we will become immortal.

INTRODUCTION

Book six, in the Chronicles of the Supernatural. The end of the prophecy as told in the book of Enoch, echoes through time and religion.

The Watchers (fallen angels), and the Jinn (the race which preceded humankind), once banished from the earthly realm by God, are now free to return, as the day of great judgement is imminent. The end of days on Earth means an ascension for humans, the time to return to the heavens. God will annihilate all evil, cleansing the earth; as foretold in the book of Enoch, *'it will be worse than the days of Noah'*.

There were seven young souls who battled to return the Emerald Tablet before the gates of Hell were flung open. Unfortunately, they failed, and evil is ripe in the world. The seven are now six. Kevin, Shaun, Rachel, Tim, Jade, and Casey.

Shaun, Rachel, Kevin, Jade and Casey's mission is to save as many souls as possible, helping them find the ascension portals – even if it means sacrificing themselves. They must summon all their strength, courage, and supernatural skills to emerge victorious. As the final clash between the forces of good and evil unfolds, the fate of all existence hangs in the balance.

Time is running out, and the group has to separate. They have been to the Realm of Lost Souls, the Devil's Harvest, Separated by Evil, and met the False Prophet. Now they must battle the fallen angels, in the Rise of the Dark Realm.

Will the young heroes be able to overcome the mounting odds, or will they perish in darkness and despair?

PROLOGUE

Shaun could feel the heat of the desert sun scorching the back of his neck, face, and arms. He used his shirt to wipe the sweat from his face as he paused in his work. It hadn't taken long for Abraham to put Shaun and Rachel to work pitching tents at the Sphinx. Shaun hoped there would be enough food and water for all the people. Pilgrims were spread out across the site, taking shelter under the covers he had helped to erect. In the distance, he could see more travelers arriving, in buses and on foot. Soon the place would be overcrowded.

Everyone who had arrived at the Sphinx believed it was the Lion's Gate; a portal to the stars and heaven. In the past week, hundreds of people had gathered for the final ascension. Most believed Rachel's shared message from the stars: God was calling them home before the dark realm unleashed its fury and, on the eighth day of Leo, God would cleanse the planet for a second time.

The survivors of a plague of evil shape-shifting micro creatures that entered the brain and turned man against man — far worse than any biblical plague or the Spanish flu – had the prophecy dream, and others just followed. The idea of ascension created a reserved, skeptical mood in some. Many arrived at the Sphinx malnourished, shell-shocked, with wounded psyches. The Ammit – creatures from the world of the dead, tall as a pony, with the snout of an alligator, a lion's mane, muscular upper body, and the hind legs of a hippopotamus – had returned, and now they searched the Middle East for flesh and souls to feast upon. The Ammit had roamed in ancient times, casting judgment and condemning men to horrors worse than death, eating their physical, impure hearts before devouring their souls. They had killed hundreds along the way.

Terrible stories circulated the campsite, about attacks by giant scorpions, vipers, cobras, and black mamba, striking out at resting travelers, eating them whole, before the injected or sprayed venom had time to render their prey helpless.

Abo had arrived alone and, while he pitched tents with Shaun, related what had happened to his family. They had ridden camels through day and night. Exhausted, the people let the animals drive them into a terrible sandstorm. Abo had been lucky because he refused the camel, believing they were Jinn, even though the others thought he was crazy. Abo had not seen his family since.

There were many travelers, from many countries. It didn't matter where the pilgrims were from; all had terrible stories. The one that stuck in Shaun's mind was of an Italian woman from Abruzzo, who kept pushing her glasses up on her nose with a trembling hand as she explained in a thick accent that there had been a terrible earthquake, then the mountains came alive and ate all the survivors in her town. The story reminded Shaun of when he and Rachel had escaped the giants at Casey's estate. The giants had cloaked their appearances. They had blended into the night, making it easy to snatch up and eat members of his community, and destroy

Casey's estate. He wondered if Tim, Seth, and their families back in the United Kingdom had escaped the giants and made it to Stonehenge.

Later, as he patrolled the campsite, Shaun didn't know if he should smile at people as he passed, or keep his eyes down. He walked quietly past a family in mourning. They had narrowly escaped the Ammit, but their aunt and uncle had not, making it just outside of Egypt together before they were killed.

Shaun remembered the Ammit only too well. They had nearly killed him and Rachel the last time they were in the Middle East. They had been searching for her family, when they were trapped by the Supreme Master. No matter how vicious the Ammit were, they could be killed with a bullet. Nothing supernatural about that. Abraham had deployed a patrol to kill the Ammit on sight. The Ammit, devourer of the dead, fed on heavy hearts and souls but now also hunted the hearts and souls of the living. The joined forces of the Israeli soldiers did everything they could to protect the pilgrims making camp.

Shaun walked back towards the Sphinx, and smiled at the children playing soccer, kicking up dust. Here, no one seemed worried about the omnipresent black clouds in the distance, even though the storm surely heading their way had advanced slightly throughout the day. Lifting the binoculars from around his neck, he scanned the desert, concerned that invisible giant creatures may be headed towards them. How long could they remain unseen? He didn't know.

He headed back to the paws of the Sphinx and scanned the town. Shaun could kick himself for leaving the estate. They were his family now, and they needed to be together. Tim and Seth were going to need his help to get the United Kingdom survivors across to Stonehenge before the 8th day of Leo 2025, ten weeks from now.

Tonight, he would try to meditate, to contact Casey and get him to send Kevin back to open a portal for them, but perhaps Casey, in the midst of his grief for Sophia, might not hear him. It had only been a few days since she died, and Casey would be hurting. *Hopefully he hears me.*

Rachel had delivered the message from the stars. The community here had the military. They were well protected and organized. They didn't need him as much as the people back at Casey's estate. Kevin's family were now his family too.

1

ANCIENT BEAST: SHAUN. EGYPT.

Shaun wiped his brow and grinned at the children as he finished work on the makeshift goal he'd created for their soccer games. An hour ago, he had stopped patrolling and was now helping to make sure the orphaned children were comfortable. The three adults who watched over the children had each had a dream of saving them. They'd driven more than a thousand miles in buses, finally found the children wandering aimlessly, and brought them to the Lion's Gate.

Shaun stopped and rubbed his brow. Rachel walked along the wooden boardwalk with a bottle of water in her hand. She poured the water over her purple bandana, soaking it before tying it around her neck.

"I thought you could use a break." Rachel smiled and handed him the water.

"I wish we'd had the chance to visit Egypt together before the world had turned to shit." Shaun took the bottle.

"The pyramids and Sphinx haven't changed. They look the

same as before the apocalypse. The only difference is the people, and no one has cameras. See all those tourist buses people have turned into homes? They're the tourist buses that used to travel in and out every day."

"How many times did you visit the pyramids?" Shaun handed the bottle back, with just enough for a mouthful.

"For a year, I worked in Cairo, making beds and cleaning rooms that faced the pyramids."

"Why don't the pilgrims stay in the town? The buildings are still standing."

"They probably wanted to be as close as possible, ready for the ascension."

Shaun gazed over his shoulder towards the entrance of the Sphinx, which was guarded by a soldier. The guard stepped forward and looked up into the sky. Shaun wiped his face with his shirt and followed the soldier's line of sight. On their right, behind the tents, a ball of dust traveled down the distant sand dune, heading towards the pilgrims. "What do you think it is?"

"Maybe a patrol vehicle?" Rachel put the lid back on her bottle of water.

"It's moving fast."

"That's a wide, dense trail of dust. Too wide and long for one vehicle."

"Quickly, everyone together!" Shaun shouted.

"What's wrong?" someone asked.

"I'm not sure." Shaun pointed towards the dunes. The guard talked into his two-way radio, then raised his gun. The other soldiers moved beyond the pilgrims.

"It's a patrol vehicle. Oh no." Shaun moved into the middle of the tents and stretched out his arms. Rachel urged the people to move behind the soldiers and take cover. Tingling coursed through his veins as the icosahedron sapphire embedded in his palm illuminated. His body sparkled with electrified blue energy as power from the icosahedron surged through his being, veins bulging with power. He pushed and expanded the blue energy upward, creating an arch above and around the Sphinx until it touched the ground on all sides, encompassing the hundreds of pilgrims and enveloping the perimeter.

The patrol truck was closer, and whatever was whipping up a dust storm behind it was right on their tail.

Rachel ran over to him. "There are soldiers in the truck. You can't keep them out. Lower the shield for them!"

"I can't. You know I can't, Rachel. I can't protect them, but I can protect the pilgrims. They're soldiers, they'll understand." Shaun maintained the hermetic sphere. The patrol truck drove to the edge of the shield, a herd of Ammit on its tail. The soldiers were stuck in their vehicles. What were they thinking, leading those creatures to the camp? People cringed and screamed as the Ammit set upon the truck, toppling it over, ripping the doors and roof off, reaching in and pulling out men, tearing them apart, then the fighting amongst themselves for the body parts. Shaun turned away. Gunfire exploded around them. He glanced at his side – Rachel was gone. *No, Rachel. Please, no.* She had left the protection of the hermetic shield, but he couldn't drop it.

A couple of yards away, hiding behind a stone block from the Sphinx, Rachel cocked her gun.

Dammit, Rachel! His heart raced, his chest tightened, and his stomach churned. *Oh God. Please, not Rachel. No... please.* A young man wearing a long caftan and a turban ran up behind Rachel, carrying a missile-launcher. Rachel stood her ground and fired at the Ammit, which were tearing the vehicle apart with their alligator jaws. They ripped off the tires, pulling back sheets of metal and the exhaust from the undercarriage. The ancient beasts consumed the bodies and souls of the men still inside. The man handed Rachel a rocket. "Rachel!" Shaun screamed over the sound of the gunfire.

She set down her gun, and took the rockets. The frail man kneeled behind the stone block and rested the barrel of the rocket launcher on his shoulder. Shaun couldn't recall seeing the man on his patrol of the perimeter. He didn't look strong enough to withstand the kickback the launcher might produce. The sound of the Ammit tearing metal masked the sound of the rocket launched at the patrol truck.

It hit the vehicle, blowing what was left of it apart, including the soldiers still inside, and the Ammit. At the perimeter of the hermetic shield, pieces of men and Ammit fell back to the earth. Alligator heads, hippo legs, and the bloated torsos of a dozen lions lay burning.

Shaun maintained the shield, waiting for confirmation that all the Ammit were dead. He didn't let Rachel out of his sight. There was nothing more important to him than Rachel. But she would want him to protect the people first. He maintained the flow of energy into the hermetic sphere over the hundreds of frightened, weary travelers.

Ashamed, Shaun regarded their faces. His eyes locked with those of an old man. Shaun blinked, afraid the old man could read his thoughts of abandoning them all just to save Rachel. The gratitude in the people's eyes shamed him. He tilted his head down towards the sand, and prayed for strength, and in that moment, silence shrouded him. The self-loathing emotions cleared; calmness washed over him as magnificent colors radiated, sparked from the sacred platonic stones in his pocket. The hermetic shield turned into a rainbow of vibrant colors. Shaun didn't know what the platonic gemstones were capable of, or the significance of the rainbow, but it all reminded him of being immersed in the membrane of Kevin's portals. He bathed in the silence amongst the chaos, determined to keep the shield in place. Nothing was getting in.

A tug on his shirt brought him out of the peacefulness. One girl, who had been playing soccer before the attack, was trying to pull his arm down. Her brown, shiny, clammy face highlighted her bright blue eyes as she smiled. Shaun had never before seen someone with brown skin and rich blue eyes.

He checked his surroundings. The soldiers had lowered their guns. They were safe again. Rachel stood at the perimeter, waiting for him to let her in. The weak man had left the rocket launcher on the stone block.

Shaun lowered his arms, wishing he could control the shield with the power of his mind, like Casey could. Once it was gone, people moved like a wave towards the carnage. The little girl ran over to her father. Shaun followed her and put out his hand towards the man. "Thank you. Where are you from?"

"No – thank *you*. This is my daughter, Aberash. I am Bongani. We're from Africa." The man smiled, hugging his daughter to his side.

Rachel gently touched Shaun's shoulder before following the sea of pilgrims, hoping that there were survivors among the soldiers. It was impossible, but they still hoped. Everyone knew the soldiers were gone, but still they searched. Two more patrol vehicles sped over the sand hills, heading straight for the camp. The soldiers jumped out of their vehicles before they came to a complete stop, instantly blocking the crowd and moving them away from the wreckage. One slapped the hood of his truck in frustration, too late to help his fellow soldiers.

A crowd of people surrounded Shaun, calling him the blue

angel, and thanking him for his protection. They reached out and touched him for good luck. The attention and the accolades troubled Shaun. He wanted to leave the crowd and find a quiet place. Rachel was talking to the commanding officer and she must have sensed him looking at her, because she ended her conversation and made her way towards him, excusing herself as she weaved through the crowd.

"Hey, are you okay?" Rachel hugged him. Somehow, she knew he needed to feel her in his arms. The crowd dispersed.

How quickly things change. Fifteen minutes ago, he was helping the children; people had felt connected, some excited, believing they were on a spiritual journey. For a short while, Shaun had even forgotten the smell of death.

THE COMMANDER and his men collected blankets to cover the human body parts before they carefully placed the dead in the back of the military trucks. A child with a rifle poked the still-sizzling torso of one of the Ammit. The boy fired the gun. Everyone ducked. Shaun quickly snatched the weapon from the boy as smoke trailed off the burning carcass.

"Enough!" Shaun glared at the boy. His first impulse was to slap him across the face, to knock some sense into him, but he stopped himself, instead emptying the gun and throwing it at the boy's feet.

The boy pushed and kicked Shaun with such fury that it hurt. The boy snatched up his gun. Rachel grabbed the boy by the upper arm and scolded him in Hebrew.

"Commander, how can I help?" Shaun said to the soldier, leaving Rachel to deal with the boy.

Everybody from the underground city of Olivet recognized Shaun. He didn't need to introduce himself.

The commander took his cap off, pushed his hair back off his face, and smiled at the boy. "It is a mess, but the boy is just being a boy. It's natural for boys to poke at dead animals. You're from Australia, no?"

Shaun nodded.

"Have you never poked a washed-up jellyfish?" The commander walked towards the soldiers moving the dead.

Shaun walked at his side. "It's the gun. I'm not comfortable around guns. I don't know why."

"It's because your desire is not to kill. You want peace and tranquility. You are the Tekhelet Malak — the blue angel, no?"

"I'm no angel. I'll go talk to the boy." Shaun turned back to the child.

There was a time when Shaun wouldn't have hesitated to shoot someone, and he probably still would if anyone he cared about was threatened. But inside he had changed.

The boy who had poked the carcass was scolded by his mother, but as Shaun walked over to him, Aberash took his hand and pulled him away. She was about eight, the same age as Rachel when he had first met her – abandoned by their fathers, they had sat in the Judean Desert on top of the rock, watching a distance sandstorm roll over the sand dunes. The stars had disappeared, and the world had changed forever. That was a lifetime ago. Back then, Shaun had a sense of curiosity and adventure. He could understand how the boy might be feeling. He went back, taking Aberash with him.

She tugged at his arm. "Can you watch over us while we play soccer? Please?"

Shaun got down on one knee and looked into her beautiful eyes. "You'll be fine. It's safe now. I promise. I'm going to help clean up." Shaun looked over the heads for her father, saw him near the boardwalk, and gave him a wave.

"Aberash!" Bongani called out to his daughter, as if he had been searching for her. She hesitated, but then let go of Shaun's hand and waved goodbye before running off to her father.

Shaun went to the boy, who was studying the grains of sand around his sandaled feet. "Do you want to help?"

The young boy nodded, but said nothing. Shaun wasn't even sure if the boy understood English. He put out his hand, and the boy looked up, refusing the hand but stepping forward. The boy turned back to his mother, and she nodded her head, giving him the permission he sought.

"It's okay. Let's work as a team." Shaun was determined not be like his father. He would show kindness to the young boy. Shaun recalled a time before he grew up and realized that he despised his dad, when all he had wanted from his father was a hug, or a smile. The strongest memory Shaun had that made him think about who he was becoming was when his dad passed out drunk on the floor, blocking the doorway to the kitchen. Shaun had to stop himself from stomping on his father's head. So much anger and resentment had grown inside him that he had ended up behaving with the same contempt for other kids in the street.

The boy nodded at Shaun's words, but refused to smile.

"We're going to help bury the Ammit body parts. We need shovels." Shaun made the motion of digging. Rachel had made herself busy, collecting military identification tags from the ground.

The soldier in charge of the Ammit remains, picked a spot away from the camp, and Shaun and the boy started digging. The boy didn't complain about digging, nor picking up the parts.

"They're really ugly."

The boy nodded.

"Back in Israel, Rachel and I were chased by the Ammit."

The boy held his breath and his eyes opened. "You escaped? How?"

It was the first time he had spoken. Shaun smiled.

Shaun stretched out his arm, aiming his hand towards a mound, and pushed the icosahedron's energy outward. The sapphire pulsed. A ball of energy blasted from his hand and slammed into the embankment, sending sand flying into the air. The boy jumped back and covered his eyes. Shaun laughed and coughed at the same time. "I blew the first Ammit right off its feet and it tumbled backwards into the rest of the pack, and they went down like dominoes. It gave Rachel and me enough time to escape. We were in Jerusalem and all the shops were boarded up with wood, or iron sheets. A boy slipped behind a sheet of metal. We followed him into the front of a pizza shop. The boy wasn't alone. His grandmother was there too. We hid inside, but the boy kept a gun on us until we left."

"Didn't he know you are the Tekhelet Malak?"

Shaun was no angel, but he decided not to bother correcting the boy. "I didn't know what this stone could do. It wasn't embedded in my hand then. It was in my pocket." Shaun held out his hand, showing the boy the icosahedron.

He let the boy touch it.

"Were you scared when the Ammit attacked?" the boy asked.

"Yes, terrified."

"But why? You have magical power."

"Even though I was scared, I was worried for Rachel's wellbeing, and my desire to protect her was greater than my fear of the Ammit. Before the apocalypse, I was a bad teenager. I hurt people, and didn't care about anyone. I never want to be that person again." Shaun shook his head, thinking how much of an asshole he had been, and how grateful he was to have found Rachel again.

"And now you care and protect everyone!"

"What's your name?"

"Umair."

"Come, Umair, you've done enough work for today. Go have some fun with the others."

Shaun escorted the boy back towards the campsite but Umair stopped abruptly and picked something out of the sand. He held it up for Shaun to see.

"What is this?" Umair asked.

Shaun took it from his hand. "A tooth. It's much bigger than a human's. Could be an Ammit's." The boy peeled his eyes away from his new treasure, turned to Shaun, and smiled as he stuffed the warm tooth into his pocket as a souvenir.

In silence, they walked back to camp. Umair never took his hand out of his pocket. When he was back with his mother, Umair pulled out the tooth and showed her. Then he smiled at Shaun and ran off to the other children, who had resumed their game of soccer.

They stopped playing as Umair shouted something in Hebrew, and he waved his arm in the air for the children to gather around. As the children circled Umair, Shaun imagined the story he would be telling them. Huddled in a circle, they studied Umair's souvenir before heading back to the game as if nothing bad ever happened. Aberash had the ball and passed it to Umair first.

"That was nice," Rachel said.

Startled, Shaun pivoted in surprise. "Don't do that."

Rachel kissed him on the cheek as the kids played soccer.

"Do you like soccer?"

"It's football." Rachel put her arm around his waist.

The wind picked up, and the smell of death stalked across the campsite.

"You need a wash." Rachel crinkled her nose.

"You don't smell so great yourself. What are you thinking about?"

"Tim and the others. I hope they are alright and escaped the giants."

"I wonder how Billie and Ernest are holding up after seeing their dad eaten by the giant ogres, like barbarians."

"Is that what they were – ogres?"

"I don't know what they were, but when they materialized from their invisible shield, they reminded me of cyclops, with three eyes instead of one. They were ugly, like ogres, or giant, shirtless, hairy Vikings." Shaun scanned the landscape, searching for giant ogres, but all he saw was people forming connections; strangers being drawn together by an invisible web of hope. There was a unity that he'd never known or seen before, except with Kevin and his family. Shaun's thoughts stayed with Kevin, until his attention was drawn to a family sitting in a circle, cooking – it seemed so natural, a spark of hope. Shaun encapsulated the image and imagined projecting it to Kevin. Transmitting an emotional image wasn't easy. He hoped Kevin could receive it, and be prompted to open a portal to the camp; a place he had never been.

"Let's wash up," Rachel said.

They headed to the tent that served as a wash station. The two women officers in charge told them to wait for an opening on the bench. Women on one side and men on the other. A man finished washing and threw the dirty water outside the tent. The closest woman handed Shaun a bowl with fresh water in it. He took it to the bench and rinsed his face and neck, then cleaned his hands. Shaun copied the previous man and tossed the dirty water outside. He waited while the sand soaked up the water.

He stood outside, waiting for Rachel, smiling up at the sky, wishing he could call Kevin. He shook his head, feeling silly for trying.

Rachel pushed the flap of the tent open. Her face was shimmering with water. She had also run water through her hair and pushed it back off her face. Shaun admired her long neck. She was so beautiful.

"The chopper will be here soon… Why are you looking at me like that?" Rachel said.

"Like what?" Shaun felt a little embarrassed. "I was admiring your natural beauty. How long is soon?"

"Half an hour. We can talk to Abraham and see what he wants us to do while we wait for Kevin. Soon as Kevin returns for us we'll head straight back to England."

2

───────

LETTING GO: KEVIN. BLACK MOUNTAIN, NORTH CAROLINA.

Kevin didn't want to stay at Black Mountain and watch Jade and Mingan bond. It was too painful. He had imagined traveling with Jade; through portals to unknown realms, exploring galaxies, until they settled down and lived happily ever after on a foreign planet, so he had ignored the warning signs of fear, anxiety, and a sense he was about to lose something precious. Why didn't he listen to his intuition? The foreboding emotions had heightened the memory of his grandparents' death. He was just grateful that the unsettling feeling he had experienced at the estate did not come to anything. He didn't lose anything precious for a second time, although he nearly had, when the estate basement ceiling collapsed in and the refrigerator from the kitchen above fell, pinning Jade to the floor. Kevin had frozen, believing his premonition had come true, just like when his grandparents were murdered. Seeing Jade motionless under the weight of the debris, he was sure she was dead. He had sensed her spirit traveling through the astral realm, moving further and further away from her body, and from him. His heart was in his mouth, and he had pleaded with God to heal her.

As Kevin tried to free Jade from the wreckage, dark, shadowy entities were coming for her soul. Casey with his telekinesis managed to raise the refrigerator off Jade's broken body, and lifted her into his arms. Kevin generated the portal and Casey jumped into the its healing membrane with Jade still in his arms. Outside, in the paddock, Kevin collapsed the portal and went weak at the knees as Jade stirred. Her disjointed limbs were repaired.

That was less than twenty-four hours ago, and Kevin had accepted that if Jade wanted Mingan, he would have to let her go. He was just grateful she was alive. For the past few hours, he had tried to ignore Jade's subtle surge of excitement, and curiosity, as her energy bubbled over in Mingan's presence. Kevin couldn't block the emotions, so it was surely best to leave. Casey had her back; he didn't need to stay. So, when the very subdued image of the pyramids floated into his mind, he wondered if Shaun had consciously sent it. Trying not to think of Jade, Kevin connected with the image, curious where it would lead. He moved his hands through the air, collecting the particles and compressing them until the multidimensional energy waves of color formed and crackled into life as the portal opened.

Kevin touched the cool membrane and stepped in. Reluctant to leave the harmony of the portal energy, Kevin forced himself through, and stepped out under a dusty sky, in front of an unsuspecting family who were sitting in a circle with a pyramid rising ominously in the background. The family stood up, mesmerized by his sudden appearance. He closed the portal and the flashing waves of lights disappeared. Kevin smiled at the family. The scene before him was identical to the image in his head. He had taken a risk, and it had paid off.

Shaun jogged towards him. "Hey, Kevin."

Kevin was curious about how Shaun had led him to this very spot.

"Incredible!" Shaun pulled Kevin into a hug, giving him a manly slap on the back.

"Are you okay? Is everything alright?" Kevin looked around the campsite, trying to hide his emotions as he felt a surge of heat warm up his cheeks. "What's that smell?"

"We had trouble earlier with the Ammit, but all is well. We're about to head to Olivet. Etain is flying in with the chopper. He'll be here in about ten minutes. You've got great timing. This is crazy!"

"Are you sure you're okay?" Kevin asked, feeling a thumb in his chest, as if his heart was racing. Stepping out of his own emotions, he could feel Shaun's adrenaline racing through his body. *Something has happened.*

Rachel spotted him and stopped playing soccer with the children. With a smile, she ran over to greet him.

"We're so glad to see you. Shaun's worried about Tim and the others."

"Me too," Kevin said, looking at them sideways.

THE SAND LIFTED and scattered over the roofs of the tents as the chopper blades built up momentum. "Is the sky always caramel?" Kevin buckled his seatbelt, excited to be in the chopper.

It was hard to hear Rachel's answer over the sound of the Black Hawk's engine. She pointed to the headset on the panel next to his seat. In awe of seeing the pyramids from the sky, Kevin had forgotten about that. He quickly put the headset on and adjusted the microphone. The last time he had been in the sky, he had flown his grandfather's Piper PA 28 Cherokee plane into a portal and crash-landed on the lawn of Casey's estate. It seemed like a lifetime ago.

"No. Only after a sandstorm, and there's been two in twenty-four hours," Rachel told him.

The size of the pyramids and the Sphinx mesmerized Kevin. The tents flapped in the wind, like discarded tissues.

"You haven't told us why you came back," Shaun said.

"You brought me here." Kevin turned his head and looked away so Shaun couldn't read his face. Sometimes Kevin forgot that not everyone was like him, able to read and feel another person's or an animal's emotions.

They wanted him to say more; he could feel them staring at him, waiting. When he didn't answer, they leaned into each other and let him be.

Kevin noticed a change in his friends' energy. He turned and pretended not to look directly at Shaun or Rachel. They were on a natural high. They squeezed each other's hands. Kevin didn't know what was going on between them; it was their business, but he sensed a state of bliss, which he didn't want to ruin with his own troubles with Jade. It was mind-blowing how Shaun, the town bully, had changed into the hero. Kevin had always felt there was something more, deep inside Shaun, his exterior just a front to hide the pain he carried.

Casually, Kevin folded his arms across his body, covering his solar plexus and preventing any more deep, private emotions passing from them to him. It was something he had to practice more often. He wished he had never sensed the giddy feelings Jade had whenever Mingan was around. It had drained him and now it made him tired just thinking about it. Mingan had a strong desire, too, and Kevin didn't want to know any more. It was easier to remove himself, rather than unintentionally read their body language and pick up their emotions. Being an Empath sucked.

Kevin cleared his throat and blinked rapidly, trying to forget Jade for a while, and hoped his lack of enthusiasm went undetected.

He liked the smell of aviation fuel. "So, what's next? You two ready to head out? I suggest we try and stay ahead of those storm clouds. They look and feel nasty."

"Yes, but no. Not yet. Abraham and Delilah have sent out military patrols to find more survivors," said Rachel. "The survivors will have the opportunity to stay in Olivet, the underground city, for the next ten weeks, and in the last week before the portal opens, they can continue their pilgrimage to the Sphinx in time for the 8th day of Leo. Otherwise, they can get a ride straight to the Sphinx. The underground city is the safest place to be, and close enough to the portal. The people can rest and prepare for their last walk to the Sphinx."

"I was thinking of bringing everyone from around the world here. We can ascend together from here. What do you guys think?" Kevin said.

"It's not a bad idea," Shaun said.

"How will they get here?" Rachel said.

"That's some heavy lifting, K."

"I can do it. We need to find people, and we'll need to travel through the portal to different countries to do it."

"You tire, opening and closing portals," Shaun said.

"Shaun's right. If portals across the world are going to be activated, it's best the people make their way to their closest portal in their own country," Rachel said.

"What if there isn't one? The sun will energize me. Sometimes I just need a bit of a boost. We can make sure people know about God's ascension, and they know where they're headed to, and if they don't, we can bring them back here. We've ten weeks, right? Simple," Kevin said.

"Yeah. Okay, why not? Let's focus on finding the survivors and offer them a choice to make a pilgrimage to the portal in their country, or to come here and join us at the Sphinx," Rachel said.

"Back at Olivet, we can find people who have travelled to different countries before the apocalypse, they can help you with their emotional memories to generate portals to specific places around the world," Shaun suggested.

Kevin agreed. "Okay. It makes sense."

"It's good that you came. It might be hard to convince people to believe the message from the stars is from God," Rachel said.

"I never thought of it like that. How can we save them from the coming purification, the total annihilation of the entire planet, if they don't believe in something greater than themselves? Do we tell the Buddhists that Buddha sent the message?" Shaun asked.

Tension gripped Kevin's stomach and fear ascended into his throat. "What's that?" He pointed out of the chopper's side-panel window. Deathly, smokey creatures flew through the sky at an alarming speed.

"Hang on," Etain said over his shoulder.

The chopper banked right, then left. Kevin did as he was told as Etain employed tactical maneuvers to avoid a dark figure tailing the chopper, matching its speed.

"Etain, what are they?" Rachel pushed the headset microphone closer to her mouth.

"I'm not sure. They dropped out of the storm clouds on our flank."

The ghostly charcoal figures increased in numbers as Etain tried to out-run them. He pushed the chopper to its max, but still the entities were gaining. The veins in Etain's forearms bulged as he held tight to the chopper's oversized joystick. The computer chimed – pull up – pull up, pull up. Etain pulled back on the controls. Kevin worried the engine was going to stall if they elevated too fast.

"What is it?" Shaun pressed up against the window and studied the object.

Etain pulled up and flew diagonally across the sky. "I don't think I can outrun it."

"It's some kind of intelligent life force," Kevin said.

"Kevin, help us!" Rachel demanded.

The emergency beeps were loud and demanding; even with the headset on, Kevin could hear them. Rachel unbuckled her seatbelt and moved to crouch in front of him. He placed his hands on her temples and stepped into her mind. It was calm, optimistic, as he connected to the image she wanted him to see. A gold circle with a giant H. A helipad. Kevin focused on a point outside the window and opened a hole in the universe, creating a portal. He had to stretch it out wide for the Black Hawk to pass through. He wasn't sure if it would be big enough. Better too big than too small. "Etain, bank left." It sounded like he was panicking. The embarrassment surged to his cheeks, making them burn red.

Etain glanced at Rachel for confirmation. She nodded, returning to her seat and buckling her seatbelt. Etain swooped sideways, entering the shimmering portal, and pulling up the chopper when he recognized the helipad.

As soon as Kevin spied the markings that represented the helipad, he collapsed the portal. The chopper landed with a heavy thud.

Relief and wonder washed over him, and circulated inside the chopper. The one good thing about being an Empath was when the joy of others touched him, filled him up, even when he was emotionally unbalanced. It felt good, like a warm bath. Etain took off his headphones and locked eyes with Kevin. He reached out his hand. Kevin took it.

"Thanks! You have some incredible friends, Rachel."

Kevin turned away. He didn't deserve praise. He was only using the gifts God had given him, and they could easily be taken away. A thought of Jade entered his mind, and his emotions clouded with jealousy. It was an emotion he disliked feeling from others, and it was worse when it was his own. He was annoyed he felt so worthless and betrayed, and, as his emotions spiraled out of control, it was like being pushed into a black pit.

"Kevin, Kevin!" Shaun screamed into his face.

"Yeah, yeah."

"We're did you go, pal? Your face looked so gray. Are you sure everything's okay?"

"I'm fine," Kevin snapped.

* * *

From the roof, Kevin couldn't tell how big the bunker was. Shaun had said it was the size of a city. The rooftop helipad was big enough to accommodate four choppers.

"What was that?" Etain asked, shutting down the chopper.

"Whatever they were, they had intelligence and emotions." Kevin unbuckled his restraints and opened the door. He turned around in his seat before standing to see behind him. "What's wrong, Shaun? Did you feel something?"

"I'm not sure. When those ghostly creatures turned towards us, I noticed the atmosphere changed. It thickened. Heavy. Bleak, almost. It reminded me of my dad when he arrived home drunk and the air would change. I would have to be super-cautious of his moods, not sure what to expect: his tears or fists." Shaun twisted his hands together, then opened his palm and touched the embedded icosahedron sapphire. It pulsated into life and Shaun had a blue tinge around his body. The stone sensed Shaun's concerns and instantly protected him. Kevin stayed in his seat and searched for what Shaun felt.

Etain cleared his throat. "Maybe those things are Jinn. But Jinn are supposed to be unseen. When I studied with our Rabbi, he told me about the Jinn that surround us every day."

"That's the second time someone has mentioned the Jinn. What are Jinn?" Shaun asked.

Kevin sensed Shaun's caution and fear. Shaun asked the question, but from his hidden emotions, Kevin sensed he didn't want to know. The unseen and the supernatural scared him. Kevin tried to block out Shaun's fear as his stomach churned with energy, which was making him super nervous. *The sooner the heavens open the portal, the better. We can only avoid the evil for so long,* Kevin thought.

"Let's get inside and tell Abraham what we've seen," Etain said.

IT WAS surreal to be inside an elevator again. Kevin couldn't have imagined the size or the opulence of the underground bunker. The glass elevator continued down into the heart of the city. In the atrium below, there were shops, theatres, and worship halls which surrounded parkland and walking tracks. A clean-up crew was trying to put the gardens and waterfall back in order. The children's play equipment was covered in debris. It was as if a tornado had passed through.

"That's what Shaun did," Rachel smirked, and slapped Shaun playfully on the buttocks.

"So, this is where you blew up the Leviathan, the shape-shifting supreme master. It's hard to imagine it ruled over everyone with mind-controlling amulets."

"Pretty much." Shaun bit his lip as if to stifle a smirk of pride. He took half a step forward.

"No hugging in the elevator," Kevin joked.

It was nice Shaun had finally found his purpose in life – defeating monsters, and helping people – it was very becoming. Something his grandmother would have said. Shaun deserved the win. "Way to go." Kevin slapped Shaun on the back.

"He's being modest." Etain watched the numbers scroll down.

"Why do you both slap me, on the back and on my ass?"

Kevin and Rachel smiled at Shaun. They stepped out of the elevator, over the debris, and walked into what Rachel called the mess hall. It was more like a family restaurant.

"I could use a coffee. What about you guys?" Etain said.

A tall, muscular, middle-aged man with a ginger beard, who resembled a strong lumberjack, came out of the kitchen and hugged Rachel and Shaun.

"This is Kevin," Shaun told him.

Before Kevin knew what was happening, the big fellow threw his arms around him.

"I'm Geoff, by the way."

"Coffee would be great, thanks," Kevin said, in answer to Etain. "Nice to meet you, Geoff."

"He's still on a high," Shaun said.

"And you shouldn't be drinking coffee with one kidney. Remember what the doc said. Where is the rest of your tribe?"

"Geoff, if you don't mind…" Etain said.

Geoff raised his hands. "Say no more. I'll be back in a jiffy with coffee. And water for you." Geoff pointed at Shaun.

Etain led them to a table at the back of the room, away from the buffet, and people eating dinner.

"Are you sure you want to know about the Jinn?" Etain asked.

Slowly, they nodded.

"Once you know, you can't unknow."

"Just tell us what you know, Etain," Rachel said.

Etain leaned over his coffee. "The Jinn. They are everywhere, and most of the time they are the unseen. My Rabbi said if humans became aware of the thousands of Jinn that surround us, every day, we would go insane. It was a big concern with mental health in the last decade among the Muslim community. People believed the original virus was the Jinn, entering our minds and bodies, feeding on our souls.

"The Jinn are a supernatural race. Shadow figures. Some people call them 'the shadow men without faces'. They have a solid black shadow or a black, smokey appearance. Shape-shifters with only one intention — to terrify humans and reclaim the earth.

"I think the giant creatures the pilgrims have been reporting could be Jinn. It has been said that when they enter our realm and step into your room at night, you will hear a loud thump, as if they landed, instead of walked into, a space. They radiate a malevolence. That's probably what you were picking up, Shaun, a malevolence. They can be six to nine feet tall, and they seem to have no eyes. A few people have seen red dots that could be eyes. I've never seen a Jinn take on a solid form, so I don't know if they are myth, or truly a different race. I can only tell you what the Rabbi told me. They're solid black masses that can take on the shape of any creature, including humans."

"That's like what we witnessed leaving the estate. A mass of human figures emerged into our realm as we were leaving," Kevin said.

"Some people think they're evil spirits, or just dead people's spirits. But before humans, there were angels and Jinn. God made the Jinn from a smokeless fire, then banished the Jinn because they would not bow down to humans; Jinn are a race that can take on any form. Except the form of Hashim, God," Etain explained.

The idea of the Jinn constantly looking over their shoulders, whispering into their ears, free to roam, gave Kevin the creeps. "This is bad. Very bad. We need to warn Jade and Casey about the Jinn."

Geoff brought fresh coffee and, obviously sensing the intensity of their conversation, he didn't want to intrude so he quietly filled their cups with coffee and went back into the kitchen. Kevin glanced up at him as he left without interrupting. Geoff reminded Kevin of Joe.

A woman with an air of authority entered the room and headed straight for the kitchen. She had her hair tied tightly back, and she wore a white t-shirt, olive-green military cargo pants, and black boots. Geoff must've made her aware of their presence, because soon after she entered the kitchen, she was straight back out and heading for their table.

"This is Delilah," Rachel said.

"Hi," Kevin said.

"You lot are back early from the Sphinx," Delilah said to Rachel and Shaun, ignoring him.

"What happened? Is something wrong? Why are you talking about mythical creatures? And where did *he* come from?" Delilah demanded of Etain.

"He's the portal master. He's sticking around this time to help," Shaun said.

"Don't call me that."

"We've seen Jinn in the sky. Well, I think it was the Jinn," Etain said.

"What did you see?" Delilah sat down next to Etain.

"Solid black shadows chasing us. We were airborne, and it kept up with our tactical maneuvers," Etain said.

Rachel sipped her coffee and sat back in her seat, looking very calm. Her short dark, wavy hair framed her face. Her emotions were thoughtful. Contemplative. She reminded him of Jade.

"I agree with you, Kevin. I think that's what we encountered back at the estate in England. They were tall shadows. One wore a hat, like in old black-and-white movies," Rachel said.

"Also, there were giants that were first invisible. They moved out of the trees. They terrorized us, destroyed the estate, and ate one of our people," Kevin said.

"How did you escape?" Etain asked.

"Kevin connected with my mind and emotions, then opened a portal to here. Just outside the bunker. You know the rest," Rachel said.

Geoff brought a coffee for Delilah. "How did you know the invisible giants were there?"

"They had a shimmering look to them," Kevin said.

"The trees had distorted. Like a poor signal or a hazy mirage. Then they materialized." Shaun shuffled over, making room for Geoff to join them.

"Thanks, Geoff." Delilah took a sip of her coffee and studied the space in front of her. She nodded, as if she had come to an internal conclusion.

Before Delilah spoke, she rubbed her brow, like it ached. "This is bad news. There are different stories about three main groups of Jinn. Some take on the appearance of animals, some fly unseen in our skies, and there's those that make themselves visible as dark shadows. They come to cause havoc. Jinn have emotions and personalities not dissimilar to ours. Some are resentful towards humans because God favors humans. Other Jinn are good, and others are neutral, and don't give a rat's ass about humans. They ignore our presences like humans ignore ants. But then there are the troublemakers, intent on causing terror in our lives. Those Jinn want us to suffer. They're hellbent on getting humans back for taking their place on the planet. They're energy, like a radio frequency. We can only see them if they want us to see them. They are the unseen." Delilah narrowed her eyes in thought.

Kevin peered at the space around them, wondering if it was really empty. Everyone had finished their meals and they were turning in for the night. Slowly, he expanded his energy, reaching out into the space. It didn't feel so empty. "Could the Jinn be here, listening to us?"

"Sure. There could be one standing at the edge of the table," Geoff said.

The idea spooked Kevin. He didn't want to know. He didn't want any trouble. The image of the ghostly She-Devil feeding on his brother Alex's life essences until he died changed his mood in a heartbeat. Kevin had come up against the unseen before, but the only person who had actually seen the She-Devil had been Casey, and he described what he had seen after Kevin pestered him to tell. Now the image was always in the back of his mind, haunting him.

"I know that look. You sense something?" Rachel asked.

"Give it up, K."

"It's nothing. The stories just got me spooked, that's all. What if they're around us? How do we do anything without them knowing? We have to make peace."

"No. We have to stay focused and get our asses out of here, and up there. I've got you, buddy," Shaun reassured him, clapping him on the shoulder.

An overwhelming feeling of pride for Shaun filled Kevin's chest. He widened his eyes to dry up the gathered tears he fought to hide. Shaun had a good heart and was no longer afraid to show it. Again, Kevin was reminded, by his uncontrollable emotions, of how being a male Empath sucked. When he was a little kid, he was called a cry baby, until he learned to not blink until the unshed tears dried up. He bottled up his own emotions so much that adults thought he was stoic. But he was far from it.

"What are you smiling at? You're not going to cry on me. Bloody hell, K. Reel it in."

Other people's emotions still made Shaun uneasy. Kevin laughed as Shaun squirmed. It was good to hear himself laugh. It changed the energy in the room slightly. "In all seriousness, what are we going to do?"

Etain's voice was commanding and reassuring. "We'll inform Abraham and, like Shaun said, we stay on our current course and get as many survivors as possible ready for the ascension."

Kevin swept his fringe back. "So, I'm clear about what we are up against; are fallen angels also Jinn, or are they demons?"

"Neither. They're a race of their own. Maybe the storms conceal the Jinn. There are stories of desert Jinn that are whirlwinds, like twisters and tornadoes," Etain said.

"So, besides the Ammit, fallen angels and demons, there's Jinn out to get us, and they can take on any form?" Kevin clarified.

Etain rubbed his eyelid. "Look, I don't know what's out there. We're talking about mythological creatures, so let's not jump the gun. Stay focused on the ascension."

"Etain is right. We shouldn't spook ourselves with ghost stories. It'll just make us crazy," Shaun said.

"They're not ghost stories," Rachel said, moving out from under Shaun's arm.

The energy between everyone was jittery. Kevin wondered if they were being influenced by the Jinn. It scared him not to know. *And what about the sandstorms in the past twenty-four hours? Were they the work of Jinn?* Kevin wondered. Maybe it was best that the questions remained unanswered. At least, until his and everyone else's fear settled.

3

DARK MATTER: SHAUN. EGYPT.

S haun left the soldiers at the second roller door, topside. Kevin rode shotgun as they drove back down the steep, twisty ramp to the first level of the city. Shaun pulled up the truck in the military and communications area, and Kevin jumped out and gawked at the planes on the first floor of the bunker. Shaun waited as Kevin, with his mouth hanging open, scanned the contents of the massive hangar, which was filled with dozens of aircraft.

Kevin loved planes; it was a passion he said he'd shared with his grandfather. He'd told Shaun he would've gone into the Air Force if the world hadn't turned upside-down. There was much Shaun didn't know about Kevin, but he did know that his grandfather taught him how to fly a Piper PA-28 Cherokee, which was now in pieces, and turning to rust on the lawn of Casey's estate.

The men sitting at the compound's two-way radio communication panel were alert, in control, checking and repairing the equipment. It was early morning, and they had worked through the night. Etain had prepped three groups to enter the portals to different countries. Shaun remembered there was something Kevin would die to see. He should've shown Kevin it first up — he would have loved it. Shaun promised himself to surprise him when the time was right.

"Nervous?" Shaun asked, standing beside him.

"Nah, but I would prefer to fly one of those beauties, instead of opening and closing portals."

"Why, is it draining you again?"

"A little, but we're indoors. I always feel the absence of the sun."

"We can go topside if you like, but again there's no sun. We'll just watch out for the Jinn and the Ammit. You know, try not to die. Just pray you don't have one of those creatures sneak up on you. Maybe instead of the sun, I can help you recharge?"

"How?"

Shaun suddenly felt nervous, almost wishing he hadn't said anything. And he knew Kevin felt it. But Kevin encouraged him. "Go on, what is it?"

"What if I give you a boost, like Casey does?" Shaun picked at the skin around the sapphire embedded in his hand.

"Can you control the flow?"

"Yes, and no."

"Well, we won't know unless we try, right?" Kevin said.

Shaun focused his attention on the icosahedron. It glowed.

"Wait. Maybe we should do this outside, just in case you fire off a photon blast, reducing me to dust."

"Maybe this isn't a good idea," Shaun said.

* * *

THE SUNSHINE WAS opaque behind the caramel sky, but it was good to be outside.

"You just hang ten and keep an eye out for Ammit and the Jinn, while I practice controlling spurts of energy." But each time Shaun channeled the energy, he punched a small hole in the ground.

After half a dozen turns, Shaun stopped. "I don't think this is going to work. If I hurt you, you might not be able to open a portal. I can't risk hurting you."

"Even though the sun is covered in dust and sand, I can feel the power travel through every pore of my body," Kevin said.

They leaned against the first roller-door entrance to the bunker, and Kevin soaked up as much sun as he could. Shaun kept a look-out, while Kevin closed his eyes.

"What are you thinking?"

"I'm imagining I'm on the beach," Kevin told him.

A dark cloud blocked out the warmth. Suddenly, something like a giant moth swooped down, and Shaun pushed Kevin behind him, hard up against the roller doors, as he fired random balls of blue light from his hand, blasting the dark matter that moved like a moth.

"Bloody Jinn!" Each time it broke apart, it just reformed. "Bloody hell, back inside!" Shaun shouted.

Kevin raised the door a few feet, so they could roll under. He slammed it behind them.

"What are you two doing?" Rachel asked, opening the next roller door to the bunker. She was heading out in the Jeep, the engine idling while she opened the connecting roller door.

"Where are you going?" Shaun said.

"To search for survivors. I thought you guys were getting ready to leave."

"You can't go out on your own." Immediately, Shaun knew it was the wrong thing to say. Her hands went straight to her hips, and she chewed on the inside of her cheek, twisting her mouth. He quickly tried to salvage the situation. "What I meant to say was, we narrowly escaped an attack by a Jinn. It's still out there."

"The Jinn might know where we are. We better tell the others. Get in."

Rachel held the driver's door open, ready to jump back in. Shaun headed for the driver's side and, for a moment, they stared at each other. Shaun smartly doubled back and sat in the passenger side. They drove down the spiral driveway to the military section, a mile underground.

As they jumped from the Jeep, Etain was waiting by the communication station. "Where did you get to?"

Before they could answer, a commotion over the radio distracted Etain. There was a problem downstairs in the civilian quarters. Gil leaned into the radio. Shaun moved closer to hear. Gill had been the resistance radio operator down in the tunnels, now he was one of the operators for the Olivet communications center.

"Repeat. Did you say dead?" Gil asked.

"Affirmative. Everyone on TAF76, Tower A floor 76, is deceased."

Rachel headed for the elevators.

"Wait up!" Shaun called, chasing her.

The elevator doors for Tower A opened. Rachel entered and pushed the button for the seventy-sixth floor. Shaun reached out and grabbed the door.

Rachel crossed her arms. "There's nothing you can do. It's best you and Kevin head off and find as many survivors as you can. I'll help here until you get back," she said.

"I'll go when I'm ready." Shaun refused to get out of the elevator, and Kevin was right beside him.

When the doors opened onto the seventy-sixth floor, there was an unusual stillness. The guards were wearing gas masks. Shaun feared the leviathan, disguised as the Supreme Master, had somehow returned.

"You can't enter until we get the all-clear," the masked guard said.

Rachel went to rush past him, but he grabbed her arm and shoved a gas mask into her chest. The elevator opened again behind them, and Abraham stepped out. Geoff handed masks to Shaun and Kevin.

"I thought I'd find you up here," Geoff said.

Geoff, wearing a gas mask, stood before Kevin and waved his hands in circles, as if performing a magic trick. He looked bizarre. "Did you pop up here?" Geoff clicked his fingers.

"Don't be such a tool!" Shaun nudged Geoff in the side.

Kevin adjusted his mask. "We took the elevator. Just like you. The air isn't polluted."

"We'll be the judge of that. Try not to touch anything," Abraham said.

It was very quiet. Shaun feared every step he took would make a sound. The corridor was cold and lifeless, as if he had stepped into a mortuary.

"All clear. Carbon monoxide levels are normal, no biochemicals were detected," the soldier reported.

Rachel left the corridor and entered the adjoining apartment.

"We shouldn't be in here. We should wait!" Shaun said as Rachel opened the bedroom door.

Shaun stepped into the room behind Rachel. There was a couple snuggled up in bed.

"Hello." Rachel stepped towards them.

Shaun glanced back at Kevin, standing in the doorway, refusing to enter the room.

"They're gone," Kevin said.

Rachel reached out to touch one of their shoulders. She pulled her hand back, as if expecting someone to lash out at her for waking them from their slumber. By no means was she skittish; maybe just hopeful they would wake up. But the couple were dead.

Rachel went into the next room. It was the family floor. She put her hand on the door, but lacked the courage to open it.

"Don't!" Kevin's body went rigid.

Shaun thought Rachel was going to ask him why, forcing Kevin to say what they all believed. But instead, she walked out of the apartment and scanned up and down the corridor, at all the closed apartment doors. "They're all gone? Every family?"

He could see the tears building in her eyes. An army doctor walked out into the corridor.

"What happened?" Rachel asked in disbelief. She shook her head. "This can't be happening!"

The doctor and Abraham walked down the corridor towards them. "Sadly, it is. It's Sudden Unexplained Nocturnal Death Syndrome, but we'll need to run a few more tests to be sure," the doctor said, more to Abraham than Rachel.

"The entire floor?" Rachel stepped into the doctor's space, forcing him to acknowledge her.

"Rachel, you can't do anything. Report to Delilah. I've got this," Abraham ordered.

"I'm not a soldier anymore. I don't have to report to anyone." Rachel turned her focus back on the doctor. "How is that even possible?"

"It's unusual, but it's happened before, in other places around the world. SUNDS was first recognized in 1984, when eighty-one men in Oahu country died during the night. Every man, woman and child on this floor has died in their sleep. I'll perform some autopsies, but I don't think we'll find anything suspicious," the doctor said.

"It's the Jinn." Rachel looked at Abraham, as if expecting him to take action.

"Now just wait a minute, Rachel. You can't jump to conclusions. If the survivors think they're not safe in the bunker, there'll be chaos," Abraham said.

"Why are you so complacent?"

"That's enough!" Abraham said.

At the communication level, the elevator doors opened, and Mama Bina and her adult daughter, Leah, walked out. The Supreme Master had trapped Leah under the influence of an amber Eldritch pendant. Shaun was still getting used to seeing Leah without it. Her mother, Mama Bina, had been down in the resistance tunnels, caring for the resistance's children under the city. Arm in arm, they walked through the lobby of the seventy-sixth floor. They paused, hugged Shaun and Rachel, and continued to the end of the corridor. They entered the very last apartment, at the end of the corridor. Abraham followed, but waited outside. Mama Bina exited the apartment, wiping her face, and she nodded at Abraham before entering the next one.

Rachel didn't hesitate to pursue Abraham. Shaun stayed close. "What's that all about?" Shaun asked.

"Never mind. You three have enough to worry about. If I need you, Shaun, I'll let you know. For now, don't mention it to anyone," Abraham said.

Geoff held the elevator door open for them. "Come on, guys."

"Do you really buy that bullshit? Sudden Unexplained Nocturnal Death Syndrome?" Rachel asked, as they went up towards the surface.

"Anything is possible these days," Shaun said, thinking about

Kevin's little brother, Alex. Shaun had loved Alex as if he was his own brother. Alex died laughing in his sleep. No matter how much they tried to wake him, they couldn't.

"It's possible." Kevin pushed his hair off his brow and sighed.

"We can explain Alex's death. It was the She-Devil – she wanted his soul." Shaun avoided making eye contact, focusing instead on the closing elevator doors. He didn't need to be an Empath to know that the mention of Alex would hurt. The death of Alex had emotionally paralyzed Kevin. He had been unable to open portals for three months because of the depth of his grief. Now wasn't a good time to remind him of his losses. Shaun could kick himself for mentioning it.

Rachel and Geoff stepped out of the elevator. Shaun could see the soldiers in groups of four, ready for the operation to search the planet for survivors.

"Tell those men to lose the weapons. You know they won't go through the portal," Kevin said to Rachel.

"I forgot. There's something I've been meaning to show Kevin. Give us fifteen minutes," Shaun said to Rachel while pushing the button down.

"Where are you going?" she asked as the doors closed.

"Where are we?" Kevin asked when the elevator doors opened.

Shaun guided him along a corridor that led to the sorting room, where the Supreme Master selected his harvest victims. Kevin started touching the gunmetal wall that was covered in rivets. He was already noticing there was something odd.

"What is this place? It's different from the rest of the city. The energy feels strange; foreign," Kevin said.

"You got that right. Here, I'll show you." Shaun stood in front of a huge metal door with a spiral, and octopus arms that moved when the lock disengaged. Shaun pushed the heavy door and it opened a fraction, enough for them to slip through. "When I first entered this room, it was dark. Reis warned us not to open our eyes, no matter what. I had taken a few steps when giant wet tentacles reached out and covered me in slime. It was called the sorting room. Everyone under forty went in, but not everyone came out," Shaun said, pushing the door all the way open.

"What happened to those over forty?"

"Terminated."

Kevin shivered. Shaun studied his face. "What are you picking up?"

"What aren't you saying? I can feel the slimy tentacles, it's as if I'm in the person's shoes; an older guy, bit of a pot belly… he is so scared, I feel warmth in my base chakra… strong, violent, ghostly energy surrounds him before he decomposes into slush." Kevin stopped talking and touched the wall again.

"This isn't a human craft, this is alien."

"You're damn right it is," Shaun said, putting his hand on Kevin's shoulder to ground him. Kevin's face went pale and for a minute Shaun thought he was going to puke all over him. "Are you alright? You're looking a bit pasty." Shaun let the energy of the sapphire flow through his palm into Kevin, until a protective blue haze surrounded him and Kevin's color returned.

Kevin shoved Shaun's hand away. "I'm fine."

"Keep your shirt on."

"Stop patronizing me." Kevin said, turning away.

"I'm not." Shaun reduced the light of the sapphire and continued as if Kevin hadn't said anything, hoping Kevin would tell him whatever was bugging him.

"Since it was discovered when I spoiled the Devil's Harvest, the scientists have been working non-stop, trying to figure out how the craft operates."

Inside, soldiers stopped them from proceeding. Shaun held up his hand, showing them the embedded sapphire, his all-access pass. As they stepped aside, a part of the wall disappeared, creating a doorway which led into another corridor made from the same metal. Kevin dragged his fingertips along the walls, as if feeling the pulse of the ship. It reminded Shaun of a jockey stroking the side of a horse before a race, calming it down, connecting. He'd also seen motorcycle riders before a Grand Prix connect with their machines. Kevin was connecting with the spacecraft.

"Everything is seamless. There are different rooms and levels. They haven't discovered how to open the other doors," Shaun said.

"This is incredible."

They had come to a dead end when, suddenly, a part of the wall disappeared again, creating another entrance. Inside, two men dressed in white coats – possibly engineers –analyzed the advanced alien control panels. They turned to see who had entered and broken their concentration.

"It's just me: Shaun. I hope you don't mind if I show my friend around. He's got a thing for aircraft." Shaun held up his hand, again showing the sapphire.

Kevin paused and scanned the cockpit, which was about forty-two meters square, with one enormous metal chair in the middle of the room. Panels on the armrests held controls with mathematical symbols, geometric-shaped buttons, and a crystal sphere that turned like a huge sensor; a trackball.

"It's really a spaceship! And it isn't just any bloody spaceship, it's an alien spaceship!"

Shaun could tell Kevin had a million questions circling into his mind. He smiled, pleased he had made him feel a sense of wonder. "It's incredible, but it's a bit late to know we're not alone in the universe."

"Yeah, right." Kevin touched the curved seat.

"Are you picking up anything? You've been feeling it from the moment you saw the outside hall that made up part of the corridor. They can't work out how to fire it up. Even if they do, it could destroy the entire city. So it's best not to."

"Can I sit down?" Kevin restrained himself for three seconds.

"Not a good idea," a scientist said, but it was too late.

Kevin sat in the pilot's seat for a few seconds before he jumped. "Whooo! Shit. That's bad."

"What is it?" Shaun said.

"Weightlessness. Horror. Bloodthirsty killings. Ancient hunters. Harvesting organs. Mining. Predators. They turned on each other. This is part of a bigger ship. Like a runabout." Kevin wet his lips, as if his mouth had gone dry.

Shaun waited impatiently for Kevin to finish reading the residual energy of the past occupants. "Okay, what do you know about the ship? Where did it come from?"

"It's definitely part of a much bigger ship. A being with predatory superiority traversed across universes to harvest minerals. They came to Earth for minerals, and to hunt humans for sport. They had reptilian-like skin. Humanoid trophies is what we were to one that navigated this craft. Our organs were a delicacy. Consuming them enabled it to recreate our physique, and walk undetected among us. If Casey was here, he could tell us what happened to the crew."

The scientist who had tried to stop Kevin from sitting in the metal pilot's chair was actively listening.

"It's taken us a week to gather less information than you've delivered in two minutes," the man said.

"Sorry, I shouldn't have sat down."

"Elon. Elon Geldart. I'm the chief researcher on this project. Nice to have you aboard. What else can you tell us? We could use your help," Elon said.

"That's about it. Our friend could tell more," Kevin said.

Elon fixed eyes with Shaun. "Where is this other friend of yours?"

"He's not here. He's in the States," Shaun said. Everyone at Olivet knew about the portal at the Sphinx, but not about Kevin, or his ability to generate his own portals.

"That's a shame. The human heart generates a magnetic field, releasing gigahertz or energy, and the owner of this ship could have had access through genetic coding; a biological signature that acts like a key. Maybe we humans will never be able to get it operational." Elon went back to his work.

Rachel strode into the room, her hands on her curvy hips, looking beautiful and stern as ever. It was a sure sign Shaun was in trouble. "There you are! I thought I would find you here. We need your help. Both of you," she added.

Something told Shaun it was Kevin that they needed, not so much him.

"Tour's over, K," Shaun said.

"We can go to the States for Jade and Casey and bring them here later, before we ascend. We can explore the rest of the spacecraft together," Kevin said.

"Sure thing. No worries," said Shaun.

Kevin dropped his shoulders when he mentioned going back to the States. The excitement was momentarily forgotten; he must have thought of Jade. Shaun didn't need to have special clairvoyant abilities to read his body language. When Kevin reappeared, twenty-four hours after he had opened a portal for him and Rachel,

Shaun thought he had sensed tension. There must be a reason why Kevin had left Jade.

"Whatever the problem you have with Jade, you'll sort it out," Shaun said.

Kevin's eyebrows flicked up. He pressed his lips together, expressing his doubts, and walked out of the spacecraft door after Rachel.

4

RULES: KEVIN. PORTAL JUMPING.

"We're ready to open the first portal, if you are," Etain said. A soldier stepped forward, hugged Rachel, and kissed Shaun on both cheeks. *A lot of hugging and kissing on cheeks. Back at Casey's estate, the people weren't so affectionate. It must be a European thing*, Kevin thought.

Shaun introduced the soldier as Reis Levin. Rachel had served with Reis when she signed up to the Israeli army at the age of eighteen. Her goal had been to learn the skills and knowledge that she would need to track down her father's killer and the Emerald Tablet.

Reis shook Kevin's hand. "So, you're the portal master?"

Kevin hated being called this – he was no master of anything. He stumbled through each opening and prayed he would find his way back.

"Enough with formalities, we have work to do," Etain said.

Reis stepped back into his group of four.

In the past, Reis had dived off the coast of Japan, from an island called Yonaguni Jima. His team would be the first to go through one of Kevin's portals, in order to search for survivors. Team Two was headed for Russia, Team Three to Peru, and Team Four to Canada. The fourth team leader was no soldier. It was the ginger, bearded lumberjack, Geoff.

Kevin stepped up and placed his fingertips on the side of Reis's head. The images of an underwater ruin filled Kevin's mind and excitement fluttered in his stomach. He pulled his hands away. "This won't work. It's underwater. We need to have a place on land."

"Why?" Reis said.

"Because you're not equipped to be underwater. What you think of is what I see, and where you will end up. I don't think you want to find yourself in the middle of the ocean dressed in heavy combat gear."

"Point taken. I know – Sengen Koen. I'll picture that," Reis said.

Quickly, Kevin wiped his sweaty palms and reconnected with Reis's temples. He focused on the new image that came into Reis's mind – a red Japanese Torii, a portal to the Gods, surrounded by cherry blossoms, and framing Mount Fuji. Kevin focused on the clear image until the atmosphere crackled from electrified energy waves, signaling the opening of the portal. He moved away from Reis and stretched out the portal until it was a doorway. Kevin stepped through first.

He admired the beauty of Japan while he waited for Reis and his team to show. Curious as to the delay, Kevin left the majestic view of Mount Fuji and stepped back through the portal to collect Reis and his men. The fluid movements of the membrane were cool and, like soft jelly or dense water, it was easy to penetrate. Reis and his men were still at Olivet, looking dumbfounded as to why they couldn't go through the portal membrane.

"Sorry guys, my mistake. I didn't notice. Rachel should've told you; it's your guns. You have to leave all your weapons behind. You can take tools, a knife, even a Jeep. But no guns, no grenades; nothing that has the sole purpose of killing," Kevin said.

After removing his firearms, Reis put his hand against the membrane and it sank in as if it was water.

"Ready." Kevin looked at the last guy taking off his bullet belt.

"Roger," the guy said.

Kevin stepped into the electric liquid energy, and all his worries disappeared. It was the effect of the portal. It was a sunny spring day in Japan, and the cherry blossoms were in full bloom. The soft pink flowers by the Torii were majestic. He thought it was ironic that he had passed through the portal between two posts that made up part of the Torii, a gateway to the shrine of the gods. If Jade were here, he could ask her a million questions, and she'd probably know all the answers.

Reis and the others were still taking their time coming through. Just about everybody did, whether it be their first time or the fifth time: the portal was such a nice place to be. No one wanted to leave, including him. It was like a rebirth every time. Kevin reached in, took hold of Reis's hand, and led him through the membrane, through the Torii on the mountainside of Mount Arakura. He then brought the next three soldiers through.

It was easy for Kevin to connect with his surroundings. When Reis and his men were ready to return, he could open the portal without Reis' memory, using his own instead.

It was a beautiful country. He could see a mountain with snow at the peak. Mount Fuji was more than he expected. Everything was quiet. The men established where they were, and quickly checked the surrounding area, ensuring they were no obvious threats.

"I'll open the portal in five days. Hopefully, I'll find you and your men here, with hundreds of survivors." Kevin shook Reis's hand.

As he stepped one foot into the membrane of the portal, the other remained on the ground in Japan. The ground shook and rumbled under his foot. He followed through with his motion and disappeared into the portal, but he wondered if he should go back. However, the cause for alarm dissipated inside the membrane as peace washed over him. Thoughts of Jade brushing her face with the ends of her hair came into mind as he stepped outside. He wasn't at Olivet; he was back at the Black Mountain campsite in North Carolina. It was dark, and the air was filled with thick fog.

"Dammit." He stepped back into the portal. He thought of Etain waiting with his men, and this time stepped back into Olivet.

"What took you so long?" Etain said.

"Sometimes, people don't want to leave the serenity of the membrane, and your men are no different."

"Next group is to Peru," Etain said.

Kevin connected to the team leader's temple and opened the portal to a seaside village in Peru. Once they were safely through, he told the group that he would be back in five days, then left. He did the same for the group to Moscow. As he stepped out of the portal for group four, exhaustion washed over him. He tried not to show it.

"This is the last group, headed for Canada," Etain said, looking at Geoff dressed in fatigues.

Geoff bent his head down so he could connect. Butterflies fluttered through Kevin. "It will not be painful unless you resist," Kevin teased.

"Was that meant to be funny?" Geoff's eyes darted to Shaun for confirmation.

Snowfields. Ski lodges. Twilight. Twinkling stars. Love filled

Geoff and passed to Kevin. The hum and sparks of the portal started at Kevin's feet, and a doorway opened around them. Together, Kevin and Geoff fell through the portal, landing on the wet grass. It was before dawn, and freezing.

"It should be spring, with snow on the top of the mountains on either side of the valley – Whistler and Blackcomb." Geoff suddenly stopped talking. He and Kevin had entered the space of a grizzly bear with its cub. A dozen feet off to Kevin's left, the grizzly bellowed and reared up on its hind legs. It moved its head from side to side, then ran towards them. It was fast. Kevin was ready to run, or dive back into the portal.

"Don't move!" Geoff said.

A crack echoed between the mountains. The bear dropped. Kevin stood in shock as the cub ran up to its parent, squealing. Geoff pulled Kevin down. Kevin quickly pulled the other men through and closed the portal. A blaze of light came from behind the tree line. A shadow of a man with a rifle in his hand stepped out into the open.

"They're a protected species!" Geoff shouted.

"Show me your hands," the man said.

They all raised their arms in the air. Kevin's jaw tightened, his heart skipped a beat, and he felt invisible beads of sweat covering his face; they really belonged to the stranger. Anxiety and uncertainty churned in the man's stomach, suppressing the hope he did not dare show. As Kevin pushed away the man's emotions, he glimpsed desperation for connection. *Connection to whom or what?* Kevin wondered. The man's courage was laced with fear. Slowly, the man with the rifle moved towards them. He let the gun tilt downward as he put one hand behind his back.

"He's got another gun," a soldier said behind Kevin. "I can take him out from here."

"How?" Geoff whispered.

"Knife. I can throw it hard enough to lodge it in his throat. He'll be dead before he hits the ground, just like what he did to that bear."

"Stand down," Kevin said, sensing mixed emotions of protectiveness and regret, as if it had caused the man physical pain to shoot the bear. *He is trying to protect something.*

"I'm not taking orders from a teenager," the soldier said.

"It's not a weapon. He's got a child behind him," Kevin said.

"I'm looking straight through his legs. I don't see a child."

Kevin could see the man was moving his hand behind his back, up and down. The man was jiggling a baby on his back, to keep it from crying.

"Where did you come from?" he yelled. He stopped soothing the baby and put both hands on the gun, taking their silence as a threat. He advanced on them.

"We're here looking for survivors, but you don't deserve it," Geoff shouted.

"Tell him why we're here," Kevin said.

The man relaxed at the sound of Geoff's familiar Canadian accent.

"We have good news. Is there anyone else with you?" Geoff said.

"Who wants to know?"

"Why are you here in the dark hours of the morning?" Kevin asked.

The man gave him a curious glance. Not sure if he should answer the question. He was hiding something, and Kevin knew it. "Why did you come?"

The child made a sound. The man turned his head slightly and his fear increased.

"I'm here to save your life," the man said to Kevin.

My life? Kevin thought. "No, it's the other way around. We're here to save your life, and anyone else that survived the apocalypse."

"How are you going to save his life?" Geoff said.

The man said nothing, but they all glanced at the bear. It had definitely pained him to have killed it. Kevin could feel that now.

"The cub will stay with the mother and die if you don't bring it with you," the man said.

Kevin's heart jumped into his mouth. He was sorry for the bear, but as soon as he thought his own life may have been endangered, he shamefully was relieved the bear was dead.

More people with flashlights walked out from behind the trees.

"I don't like this. It's an ambush," the soldier said.

Three men with a sled ran up to the bear and hauled it up.

"Waste nothing," the man said.

He was honoring the spirit of the bear. Kevin sensed the bear's energy clinging on to its body, not ready to leave its cub. Kevin walked towards the cub and picked it up. Its coat was softer than he had imagined. It was like having a heavy Shepherd puppy in his arms. Kevin didn't wait for Geoff and the others. He wandered over to the man with the baby. The people circled around Kevin, ignoring Geoff and the soldiers.

He hugged the cub for warmth as three men dragged its mother off behind the tree line. The surrounding circle tightened. He didn't fear these people. They had come to save him from the bear. They knew something that he didn't. He wondered about the dreams Casey had said the people in London had. Dreams of Stonehenge and the ascension, and people in Israel had similarly dreamed of a pilgrimage to Egypt for ascension. Dreams that none of them had had at the estate. Suddenly, Kevin wondered if they were abandoned.

Kevin waited for someone to speak, but they all kept staring at him. They were haggard and tired, as if they had been through hell and back. They had no fight left in them. "Is there somewhere warm we can talk?"

The circle broke up, and the man who shot the bear took the lead. The pain of the bear as it died left Kevin weak in the legs as he wondered what was going to happen to the cub in his arms.

He imagined what it would look like here in the winter, when the grass and mountains were covered in snow. He had imagined skiing when he was younger. Now, having lived through the whiteout after the apocalypse, through the middle of winter at the estate in the United Kingdom, he decided he would be happy if he never saw snow again. He'd rather the sunshine and surf back on his island home. The cub quieted in his arms. Kevin hoped Geoff and the soldiers were following. He didn't think these people meant any harm, but he didn't want to be responsible for Etain's men disappearing.

They walked between the trees that protected them from the sudden harsh wind that whipped up. They entered the first building, a holiday lodge, through a reception area where a huge stuffed bear guarded the entrance. Kevin's gym shoes were silent on the slate floor. A stone fireplace, with a stack of logs neatly arranged alongside, warmed the lodge. They waited quietly for Geoff and the soldiers to arrive. Standing in the middle of the reception area, Kevin noticed the sounds of scraping chairs and the drop of voices as they piled into the lodge and people came out of the bar. There were whispers and murmurs as he was ushered to a seat by the fire. Faces stared down at him from the upper floor. Kevin tried to gauge their emotions. The silence was like a funeral procession. He just hoped it wasn't his funeral.

A young girl of about nine appeared at his side. She wore a light apricot wind jacket and navy-blue tights covered with golden butterflies and sparkles. The cub was nearly as big as she was. "I'll take the cub from you."

"He's my responsibility now," Kevin said, trying to keep the bear still. It was like she was also expecting him, and the cub.

"But you don't know how to care for the cub. We can't take him out of the wild. You're supposed to give me the bear. We will find him a new family. I promise," the girl said.

Who are these people? Kevin wondered. It was a little creepy.

The cub was afraid. Kevin didn't know what to do. They both wanted to flee the glaring eyes. "I'll take him outside and play with him. I promise." The girl reached out for the cub, and Kevin couldn't hold it any longer. It was going to jump from his arms.

Everyone sat in the lounge chairs scattered around the room that was meant for people waiting to check in, or to pause by the fire to warm up with a drink or two on a snowy night. Alcohol was something he'd never had, and from how Shaun had described his father getting drunk and beating him up, or crying on his shoulder, Kevin didn't think he would ever touch the stuff.

The man unstrapped the ties around his waist that kept the baby securely pressed against his back. After checking the baby, and fondly touching its cheeks, he handed the little fellow to another man, before sitting down on a lounge chair.

Kevin, seated on a velvet chair, kept his hands on his lap, to avoid touching the material. Velvet made his skin crawl. Geoff nodded to him as if making sure he was okay. Kevin nodded back in agreement.

The people watching from the upper mezzanine level made him a little anxious. He didn't know if he should smile, wave, or run. Instead, he turned away and studied his hands. He felt uncomfortable. He felt their expectation, yet didn't know what they were expecting of him. He pushed down his hair and let it fall against his brow, but his days of hiding behind it were over. He needed to step up.

"You have been expecting me?" Kevin said in a loud voice for everyone to hear.

"You are the boy with the cub. My name is Logan Wood. The little girl who took the cub, that is my daughter Melody, and that is my baby boy, Brody."

Kevin waited for Logan to continue, but he didn't. If Kevin wanted to find out more, he was going to have to start the conversation. It was a long shot, but he was going to go with his intuition. There was a recurring pattern of prophecy dreams. In England, it was to Stonehenge. Israel, the Sphinx. It was possible this community had had a shared dream as well – one that featured him. Dreams and the subconscious mind harbor a lot more than the conscious mind is willing to acknowledge. "Did someone see me in a dream? You were waiting for me because of a dream?" Kevin asked.

Geoff walked between the chairs and sat next to Kevin, who was so grateful for this strong, protective attitude. The people peering down from the second floor made him feel small and uncomfortable.

"Yes," Logan said.

Kevin wondered who amongst the people had the dream. He wasn't picking up any additional spikes of emotions. Geoff followed his gaze.

"Who?" Kevin said.

Logan scanned the people, and each one nodded in approval. "Everyone," Logan said.

Kevin's stomach turned upside-down. Suddenly, there were too many emotions for him to process. It was unsettling, and draining.

He was getting hot and needed space. He removed his jacket and shoved it down beside his leg and onto the seat. The heat inside his body increased – he had to get out. He excused himself and exited the building, leaving his coat behind.

Outside, he stepped into the fresh morning air. The sun still had not risen. Melody giggled as the cub licked her face. Together, they rolled around the courtyard on the pavers, near a cluster of gray, vertical rocks that resembled stalagmite. Melody placed her hands over her face, as if hiding from the cub, which tried to get behind her hands, to lick her face. When Melody became aware of Kevin's presence, she pushed her matted hair off her wind-burned cheeks and red lips. The cub seized the opportunity and gave her a long lick. "Do you want to play?" she asked, wiping her mouth.

Kevin glanced back through the doors at the room full of people.

"It's okay. They know you won't be long," Melody said.

Her self-assurance was nice. Something he had lacked during his first couple years in high school. The cub wrestled with the lower part of Kevin's black cargo pants, which were still wet from the long grass. It tried to climb up his leg. He reached down to gently push the cub aside, but it playfully latched its claws onto his forearm. Kevin wrestled the cub off. It toppled and rolled into a ball. "As much as I would like to play, I must go and talk to the grownups," Kevin told Melody.

"Okay. Nearly everyone is ready to go. We didn't know you were coming today, but we knew you would come," she said.

Kevin brushed the dirt off his arm. He pushed back his hair before tucking his hands inside his pockets. "Go where? Where are you all going?" Kevin asked.

"To the stars. With you. To see my mom and uncle again," she said, kicking the few pebbles off the pavers.

5

SERPENT: SHAUN. EGYPT.

"I'll be fine," Shaun said, pressing his lips against Rachel's.

"It's insulting that Abraham has put me on the base comms!" Rachel snapped.

"At least one of us will be safe," Shaun said.

"If he wants to keep anyone safe, it should be his daughter Mia, or you. You're not even military trained. I am. I don't get it. This is ridiculous," Rachel said.

Gil stood up and relinquished his seat and headset for Rachel to take over. It was unusual for him to leave his seat.

Shaun hoped Gil's son Theo was okay. "Everything alright, Gil?"

"Just need a break. Theo was a little spooked. He's been listening to the stories of giant creatures circulating around the campsite at the Sphinx. I've banned him from going out with the water crew. Then today, waking up to the terrible news. All those poor people on the seventy-sixth," Gil said.

"Isn't your apartment on the seventy-sixth floor?" Shaun asked, putting his hand on Gil's shoulder.

"Yeah. I stayed here last night, and Theo slept under the communication panel. He's scared, but won't admit it. I needed to keep an eye on the storm. We went to have showers this morning, and, well – you know the rest." Gil adjusted his pants, avoiding eye contact.

"How did Theo find out what happened? Did he see any bodies?" Rachel said.

"You know what he's like, always curious, and eavesdropping. Curiosity will kill the cat. I keep telling him to mind his own business. His mind runs wild. Maybe you could talk to him? He looks up to you, you're his Tekhelet Malak," Gil said.

"Sure – any time. But I'm not a blue angel, or an angel of any kind. I'm far from it. Don't know what I'll say, but I'll give it go," Shaun smirked, recalling the first time he had met Theo in the Resistance tunnels — a dirty, tired, skinny eight-year-old, lugging heavy water bottles through the tunnels for the men. He was a good boy.

"Well, Theo calls you Tekhelet Malak, on account of your glowing blue aura," Gil said.

"Alright, alright, enough, Gil. Let's get a move on." That blue angel talk always made Shaun feel uneasy.

Yehuda, leading a patrol of five soldiers, including Mia, was ready to leave.

"Got to run, babe," Shaun said, signaling to Rachel.

Frustrated, she adjusted the side lever and raised Gil's chair. "Copy?" she asked.

Her voice came through, clear and commanding. Shaun adjusted the earpiece. "Copy." They all confirmed their radios and headsets were working. Shaun jumped into the back of the truck, behind Mia, and hung on as the truck sped around the ascending spiral ram that led topside.

Mia and the soldiers enjoyed the ride as if they were at a carnival. It was kind of fun. As soon as they passed under the last roller door of the last checkpoint, it closed firmly behind them.

Outside was a sandstorm. The cheers and boyish hoopla died down. They all put on oxygen masks and night-vision eyewear, exited the truck, and entered the storm.

"Homebase. We have a sandstorm topside. A heads-up would've been good," Yehuda said to Rachel on comms.

"Base here. No signs of a storm on radar. Keep an eye out for Jinn. Over."

"Yehuda to base, did you say Jinn?" Yehuda pushed on his earpiece.

"Roger that."

"Copy," Yehuda said.

Each of the soldiers carried an M16. Shaun had his stones. He held his arm out, palm open, ready. The sapphire sparked like a snake's tongue tasting the air.

"What does a Jinn look like?" Mia randomly asked the soldiers.

"I think Rachel is pulling your leg. There's no Jinn. It's a myth," a soldier said, walking off behind Yehuda.

Yehuda made hand signals, and the other men reacted. Shaun was in front of Mia, who covered the tail end of the squad. They walked behind the truck. The earth trembled.

"Earthquake! Take cover," Yehuda spoke clearly into the radio attached to his shoulder.

They all took cover behind the truck, and waited for the tremors to stop. Three seconds… ten seconds… thirty seconds. It was more than a minute. Suddenly, the truck they'd just vacated was flung across the street, smashing and grinding along the side of the building across the road.

"I can't see shit!" Shaun said into the radio. The earth swelled around them. Mia pushed Shaun to the left, away from Olivet. They followed the other soldiers as the ground bulged. Something was surging up.

"This isn't a normal earthquake!" Yehuda dodged falling debris.

Shaun had no time to reply. The ground moved in waves, creating peaks twelve feet high right under the soldiers' feet, lifting them up into the air; they fell to the ground. An arch formed, separating Shaun and Mia from the others.

"How is that even possible?" Shaun asked.

Mia pushed Shaun forward and through the archway before it collapsed. They advanced under the contracting, rolling belly of a giant snake.

"What's going on out there?" Rachel had lost all sense of formality.

"It's a snake."

"Well, kill it, and get a move on," Rachel said.

"It's a giant fuckin' snake, babe."

"Come again?"

"Yehuda to base. It is not an earthquake. I can confirm it is a giant cobra. Repeat – a giant cobra." Yehuda's radio went quiet, then someone close to Yehuda screamed.

"Mia. Shaun. Eleven o'clock. Soldier down. Pick him up. Then head twelve o'clock from his position, and to the alleyway across the street," Yehuda ordered.

"Roger that," Mia confirmed.

Shaun tripped over the soldier before he saw the guy. Quickly, he helped the man to his feet. Through the wind and sand, they made it to the alley where Yehuda and his men waited.

"Apep will be just as blind as us," Mia said.

"Who's Apep?" Shaun pressed up against the building.

"Apep is a giant snake from the underworld. It comes to destroy light, and divine order. It desires nothing but chaos and eternal darkness."

"That's just a myth," Yehuda said.

"Well, it looks pretty real to me," Mia said, looking up.

"Base to Yehuda, come in," Gil said.

"Go ahead, Base."

"We need you to lure it away from Olivet."

"Roger that."

"Make your way to Main Street, where the checkpoints are. Near the motels. Then head southwest," Gil directed.

"Copy. We'll report back once we get to the abandoned buses, a mile and a half from our current position. Let's see if it follows," Yehuda said, and the headset went silent.

Shaun readied himself for Yehuda's signal to move. A chopper flew overhead. It hovered over the helipad, attempting to land, when the giant cobra reared up, expanded its hood, and snatched the chopper out of the sky, sending it crashing into the buildings at the entrance of the alleyway.

"Go. Go. Go!" Yehuda yelled as the chopper blades turned sidewards and entered the alley. The snake took a dive and went underground. The earth trembled as they fled, and the ground behind them surged upward again.

"Faster!" Mia yelled.

Shaun turned and fired a blue photon blast at the rising mounds, but the snake continued to travel under the surface towards them. Rounding the corner at the far end of the alley, they entered Main Street. The ground had stopped trembling, and the blade had lodged in the alleyway.

Visibility was good here. They pulled down their goggles. The revs of a motorcycle rounding a corner drew Shaun's attention. He glanced back, and it did not surprise him to see Rachel – wearing no helmet. *Dammit, Rachel,* he thought. Shaun ran in the opposite direction to the soldiers and headed for her. Mia followed, and so did the giant snake. Mia pushed off with her feet and rolled to the side of the road as a mound of dirt divided them. "Mia! Go with Yehuda."

The motorcycle came to a sliding stop. Rachel reached around her back, pulled an M16 forward, and started firing upwards over Shaun's head.

"Get on. Don't look into its eyes!"

Shaun turned as he threw his leg over the backseat of the motorcycle and Rachel fired on the giant snake Mia called Apep. It stood taller than the building and spat venom at them. Rachel skidded the motorcycle around and the venom hit the ground where they had been standing. It would have been a direct hit if she hadn't moved. The venom sizzled on the road like acid.

"Get us out of here!" Shaun yelled at Rachel, as the snake reared up stories high, blocking the sun and casting a shadow over them. Shaun could hear gunfire from behind. He quickly glanced over his shoulder to see Mia alone, shooting at the creature. Her bullets enraged the giant snake. Shaun leaned towards Rachel. "We have to go back for Mia!"

Rachel turned a corner. She kept heading west, then entered a hotel parking lot and slammed on the brakes, skidding to a halt before the exit on the other side of the building, back to the street where Mia was. Shaun jumped off, and Rachel rode out of the parking lot and under the arching snake.

Yehuda and his men took cover behind a cement roadblock and began firing at the snake, providing cover for Rachel. Mia readied herself and was quick to fling herself onto the back of the motorcycle.

Shaun ran through the parking lot, keeping Rachel in his sights, and joined Yehuda's men behind the barrier. Secure, Mia jumped off the motorcycle, re-joined her team, and fired on the hooded Apep. It seemed nothing could stop it.

Shaun stretched out his hand and pushed the icosahedron's piercing blue laser energy. He aimed for the snake's neck as it towered over the barrier. The snake roared. The sound was so fierce and terrifying, he wanted to cover his ears. The earth swayed, knocking them off their feet. The laser beam hit the snake in the head.

Pieces of flesh rained down over them and turned into thousands of smaller snakes. Shaun pulled back the blinding blue light, and they jumped over the concert barrier onto slithering snakes, which were drawn into the center of the road like liquid silver, combining into another giant snake.

"Mia! is there anything that can kill this thing?"

Yehuda signaled for them to follow and take refuge behind the buses. Rachel ran by Shaun's side and as she passed him he could see blood coming from her ear. He opened and closed his mouth, then pulled down on his earlobe, trying to clear the blocked feeling and the reverberations that bounced around in his inner ear.

The soldiers started firing. Shaun was still a few feet away from the safety of the buses when he was suddenly cloaked in darkness and lifted off the ground.

Blind and deaf, he tumbled backwards. His hands touched spongy, wet walls as he slid headfirst, and tried to grab hold of something to stop himself from sliding. Goo collected between his fingers. The walls contracted and squeezed like muscles. Shaun stopped struggling, and created a hermetic shield. The blue light glowed, revealing red, muscular walls contracting as he was swallowed alive.

Inside the belly of the snake, Shaun channeled his energy into a laser beam and blasted his way out. Through the hole he'd made, he spilled out on a wave of slimy snakes, landing on the road.

Apep fell to the ground and, again, divided into a thousand slithering snakes. A cobra reared up and spat. Shaun ducked, and the venom skimmed the surface of his hermetic shield, sailing twenty yards and hitting a soldier in the arm. The soldier dropped his gun, and tore at his clothes as the venom penetrated the material, burning through to his skin. Quickly, the soldier poured water over the arm, but the venom trailed down to his hand, and his whole arm blistered.

"You two. Take him back. Go through the car park. Yehuda to Base?"

"This is Base. Go ahead," Gil said, calmly.

"I've got a man down, needing medical attention – venom burns to his right arm, needing medical help."

"Roger that."

"ETA ninety seconds out."

The Apep was reforming. There was no winning. This thing didn't know the meaning of death and, to top it off, the dark clouds on the horizon were getting closer.

"We have to distract it," Yehuda said.

As soon as it formed into one giant snake once more, Shaun fired the laser beam, splitting it in two, and in turn into a thousand smaller snakes , which gave them a couple of minutes to advance their position, moving further from the safety of the bunker. One more blast should do it.

Mia was watching the Apep once again reform.

"Mia!" Shaun couldn't stop her from making eye contact with

the creature. She raised her gun and froze for a couple of seconds, before turning her gun on Yehuda.

"What are you doing? Soldier! put your weapon down!"

"Mia – no!" Rachel shouted.

Shaun blasted the snake, severing the hypnotic hold as Mia squeezed the trigger, but dropped her weapon before firing.

"I couldn't stop myself."

"What happened to not looking into its eyes?" Shaun asked her as they ran.

They had a lead of about thirty seconds, but there wasn't anything they could do to stop it from reforming. They were tiring, soon to become easy prey.

They moved further and further away from the coast and the bunker. The earth rumbled as they moved — the snake following underground, moving away from the thousands of people at Olivet. Shaun took the earpiece out and stuck his finger in, to try to clear the crackling. His finger was covered in blood.

Yehuda continued to make hand gestures. He wanted them to hold the position. They could see a mile or so down the road. There were vehicles headed their way. A convoy of pick-up trucks, a bus, and cars. The rumbling from behind them stopped. The snake had momentarily lost their scent, or stopped feeling their vibrations. Either way, it wasn't moving. Then the oncoming vehicles were bigger and louder targets. The ground trembled. It was right under their feet, knocking them off-balance as it headed for the convoy of survivors.

The first two vehicles were pickup trucks. People were standing on the beds and waving at them, when Apep erupted from the ground. The people screamed as their trucks flipped over.

Yehuda signaled for them to advance. "Move. Move. Move!"

Keeping low, they checked the passengers and moved them into two groups – alive and dead.

"Ammit! Ammit!" a woman called, trying to drag her dead husband out from under the tipped truck. Shaun fired at Apep, which was the worst thing he could have done. It broke down into a thousand venomous snakes, which struck out at the survivors. There was so much chaos and carnage, he didn't know who to help first.

"The Ammit. Shaun."

Mia and Yehuda, along with able bodies, moved as many survivors from the wreckage as they could get onto the convoy's bus.

"Shaun!" Rachel shouted.

He turned and fired at the charging Ammit as Rachel helped the woman get her husband out from under the truck and onto the bus. The engine stalled, kicked over, then spluttered into life. Apep had reformed and its thick, dark brown, scaly body slithered past him, so close that he could've measured the width of its yellowish crossbars.

It was headed for the bus.

Shaun couldn't take his eyes off the Ammit. There were so many of them. It was as if the dark realm was calling up its armies.

"Hell no!" Shaun blew up dozens of them. He was covered in their blood. Thunder and lightning filled the sky. He gave up killing the Ammit and covered himself with the hermetic shield. The sound of the bus was moving away. Hoping to confuse Apep, he fired his photon blasts down at the ground as the convoy hurried towards Olivet, with Rachel and the soldiers on board the bus. It seemed to be working but suddenly the giant son-of-a-bitch reared up out of the ground and slammed its head down, flattening the last car.

Before Shaun could get a clear shot, Apep swallowed the bus. Shaun stopped and watched in horror as rain poured down and washed the blood off his face. The sky darkened. He ran at the beast, and whispers of clouds peeled away from the dense storm cell, flying down towards him like dark, ghostly beings. *The Jinn.* Shaun fired on the snake and missed. "Rachel! God, not Rachel, please!" He would never forgive himself if anything happened to her. He bolted into the parking lot for cover. Nothing they were up against was beatable. No wonder the message Rachel had brought back from the stars was to find survivors and ascend. At least the Ammit died, but Shaun couldn't think what was required to destroy the giant snake, or the Jinn. He was outnumbered. Every time he blasted either one of them, they just reformed. But for now that would have to do. "I'm coming, Rachel!"

Shaun fired on the giant snake again and it shattered like glass into a thousand smaller snakes. Shaun held his breath as he watched the bus tilt from side to side. It was going to tip over. It stopped rocking and remained upright. Slimy snake guts covered the bulk of the bus. The rain continued to wash blood from Shaun as he ran out into the open, screaming. "Rachel, Rachel!" Shaun ran with his hermetic shield up, through the interlacing snakes. He could see her in the driver's seat. He doubled over and rested his hands on his knees, just grateful she was alive. He surveyed the bus. It didn't look good, the sides were crushed, the roof buckled inward, and the windows had shattered from the force as the snake had tried to digest it.

The engine coughed to life. Rachel ground the gears, and the bus lurched forward. The door was opened. Shaun reduced his shield and quickly jumped onboard as a rocket whistled overhead and blew a hole in the ground behind them. Shaun ducked under the buckled roof to see out the broken back window. He cheered with a loud "YES!" as he beheld snakes falling into the pit left by the rocket. The joy was short-lived, as Apep's head rose from the hole.

"Faster!" Mia kept pressure on the stomach wound of a young woman.

Again, a rocket raced across the top of the bus. Ahead, he could see a tank. It fired another rocket. His radio squawked into life.

"Base to Yehuda, come back."

"Go ahead, Base."

"Leave the snake and Ammit to the men in the tank. Get your casualties back to base."

"Roger that."

Shaun assumed Yehuda must have called ahead, notifying Gil of the situation. He was only too happy to follow the orders. He just hoped Rachel would be, too.

RACHEL AND MIA worked well as a team. Shaun was soaked through as he helped unload the casualties. When Abraham ordered him to get cleaned up, he didn't need to be told twice, and headed straight for the apartment and the shower.

The hot water over his body was a such a blessing he thought he was in heaven. But he couldn't fully enjoy it, knowing there was mayhem outside. Shaun walked out of the bathroom and found a set of clean clothes. He picked up the towel and tried to unblock his ear, realizing he hadn't taken out the earpiece. Enjoying the feeling of clean clothes, as he left the apartment, he put the earpiece back in.

"Chopper one in need of assist," he heard Etain say over the radio.

Shaun sprinted for the elevator that would take him straight up to the helipad. The minute the doors opened, he ran outside and shielded his eyes from the sand and dust the chopper whipped up as it landed.

As Etain powered down the chopper, the snake reared up, its hood flared out. Shaun blasted the thing down to a thousand slithering snakes once more. They dropped to the pavement below.

Etain ran from the chopper, along with his crew. "I owe you one," he said.

6

BLACK FOG: KEVIN. CANADA.

The sun was rising. Tumultuous clouds boiled on the horizon around the top of the mountains. By the end of the day, the storm would break over the village, but that shouldn't be a problem. They only needed half an hour to get out, not eight. "Don't stay out here too long, a storm is coming," Kevin said to Melody. Before he went up the stairs into the lodge, he took one more look at the storm. It had a life of its own. He sensed pent-up emotions from within it. He frowned, puzzled – how could a cloud have emotions? He pulled himself away, walking up the stairs and into the lodge.

Kevin instantly felt the weight of the emotions in the room. He sat down, took in a deep breath, and attentively listened as the survivors at the ski lodge surrounded him and told him about their shared dream of his coming. It had started a week ago; the same day Jade had seen the beat-up car in front of the estate, and Casey had started drawing in his sleep; all the people in this small village had a shared dream about Kevin. He couldn't understand a calling, a vision, about him, and it scared him. He was a fraud, an imposter.

To them, killing the bear to save his life was something they had to do, because their future depended on his survival. They spoke as if he was a guiding sage. While they talked, they offered warm drinks. Kevin would have liked a heavily caffeinated fizzy drink or a hot chocolate. He declined the coffee but, to his surprise, someone brought him a hot chocolate. Kevin gratefully took the mug. "So, you all saw me arriving at the lake in your dreams? But what about the men with me?"

"We did not see them," said the man who had handed him the hot chocolate.

"Can you read minds too?" Kevin asked him.

"No. In my dream, I made hot chocolate for you," he said, walking away and sitting down with the others.

It all seemed so odd.

Kevin took a sip of the hot chocolate and welcomed the warmth running down the back of his throat. "We're here to find survivors, and Geoff here has visited Whistler Mountain in the past, and thought this would be a good place to start. So, you can all thank him, not me."

Geoff almost smiled.

"There is no need to come with us if you don't want to," Kevin continued, still gauging the emotions of the people. The smell of the fire was prominent, even though it wasn't lit. He took another sip, and breathed in the steam. "There are several sacred sites scattered around the world. There must be one here that you can access for the ascension in two months."

"We must go with you now. We shouldn't wait. We must leave as soon as everyone from the different parts of the village has arrived," Logan said. He seemed to be the spokesperson for the fifty or so people. The man's fear spiked. It was like a flutter in his chest that made his heart beat a little faster.

* * *

THE SOUND of the coffee machine making frothy milk was louder than the faint murmurs in the lobby. Lightning struck the ground close by, causing everyone to jump and scream. The soldier standing at the door said, "Heads up everyone, the storm's coming. I suggest we all pick up the pace. Kevin can do his thing, and get us all out of here before the storm sets in."

Logan headed for the window. "It's rolling in quicker than we expected."

The men and women on the mezzanine hurried down the stairs. A woman with dusty blond hair, wearing a puffy ski jacket, ran down the stairs, putting on her gloves and yelling, "We're too late! They're here. We must go now."

"I need to get my parents," a teenager said in a panicked voice.

"Wait! Everyone! Just calm down!" Geoff said.

Kevin leaned toward Geoff and whispered, "What did the woman mean by they're here? The storm has emotions. I can feel them. There is more than a storm rolling in. I know it sounds ludicrous, but there is something inside the storm. You need to tell the soldiers."

Geoff leaned in closer and Kevin's attention to detail went into overdrive, starting with the smell of Geoff's caffeinated breath, then his lips moving in the middle of the ginger beard.

"Do you think she meant… do you think it's the…" Geoff stopped in mid-sentence, as if he believed that speaking the words would call something into being. His cheeks colored, and Kevin knew he was embarrassed to be superstitious.

Kevin motioned with his finger for Geoff to lean down. "Yes, I think it could be the Jinn… the shadow people… whatever we call them is not important," he said in a low voice.

"Aren't they the same?"

"I don't know. Something is traveling inside the storm, and it's not friendly. Its hatred is all-consuming. Tell the soldiers to sweep the village as fast as they can and get back here. We'll leave as soon as we're sure we will leave no one behind," Kevin said. "Everyone, listen up. Geoff and the soldiers will help you locate everyone in the village who is not yet here. You do not need to bring anything with you. If everyone you know is here, stay put. We'll leave in fifteen minutes," Kevin said.

The murmurs increased in volume.

Geoff raised his voice. "Everyone, calm down. We'll get you all out. We need to remain calm."

"We need more time. It will take us double that to check every property," the soldier said.

"Make sure you're all back within thirty minutes," Kevin said.

The energy drained from the room. With his current energy levels, Kevin needed all he could get to hold open a portal. He should have taken the chance and gotten a zap from Shaun.

"Get them here as fast as you can," he said to Geoff and the soldiers. It was risky, but if he could get only eighty percent of the people back to Olivet, that would have to do for now. He would have to lead them through the portal, because he was the only one experienced enough to do so.

Fleetingly, he wished Tim could be with him. He missed Tim, but he was glad Tim had Seth. It was nice how Seth protected Tim. It would be good to go back to England for him, but Kevin didn't know exactly where he'd be, and he couldn't spare the energy anyway. He could go back to North Carolina and get Jade and Casey. It wouldn't take long. Either of them could lead everyone through, and Casey could give him a boost.

"Where are you going?" Geoff asked as Kevin headed away

from the fireplace.

"I'm heading back to Black Mountain for my friends, Jade and Casey. They can lead the people through the portal while I hold it open."

"I'll do it," Geoff said.

"You've only passed through once. What if you get stuck? It's so peaceful. it's easy to get caught up in the bliss."

"Why don't you just go back for Shaun or Rachel?"

The emotions welled up inside Kevin. He wanted to get Jade and Casey. He was worried about them. Subconsciously, something nagged at him, drawing his attention away from the situation at hand. Shaun should have been his first choice. "You're right, Geoff. I'll go to Olivet and get Shaun. I need somewhere private, away from all these emotions."

"Umm, over there, go through the door behind the reception. You should find the manager's office. You shouldn't be interrupted, but there's no hiding what you're capable of; that cat is already out of the bag."

"I'll meet you back here as soon as I can. Hopefully it won't take me too long."

The physical sensation of the mass behind the clouds churned his insides. He let out a deep breath. "You've got this," he told himself.

The office door was closed. Kevin knocked. "Hello?" the room was empty, and smelled of sanitizer. Filing cabinets were lined up against the left wall. A curved computer screen sat on a wooden desk, a printer to the side. There was only one wall with nothing butting up against it, except a tall, flourishing green plant. Kevin didn't know how it was even still alive. He dragged the heavy pot into the middle of the room, next to the desk. The wall was cool and, as he placed his hand against the wall, he tried to concentrate on Shaun in the underground city of Olivet. But the images of Jade kept flashing in his mind. He opened his eyes and readjusted his focus onto Shaun. As soon as the portal opened, he stepped through, and Jade entered his mind.

The air was fresh and the grass springy. All the way to the lake, the cabin lights glowed, illuminating the people in the community, but they were scared, running for their lives. Casey levitated a group of people up onto the roof of the community hall. Jade rammed a spear into a tall, gaunt, skeletal creature. *What the hell is going on?* Kevin thought.

He was torn. He wanted to get her out of there, but he couldn't risk getting hurt. The people at Whistler were counting on him. Jade didn't need him. She had Mingan, and he trusted Casey to watch over her. The anguish of not reaching out to help was overwhelming, and he had to do something. She was near the community hall, in the thick of the battle. He collapsed the portal and was running towards her when a preacher man wearing a hat magically appeared in the middle of the battle.

Dark energy flowed like a river around the man. It was the same as the feeling Kevin had sensed inside the storm. This was a supernatural entity, taking the form of a man. But inside the storm at Whistler Mountain were hundreds of dark entities. Jade broke away and ran into the woods with others from the community.

If Kevin didn't get her now, he might lose her.

He ran around behind the community hall, hoping to cut Jade off, but a beast jumped from the second floor, knocking Kevin to the ground. Mingan leaped out of the darkness and turned into a wolf in mid-air. The beast pressed down on Kevin's abdomen, trying to bite his face, but suddenly evaporated into smoke, along with the wolf. By the time Kevin got up and peeked around the side of the building, Jade was gone, and so was Casey.

Kevin resisted his instinct to look for them as he raised his hands, visualized Shaun's glowing blue sapphire, and stepped through the portal and into the bunker. He was back in the restaurant on the lower ground of the compound, and Delilah was there, as if she was waiting for him. He had underestimated the level of her connectedness.

"What do you need?" she asked urgently.

"We have a village of people to clear and transport, and I need Shaun to guide them through the portal while I hold it open. There's a storm coming, and it might be a vehicle for hundreds of revengeful Jinn. It could just be a massive storm cell, but I don't think it is."

"Homebase, copy? Come in, Gil?" They waited for an answer, but all they got was static.

"Alpha One. Abraham, you copy," Delilah said.

"Copy," Abraham replied.

"Is everything all right up there?" she asked.

"Nothing we can't handle."

"Roger. Is Shaun with you?"

"Shaun's on site. What do you need?" Abraham asked.

"Kevin's back and needs Shaun's help. Can you send him down to the Atrium?" Delilah said.

Kevin let his mind rest and focused his attention on the two tower elevators, searching for Shaun.

"He's on his way."

"Thanks," Kevin said to Delilah as she walked over to him at the window.

He fixed his eyes on the closest elevator, waiting for Shaun to step out.

"I'll meet him at the elevator," Kevin said.

"You've got this," Delilah said.

Just hearing the words made his heart skip. Tim was the only one who ever said that to him. In that moment, Kevin feared for Tim's life.

"Why did you say that?" Kevin pushed his hair off his face so he could read her eyes.

"It just came to me. I see you beyond the here and now. I see you traversing the galaxy. So, for that to happen, whatever is happening now is only a stepping stone for you."

"What do you mean by traversing the universe? Why did you use those words, 'you've got this'? Why those exact words?" Alarm bells went off inside his head. There were too many people he cared about scattered around the world. He couldn't keep them safe. He had to hurry and get everyone back together again. They had to stick together. It was too risky to be so far apart.

"Like I said, they just came to me. Are you alright?" she asked.

"Yeah. Yeah. Thanks. I see Shaun. I've got to go."

Kevin jogged towards Shaun. "I need you to come with me. Can you do that?"

"Sure. I'm all yours. What's wrong?" Shaun was covered in dust.

"We found at least fifty people alive, and they're ready to come to Olivet. They're waiting for us to return."

"Waiting for you? Is Geoff okay?" Shaun said.

"Geoff's okay, as far as I know. He was when I left him. But I don't think Jade and Casey are. I'm worried about Tim, too. I feel like my insides are being ripped out." It surprised Kevin how easily he surrendered his emotions to Shaun.

"Take it easy, K. One thing at a time. Let's get those people back here, and then we can check on Jade and Casey. Focus, K. Take me to Geoff."

Trying to calm himself, Kevin exhaled, as if blowing through a straw. The image of Geoff bending down and his lips moving between the slits of his ginger beard came to mind, along with the office with the row of filing cabinets against the wall. He managed to open the portal back into the office he had left.

Kevin led Shaun out from behind the reception desk. People were rushing around, yelling, and boarding up the windows.

"What the hell's going on?" Shaun asked.

"There seems to be a force hiding in the storm; possibly an army of shadow entities or Jinn, heading for the village. I'd bet my life on it." He wanted to take back those words. He was never a hundred percent certain. But he had to trust himself if these people were going to have a fighting chance.

Geoff came through the front door of the lodge with a small child in his arms and a woman pushing a wheelchair. It was the woman in the puffy ski jacket, who had panicked before he left. Geoff helped to get her family and bring them safely to the lodge. The wind howled through the building, sending a shiver up Kevin's spine.

Geoff put the child on the couch by the fire, and marched towards them. He stretched out his hand to Shaun. Kevin could feel the love and admiration Geoff had for him. The feelings were mutual. "It's good to have you here." Geoff pulled Shaun in for a bear hug.

"I'm glad I can help. What's the status?" Shaun moved out of the embrace.

Shaun forever amazed Kevin. He loved him like an older brother; he was so proud of him, it made him tear up. Quickly, he hid his tears and forced his eyes to stay open until the unshed tears dried up.

"You need to do your thing and start transporting people out of here. The west and central areas of the village are clear. But the storm cell is about to touch down," Geoff said.

"Do we know how many entities? Or what type is inside the cell?" Shaun asked.

"They're not friendly. It's not coming to protect us. Whatever they are, they think they have the element of surprise. They reek of revenge. That's all I can tell you. I don't know how many, but it feels like an army," Kevin said.

"I should've brought Etain. Let's get these people out of here," Shaun said.

"What do you want us to do?" Geoff asked.

"Get everyone to form a line. Make sure they are clear about no weapons."

"Shaun, help Geoff while I open the portal." Kevin searched for a discreet place to open it, but it didn't matter where; they all had dreamed of him getting them out of here. They all probably dreamed of the portal. He should have asked.

Kevin placed his hand on the stone wall of the fireplace – as good a place as any.

As people lined up, there were murmurs of concern for those that had not yet arrived, worry their friends and family were going to be left behind. It reminded Kevin of the days when they had queued at boarding gates at the airport, waiting for a voice on the PA system to tell them it was their turn to board. Those days were long gone.

The woman pushing the wheelchair spoke softly to the child Geoff had carried into the lodge. Her demeanor had changed considerably now that she had her family with her. The child clutched a doll. Kevin got to work, and drew in the energy from the atmosphere. The memory of flying over the pyramids came into his mind. It was like they were calling him. He thought about it for a moment, but the sounds of the frightened people behind him helped him to aim his focus on the bunker. It would be best to take them to the bunker, rather than the campsite outside the Sphinx.

As he built up the energy, the vibrant membrane of the portal took form and people suddenly went quiet. Kevin turned around. They were all mesmerized by the colors and the sparks of the energy waves. The line of people wormed around the lodge and down into the bar area.

"Ready?" Kevin said to the little girl.

"Ready!" she said, holding on to the side of the wheelchair.

"Shaun!" Kevin yelled. Shaun, at the back of the room, flicked his head up, registering Kevin. He excused himself, and hurried to the front of the line.

"What's up?"

"I'm ready. First, I'll go through with this girl and her family, and make sure it's the right destination, then I'll come back. Be ready with the next group of people," Kevin said.

"No worries, K, all good."

"Everyone, listen up! Keep your children close. Put your hand on the shoulder of the person in front of you. Parents, hold your children's hands tight. Carry them if you can," Kevin said. There was a murmur of concern. "There's no cause for alarm."

The roof groaned, as if it was being pulled up by the sweeping storm. Kevin shouted over the noise. "I'm asking you to do this not for safety, but speed. The portal's energy feels so good, you'll never want to leave. All your ailments will disappear." The murmurs turned into eagerness.

A guy on crutches moved out of the line and shouted to Kevin, "Can I come up the front?"

The man was in his early thirties, and had a young woman with him.

There was no need for Kevin to answer, as the people graciously made room for the couple to move to the front of the line. Kevin took hold of the little girl's hand; it was hot and clammy. He smiled at her. "It's going to be okay," he said as he pushed the wheelchair with one hand and together they stepped forward into the portal's membrane.

Kevin could feel the goodness flow through the little girl and him. He tugged them out the other side, into the bunker where Delilah waited. She helped the people orientate themselves and find seats before they began taking their names. Healed, the old woman in the wheelchair pushed her gaunt body up out of the chair with a new lease of life. The man with the broken leg propped his crutches against the side of the table, sat down in a chair, and pulled the plaster from his leg.

Kevin went back and held open the portal for Shaun to lead the next group through. Hands on shoulders, people followed each other, and quickly entered the portal. The lodge door burst open with more survivors.

"Is that everyone?" Geoff asked the soldier.

"No. sir. There are people caught up on the eastern side of the village. We moved towards their cries for help, but we couldn't find them. The storm is getting stronger, and there's – well, I don't know what they are, but an army of shadows materializing from the fog."

"Get them through the portal," Geoff said.

"Melody! Has anyone seen Melody?" Logan shouted.

Panicked, Logan shouted out Melody's name. Kevin recalled he had seen her outside, playing with the cub.

"Maybe she went through with one of the others?" Geoff said.

"I can't leave until I find her. And my sister and her children aren't here, either. They're on the eastern side of the village." Logan removed baby Brody from his pouch and handed him to Geoff.

"I'll get them. It will be all right." Kevin, conscious of his body language, worried he would reveal the hopelessness he was picking up from Logan.

But the man put on a brave face, kissing baby Brody goodbye in order to go find his missing daughter and his sister's family. It was a tug-a-war of emotions, which he tried to dismiss and hide from the others.

"Geoff, join the line. Once you're through, I will collapse the portal, and I'll help find Melody, and Logan's sister," Kevin said.

"I'm not leaving without you," Geoff said.

"You have to." Kevin could feel his energy draining. Suddenly, the portal collapsed. Kevin pushed his hair back off his face and pushed out his hands to create a new one, hoping the last person had made it through okay. He was sweating with exhaustion. He could use a zap of energy from Casey right about now.

As soon as the portal was open, Shaun stepped through. He must have seen it collapse and reform.

"What's wrong?" Shaun said, searching the almost-empty foyer.

"It's all good. I've got it sorted. Get these last few people and the soldiers through," Kevin said, trying to hold it together.

"I'm not leaving you. Something's wrong."

"Geoff, you go. Take them all straight through. Got it?" Shaun said, looking at Kevin.

As soon as the last person went through, only Shaun, Kevin, and Logan remained.

Black fog drifted in and out from under the main entrance. The fire went out and black smoke billowed down the chimney.

"It's the Jinn," Kevin said, exhausted.

"What the hell!" said Shaun.

7

—————

SHADOWS OF THE UNSEEN: SHAUN. WHISTLER MOUNTAIN.

"This way," Logan said.

Shaun waited for Kevin, who had his head in his hands. He wasn't moving, and had expelled way too much energy. Shaun grabbed Kevin's arm, wrapped it around his shoulders, and then followed Logan down a flight of stairs. "Where are you taking us?"

"The parking lot. We can take a car. There's plenty down there."

"What makes you think we can see through the black clouds out there? And what's going to stop them coming through the vents into the car?" Shaun stopped on the stairwell landing and sat Kevin down against the wall. "Take my hands." Shaun crouched in front of him.

Kevin reached out his very pale hand.

"What are you doing? We have to keep moving," Logan urged.

"Just wait a minute. Kevin used up all his strength, opening a portal to save your community. You can give him a few minutes to recharge," Shaun snapped, igniting the icosahedron sapphire in the palm of his hand. Blue light traveled from his hands into Kevin's entire body, creating a massive boost of energy.

"Thanks. I needed that. I'm glad you didn't blast me to pieces."

"So am I. But it was worth the risk." Shaun gave Kevin a cheeky smile.

"You good to go?" Logan asked.

"Yeah. We're good," Shaun said.

Logan was right about one thing: the lot had plenty of cars. Shaun guessed the occupants had become infected at the beginning of the apocalypse, and had died on the mountain. Logan turned around, probably because he couldn't hear their footsteps.

"How many people made it out of here?" Shaun asked.

"I worked on the lifts during the winter and my family, and my sister's family, came too. My sister, Rebecca, lost her husband, and I lost my wife about a year ago, to the virus. My sister doesn't want to leave. She hopes they'll come back.

"Melody might have gone to get my sister and her boys. She acts more grown-up than her aunt sometimes. Melody had a dream about you, but Rebecca didn't. She woke up screaming, waking her two boys. When they entered her room to see what was wrong, she said it was like a spell had been broken and then she'd woken up. Rebecca said she dreamed of an army of black shadows coming for her. During the night she would wake paralyzed, and said a shadow of a man stood in the doorway. She believes one dream is a calling from God, and the other a calling from the Devil." Logan kept testing car doors.

"What dream did Melody have?" Shaun was thinking of the people in the Middle East.

"It was about him."

Shaun turned to see that Logan was pointing at Kevin, who had wandered off. "K, what are you doing?"

"There has to be an office where the car keys are kept," Kevin said.

"Shit. Why didn't I think of that earlier?" Logan exclaimed.

"You're worried about Melody."

"The keys are upstairs in the lobby," Logan began heading back to the stairwell.

"Wait. I'll go. Just tell me where they are," Shaun said.

"Near the front door, there is a lectern where the stuffed bear is, and behind it is a door to the concierge's room, where car keys and luggage are stored," Logan told him.

"Do I need a key to get into the room?"

"It's not locked," Logan assured Shaun, as he jogged to the stairway they had just descended.

"Stay here, K, I'll be right back." Shaun ran for the door marked 'exit'. When he had first arrived at the underground city over a week ago, he had searched for such a door. Now he wished he were back at the bunker. It was a lot safer than being out here. Shaun touched the door with his hand. It was cold. He scanned the bottom of the door for the black fog he had seen drifting under the entrance to the lodge. Nothing. Slowly, he opened the door and peered into the lobby. The black-and-gray clouds were pushed against the outside of the unboarded windows.

Shaun spotted the bear and the lectern in front of the concierge's door. Inside, he grabbed as many keys as he could, knowing that just because they had the keys didn't mean the cars would start. The fuel could be bad. There was plenty of electricity, so he took a key with a symbol that resembled the shape of a cat's nose. Shaun hoped the car it belonged to was there and would work. He had wanted to ride an electric motorcycle, which would never happen, but an electric car would be fun too. It was such a different world, and he wished he had made different choices growing up. *It is what it is,* he thought. He was just born at the wrong time. Or maybe not.

A door banged closed. The wind whistled under the door. Something clattered to the floor. "Who's there?" Shaun peeked out of the concierge's room.

There was the sound of another door banging closed. He twisted around, and scanned the room. The main doors had opened. He could see the stuffed grizzly out of the corner of his eye, as a man's shadow took residence in the doorway. There was no visible man to cast such a shadow. In the likeness of a man, the shadow stepped forward, then another appeared, and then another. The first was taller, bigger, more dominant, and the others slightly smaller and hunched over. The tones and density of the shadows were different, like ink smudges.

Evil had arrived.

Shaun froze. He willed himself to move, to run. His heart beat so fast he thought he was going to die. He clutched the keys tight. The only thing he could control was his thinking. Shaun connected with the icosahedron embedded in the flesh of his hand, and a blue haze surrounded his being in a flash. His shoulders dropped, and he moved his neck from side to side, cracking it before sprinting for the exit to the stairwell and leaping down the first set of steps, dropping car keys.

As he burst through the door to the parking area where he had left Kevin, he pushed the key button with the shape of a cat's nose, hoping it would work. Kevin and Logan were waiting in the middle of the car park as Shaun searched for the car's flashing headlights. "Over there!" he pointed.

Kevin and Logan ran over to the unlocked vehicle. "Get in." Shaun jumped into the driver's seat.

"Wait," Logan said, and grabbed the car door before Shaun closed it. "Do you know where you're going?"

Seeing Logan's point, Shaun jumped out and ran around the back, nearly tripping over Kevin, who was detaching the charging hose from the charging station. Kevin jumped into the back of the sedan and Shaun climbed into the front passenger seat.

"Man. You know how to pick them. What happened upstairs? Your heart is racing," Kevin said, buckling up.

"Dark fog entered the lobby – shadow men, or maybe the first of the Jinn army. The storm outside the lodge sounds violent. Visibility will be bad." Next to a pair or violet mittens near his feet was a map of the village. Shaun picked it up and handed it over the back of the seat to Kevin, who snapped the map open.

Logan drove up to the yellow box with a silver button that controlled the opening and closing of the lot's parking arm, blocking their exit.

"Please don't tell me we need a fucking code to drive out," Shaun said, pulling the visor down and staring into the mirror. Kevin had his head down, reading the map, making it easy for Shaun to see out the back window. The ghostly figures that moved and looked like shadows hadn't followed him down into the underground parking lot.

"What do you think they want? Maybe we could reason with them," Logan said.

"I think it's best we pray to God they don't catch up with us," Kevin said.

Shaun never had much faith growing up. Not after his father stole the Emerald Tablet from the tomb of Thoth. That was the catalyst for the beginning of the end. Not just for him, but for all mankind.

What a legacy. His father had released the first wave of evil and, soon after, his mother had died of cancer. At least she didn't suffer the plague of evil. Shaun lost all faith that day, and believed God was a cruel joke. But Sophia had changed his mind and heart. Her faith in God was so strong that she literally walked through fire to save the world from a fate that had been decided millennia ago. Like everyone else, Shaun missed Sophia. The absence of her physical presence was very real. "You've got to have faith in something," Shaun said to Logan.

"Yes, I do. Him. I dreamed of you, Kevin, and you're here. Never have I seen any sign that God is with me."

"He's the silent partner in our lives that's always supporting us," Kevin said.

Shaun could tell that Logan was getting uncomfortable talking about spirituality. "Let's just get the fuck out of here and get back to our mission to find the survivors."

The garage roller doors opened. An ominous dark cloud covered the exit of the car park. Lightning sparked inside the churning clouds that had touched down like a tornado. The car lights and fog lights came on automatically. The car didn't make a sound; it didn't even purr like a kitten. Logan let the car idle.

"I'm going to floor it straight through the clouds. I know the road and its curves."

"Wait, where are we on the map? We need to have a sense of direction before we take a leap of faith into that!" Kevin said, pulling his seatbelt at the shoulder, moving forward and placing the map on the armrest between the two front seats, for Logan and Shaun to see.

Logan put the car in park and took the map. He turned it sideways. "Here, building number five, south of the village center. We need to go here, the upper side on Blackcomb Mountain – it's east of here, building number seventy-eight." Logan tapped down hard on the map.

"That looks easy enough," Shaun said.

"It shouldn't take long at all. I'm going this way." Logan traced his finger along Whistler Way. "We'll go north around the village and onto Village Gate Way, then onto Blackcomb Way, which will take us right to lodge seventy-eight. It looks like the long way around, but it's our best bet."

"We're in your neck of the woods. We'll leave it up to you." Kevin let go of Shaun's seat and sat back.

Logan released the handbrake, took a few breaths, and sped out of the underground parking lot. Shaun braced for the impact.

8

INSIDE THE DARK REALM: KEVIN. CANADA.

From the moment they left the parking lot, it was like being at the heart of a storm. Black clouds churned above so that it was as if they were underwater, looking up, everything in shades of gray and black. Desolate. The world had lost all its color. It reminded him of Jade's description of the Realm of Lost Souls. It would be very easy to get lost in a place like this. The air on his tongue tasted like cardboard. The trees had lost their color as if doomed, left to wither and die.

"Stop the car." Kevin unlocked and opened his door before the car came to a complete stop. "What is this place?" He took a few steps away from the car. Snow fell, and he held out his hand and touched the flakes with his index finger. Ash. Not snow. Ash was falling around them. Under the clouds, the world had gone silent. The life, sucked away from the atmosphere. The ash was building up along the street, like snow.

"K, get back in the car. It's not safe."

"It feels like nothing, like limbo, worse than death. Purgatory."

Kevin coughed, his lungs rejecting the thick soot-like air. He coughed and choked, and wished he had a mask to filter the air. Whatever lived in this energy was not truly alive.

Kevin stepped back, touched the car door, and climbed back into the car. Logan revved the engine and the car skidded as he made a right-hand turn. In the storm, sound was muted, flat, like listening through walls with a glass. The car spluttered as if the engine wasn't getting enough air or fuel, its pipes clogging, like a plane's engine in the fallen ash of a volcano. But the car was electric, and didn't have an air filter.

The storm reminded Kevin of a pyroclastic cloud. They were under an ocean of pyroclastic evil.

Everything was the color of gunmetal gray, smoky gray, blue-gray, black-gray, silver-gray. It was like just before the whiteout, when they were stuck in a parallel world, witnessing life return to New York. It, too, had been multiple shades of black and gray before the color returned.

"We're in a different realm, but how?" Logan said.

"How do you know that?" Shaun said, turning around in his seat, as if he could gauge from Kevin's facial expression what he thought about what Logan had said.

"I think he's right. It's a merger. But I thought we would have more time. We've got weeks to go. Let's just pray this is an anomaly. It hadn't begun back at the campsite, or at Olivet. Maybe this is the first," Kevin said.

"Let's not waste time speculating. Let's get the others and get out of the lodge," Shaun said.

The car jerked, labored, then stopped. Logan pushed the ignition.

"Have we run out of juice?" Shaun asked.

"No, it's fully charged. I think we'll have to go on foot from here."

Ash settled upon Kevin's face. He lifted the hood of his three-tone jacket. White, black, and gray. How appropriate. The white would soon look gray, and he would blend perfectly into the dark realm. He trudged through the mounting ash behind Logan, feeling everything in this dark realm was the embodiment of the living dead. Logan checked the vehicles along the way, to see if any of them worked.

"Dozens of people used these cars just this morning. I don't understand it. They were running perfectly fine. It'll take us about thirty minutes to walk along the road, but there's a quicker way." Logan pointed to a gray stone building which said 'mountain bike rentals and lessons', in bold white letters. "Can you ride?"

"Yeah." Shaun said.

Desperate to find his daughter, Logan stood outside the store and started yelling her name at the top of his lungs. "Melody! Melody, where are you, baby girl?"

In the dark realm, Logan's voice didn't travel very far, no matter how loud he called. If she was in the dark realm, she wouldn't hear him. A bird fell off a pine tree next to the bike track. More birds, trapped under the storming clouds, dropped from the sky. Empty gondolas hung motionless.

Kevin turned and pretended to be interested in the mountain-bike track and mounds for jumping and tricks; anything to distract him from the dead birds. He could feel Logan's blood pressure surge, and the tendons in his neck suddenly went taunt. Logan's emotions were spinning out of control, and rapidly draining Kevin, who didn't know if he was going to be able to find the stamina he would need to push back the painful emotions and the negative energy in the dark realm, never mind ride a bicycle up a mountain. "Logan, take a minute."

"Logan, can you imagine the villa where your sister is staying?" Shaun glanced at Kevin.

"Of course. She was supposed to get my nephews up and ready to go by three this afternoon." Logan opened the door to the mountain-bike rental store.

It was bathed in color, the atmosphere clear and light; the ugliness of the dark realm had not yet entered the building. Kevin looked around, trying to work out why, what prevented the dense fog of the dark realm from entering the building.

Logan waited to catch his breath while Shaun sized up the bicycles, picking out one for himself. Kevin didn't think Shaun had ever owned a bicycle growing up. He'd had only the ones he had stolen, and Kevin could never understand why. Shaun's dad was loaded; Shaun could've had anything he wanted. But over the past few months, Kevin realized that all Shaun really wanted was a family. A father who didn't resent him for looking too much like his dead mom.

Kevin picked out a mountain bike for himself, and checked the tires were firm. He found some bandanas and gave one to Logan. "This might help us keep the ash out of our lungs."

Shaun tested his bike. "Why don't you open a portal to the lodge where Logan's sister is? It's worth a try."

No matter how much he would like to open a portal, and no matter how optimistic he was, he could feel he didn't have the energy. His muscles were like jelly. "No harm trying."

"But shouldn't he conserve what energy he has, to get us all safely out of here?" Logan asked. "If it takes half an hour to walk, then it should take less than ten minutes to ride up there. Then, those that we find can help search for Melody. I just pray she hasn't gone into the woods to find a family of bears to adopt the cub. We can't search the woods on our own. We need help."

"I could give you another boost."

"I'm eager, but not that eager. Save it for later." Kevin unrealistically imagined the boost would blast him across the room and his hair would end up smoldering.

He focused on the energy in the room. With his hands outstretched, he touched Logan's temples, drawing on the image in Logan's head. The air crackled around them as the portal opened. Kevin strained to gather the speckles of light and compress them. He could feel the tendons in his neck tighten, and the tension in his forehead as he willed the energy in the atmosphere to split and open a doorway to the lodge, where Logan's sister was waiting. It was too difficult. He let his arms drop. His shoulders slouched. "We should just ride. This way, we can search for Melody along the way."

Shaun had already thrown his leg over his chosen bike, and pulled the bandana around his neck, up over his mouth. "I'm good to go."

Logan readied himself. "If we find it hard to breathe, we can stop at the first aid and medical station for oxygen."

"That's a good idea," Kevin said.

"You're going to get us all out of here, aren't you?" Logan's knuckles turned white as he gripped the wide handlebars.

"I'll do my best." Kevin folded the map Shaun had found in the car and tucked it into the zipper pocket on his left arm. He loosened the strap around his right leg, which secured his bowie knife. Shaun wasn't wearing his sheath; he had left it back at Casey's estate. "Why didn't you bring your bowie knife?"

"I've got Casey's Swiss Army knife. That's all I need, because I've got this..." Shaun held up his hand, and with a slight push outward, a blue light shot from his hand and blasted the manikin that was dressed for a summer hike.

"That's cool," Logan said.

Shaun was trying not to smile, but Kevin could feel the resistance in him and smiled back. Kevin allowed Shaun's pride to wash through him as Shaun allowed his smile through.

Kevin took in a deep breath, preparing to enter the dark realm, ready for the stale air and the absence of the light energy particles he relied on. He had read that in some places, where it was often gray, dark and cloudy, people needed light therapy to aid in the relief of depression caused by the lack of sunlight. He couldn't imagine surviving too long in a place without sunlight; it was his life force.

They rolled through the center of town and, ignoring the ghostly sounds of the dark realm, they crossed a creek, stopping at a few stores and motels along the way to catch their breath and clean out their lungs, while always praying Melody was inside. Sometimes, a strange sensation crawled up Kevin's back; the emptiness of the absence of everything familiar was replaced by eerie, distant noises that penetrated the silence.

Quickly, they rode past the lift ticket booth and a sushi bar, before crossing over Blackcomb Way. Kevin's heart raced to pump blood around his body, which was feeling like soup. He rode ahead and took the lead, searching for a place to stop and making a dash up a side street, to a Holiday Inn. Shaun and Logan followed. Kevin climbed off his bicycle and set the kickstand before racing into the motel.

Once inside, he put his hands on his knees and drew in deep breaths. Shaun and Logan did the same.

Logan spat gray muck from his chest. "Dammit! My chest hurts. The thicker the fog, the harder it is to breathe. The ash is clogging up our lungs. The amount of time we can stay in the dark realm is getting shorter and shorter." Logan rubbed his head and eyes and then kicked the wall, frustrated.

"We'll find her," Kevin said.

"He's right, we'll find her," Shaun agreed.

Logan didn't wait for any more reassurance and Kevin couldn't blame him. They took in a few deep breaths, like pearl divers. Kevin had often swum underwater and could hold his breath for three minutes. The best place in the world was underwater. He jumped on his bicycle and caught up with Logan and Shaun. They rode past half-empty parking lots, and didn't bother stopping at the stop signs, or at pedestrian walkways. He imagined the trees would have been green and full of spring colors.

Kevin looked over his shoulder. Seeing flickers of movement, at first, he thought it was a jackal coming for him. He nearly fell off his bike. But it disappeared in a puff of smoke. The ash had stopped falling. They rode along the valley trail and came to a bridge. He looked down under the bridge. Had something moved at the edge of a rush of water moving like rapids?

Kevin loved water. His favorite times were in the ocean, a river, or a swimming pool. They were his go-to places. But the body of water that flowed underneath the bridge wasn't something he wanted to connect with.

Logan stopped at the edge of the bridge.

"Why are you stopping?" Shaun yelled.

"I thought I saw something moving across the footbridge over there." Logan pointed a few feet down the bank.

"There's no footbridge. I don't see anything but shadows. Ugly black shadows that shouldn't be there, because there's no sun."

Kevin couldn't agree more with Shaun. "Let's keep going. We're seeing things."

Logan put his foot on the pedal and, standing up, coasted cautiously across the wooden bridge. Shadows drifted like clouds along the bank of the creek. A flicker of movement caught Kevin's eye. Logan stood tall on the pedals, letting his bike slow down. *Maybe he sees them too?* Kevin thought.

Logan turned his body around at the waist, enough to look back. "Did you see that?"

"It's just a flicker of light," Shaun said.

So, they all had seen it.

"I can see a shadow under the water. Oh God no, maybe it's Melody. I can see her. She's reaching out for me. Hurry, help me, she's bleeding," Logan shouted over his shoulder as he ran to the water's edge.

"Wait up!" Before Kevin could drop his bike, Logan had rolled off the bridge and dismounted his bike. He let the bike drop to the ground, raced down the side of the creek, and slipped into the water. The current pulled him under. Kevin ran upstream, with Shaun after him. Logan's head popped up. Together, Kevin and Shaun reached out and grabbed him, pulling him up and out of the brown water.

Logan lay on the bank and coughed up dirty water.

"What were you thinking?" Shaun yelled at him.

Kevin didn't have the breath to say anything. He just wanted to get back on the bike, and get out of there as quickly as possible.

"I thought Melody was reaching out of the water. She was drowning. Piranhas tore at her flesh, eating her alive." Logan peered into the water. "See the blood? The river is turning red. Oh dear God." Logan went to jump in again.

Shaun caught him. "There's nothing there! It's gray. There is no blood. And there are no piranhas."

Confused, Logan pushed his wet hair back, smoothing it over

his head. "I could've sworn Melody was there. The piranhas… the blood in the river… all of it, I swear."

"Did you see anything, K?"

"Nothing." Kevin threw his right leg over the bike. "Let's get a move on. The energy of the dark realm is messing with his head." On the other side of the bridge, a faint haze moved; something invisible was standing there, watching. Logan climbed on his bike, took the lead, and headed down a bike path lined with gray and black trees that could have been hiding a thousand shadows.

They went under an overpass, then stopped and carried the bikes up the stairs. If they were going to get out of there via a portal, he was going to need a blast from Shaun and suffer the consequences. It had worked well in the stairway back at the lodge, there was no reason for him to be anxious.

They headed onto the Upper Valley Way and stopped at Merlin's Bar for a rest and fresh air. The bar did not differ from the other buildings. Logan coughed up blood, then wiped his mouth on his sleeve. Kevin pretended not to notice, and went behind the bar to find some snacks and a drink. There wasn't much left in the vending machine. The glass was smashed, but not all the food was taken. Kevin helped himself to a packet of nuts, a trail mix, and a sports drink. He reached in and just took what he wanted; something he couldn't get used to doing. Alone at the bar, he began to eat his snacks, then suddenly Kevin stopped chewing; the hair on the back of his neck spiked, his body tensed. There was a presence behind him. He swallowed. "Hello!" Kevin quickly swiveled around in his seat. "Hello, is someone there?"

The room was empty. Logan and Shaun were nowhere to be seen. Kevin turned back to his orange sports drink, and gulped it halfway down. He could feel the energy returning. This was the longest ten-minute ride he had ever done. It was the dark realm that was making it difficult.

The hair on the back of his neck rose. "Hello, who's there?" He got off the seat and tossed the handful of trail mix into his mouth as he searched the bar area. From behind the kitchen door, unseen emotions spiraled towards him. Fear.

"Shaun, where are you?" His voice echoed and Shaun yelled back, but not from behind the door. Shaun was somewhere back near the entrance. Kevin put his hand on the door, pushed it opened, and peeked inside.

Someone shoved the door back into his face. He stumbled backward, holding his bloody nose. Three men and one woman rushed out the door and started beating into Kevin. He rolled into a ball to protect himself. Pain exploded through his back with every blow. His ribs cracked. He gasped for air. Lights flickered in front of his eyes, and everything was going blurry. He was on the edge of consciousness.

"K! Kevin, what's wrong?"

Shaun's voice was far away. Too far to reach Kevin before he passed out or died. Yet suddenly, all the pain disappeared, and it was easy to breathe again. He slowly opened his eyes, and a blue angel radiated its energy towards him, covering his whole being. It was beautiful.

"Kevin, wake up!"

The blue angel was next to him, and smelled of salted nuts. Kevin wanted to reach out and touch the angel that had emotions just like him.

"Kevin, come on, dude, snap out of it."

Kevin blinked, and Shaun's face materialized over the blue angel's. Reality returned.

"There's four people in the kitchen. They attacked me. We need to leave, now!" Kevin got to his feet and touched his face, looking for the blood.

"No one is here. You were wriggling on the ground, hallucinating. No one is here but us," Shaun told him.

Kevin examined his ribs, feeling for protruding bones. He seemed to be intact, and there was no blood. Nothing hurt.

"We can't drop our guard, even out of the dark realm; something is following us and getting inside our heads. Making us see things that aren't real," Shaun said.

"It's evil; the dark realm infiltrating our minds. The longer we're in it, the more influence it seems to have over us," Logan said.

"Where is the army of shadows that the soldiers spoke of? Why haven't we encountered them?" Logan asked as they made their way back to the entrance to leave Merlin's Bar.

"Maybe we are encountering them differently. They showed themselves to me when I was getting the keys, so why not now?" Shaun reasoned.

"They want us to fear the unknown. There's more than one type of entity messing with us. Anything sinister could come out from the dark realm," Kevin said.

FLAGS OF MANY NATIONS, once a colorful display, and the symbol of the Winter Olympics, a symbol of unity, lifeless on top of awnings that covered the entrances to storage rentals and stores.

There were more stairs to ride down, and the fear of an illusion slowed their pace. The churning clouds above seemed closer the further they moved up the mountain. They passed a glitter tattoo hub, with something painted on the side that Kevin imagined was supposed to be a sparkling sailboat.

Jumping the bikes down a few steps, they rode across a mini-golf course, ditching the road.

Logan ducked as if he, too, could see the clouds getting closer. "What gives?" Shaun asked Kevin.

"I don't know." They reached a point where the clouds and the ground met.

Logan stopped. "My sister's lodge should be a few yards away, just beyond the clouds. Should we go through them, or try to find a way around?"

"Let's go through them," Shaun said.

"We'll be blinded. Damn the dark realm," Logan said.

"I think that's already been done." Shaun got off his bike. "Stay close to me and we'll walk through under a hermetic shield."

"A what?" Logan said.

Shaun stretched his arms out and created a blue hermetic shield around them. Slowly, they moved forward, pushing their bikes through the bubbling clouds. The force of the turbulent clouds barreled down, as if trying to compress the shield. Flashes of brilliant white lightning fueled the storm, as clouds rumbled around them. Strikes of black lightning, something he didn't know even existed, brought dense, gray, human-like shadows that charged at the shield, pushing them back into the dark realm. Shaun pushed his shield forward and the pocket of his jeans glowed with a brilliant white light. The purity of the energy was inviting Kevin to drink like a thirsty vampire as Shaun forged a way through the storming clouds that marked the edge of the dark realm.

9

THE FALLEN: SHAUN. CANADA.

Shaun checked their surroundings to ensure they were safely out of the dark realm before he stopped the flow of the icosahedron energy. The greenness of the trees was startling against the magnificent sky, and the blend of the earthy, natural colors filled their vision. The stone lodge was, as Logan said, a few yards away. Shaun spotted two couples frantically waving from the second-story window. Visibility changed as he reduced the shield and the platonic stones in his pocket stopped radiating the brilliant white light. The absence of the light was shocking. The sudden darkness was blinding. Shaun waited for his eyes to adjust. He focused on the couples at the window. Both men had beards.

"Do you know those people?" Shaun asked.

"Yes, the redhead is Mable. Her husband is Sam. The guy next to him, wearing the LA baseball cap, is his best mate Colin and his wife, Brenda. Brenda and Mable are sisters. Colin and Brenda had a son and a daughter, who were infected by the evil plague before the whiteout. They had a dream that led them to Blackcomb Mountain."

Shaun thought about all the crazies, and senseless murders he had witnessed at the beginning of the Apocalypse. They advanced to the main entrance and Logan pushed on the door, but it wouldn't open.

"They barricaded it from the inside. I don't understand. It wasn't like this before," Logan said, looking up at the window again.

Shaun and Kevin followed Logan around to a staff entrance, and Colin let them in. He checked behind Shaun to make sure no one was following.

"Is Melody here?" Logan asked.

"No. Isn't she with you?" Colin asked and then hurried on without waiting for an answer. "Did you see the shadows? It's dark and there are shadows. She might be with Rebecca, on the other side of the lodge. But Logan, the Norwoods are missing. The whole family just disappeared. One minute they were there, the next minute they were gone. Strange things started happening when the storm rolled down from the hill. Go look out the back. The clouds are there, too. They're on all fronts. The storm is surrounding us, as if we are somehow protected on the inside. But shadowy creatures keep popping in and out of existence. They snatched the people downstairs as they left the building. The Carsons were dragged into the storm. We tried to pull them back. I touched one of the shadow creatures and my fingers slipped through its arm like it was made of smoke."

"How long ago was this?" Kevin interrupted.

"Fifteen, maybe twenty, minutes ago."

"We didn't see anyone inside there. It's all black and gray. Dead-like," Logan told him.

"Listen, and you'll hear the screams," Colin said, holding the door open.

Shaun stepped back outside, and Kevin joined him. They stood quietly, listening for the haunting sounds of people screaming; Shaun wondered if it was just in their imagination, for there were no cries fading into nothingness, just deathly silence.

"Do you hear that?" Kevin asked him as he took a few more steps away from the building, looking up at the mountain behind them.

"I hear nothing," Shaun said.

"Exactly. There should be at least every-day sounds. The creek, frogs, and thunder from within the storm."

"Let's get back inside and get Logan's sister. This place gives me the creeps," Shaun said.

Together, they entered the building.

"What are you doing?" Colin asked as Brenda, Mable, and Sam walked down the stairs.

"We are here to get everyone to a safer place," Logan said as he headed to the other side of the lodge for his family.

"Where?" Brenda shouted after him.

"You're not still going on about the aliens coming to take us home? I know we must have sounded crazy, saying we dreamed of this place... but the stars? Come on, Logan, enough already." Colin's voice was full of irritation.

"See this guy? We told you he would come. The bear, every-thing, just like Melody said it would. Trust us. We can get you out of here," Logan said.

"We're not going anywhere. This has been our home for the past year, and we are not going to run because of a storm and a few shadows," Colin stated.

"It's not just a storm. It's an evil, dark realm you won't want to call home. If you want to leave with us, meet us in the lobby in five minutes. If you're not there, we'll go without you," Logan said, taking the elevator.

"You should listen to him," Kevin said.

There was a rattle of the windows then a crash of glass coming from a room nearby. Shaun raced to the door and peered through the glass pane. The storm had moved closer while they argued. "We're running out of time. The dark realm is closing in."

Kevin held the elevator door open, and Shaun jumped in. They could have easily taken the stairs, but what the hell? It was working, they might as well use it. As soon as they arrived on the third floor, two young boys, about five and seven years old, wrapped their arms around Logan. A woman came out of the apartment after them.

"Rebecca, is Melody with you?" Logan said.

"No. I thought she was with you."

"She was, but she disappeared when we were evacuating the lower part of the village. I'm afraid she took off into the woods to find a family for the bear cub."

The brother and sister stared at each other for a minute. They both looked frightened.

"Like in her dream?" Rebecca said hesitantly.

"Yes. I should've kept a closer eye on her," Logan said, rubbing the back of his head.

Kevin cleared his throat. "What did you dream?"

The question was on the tip of Shaun's tongue.

"This is Kevin, and his friend Shaun. They're here to help us."

"The one from the dreams?" Rebecca asked.

Shaun recalled Logan saying that his sister had dreamed of dark entities from the dark realm. He tried to work out why she would dream of the dark side instead of Kevin. "Can you tell us about your dream?"

Rebecca lowered her head, as if ashamed of what she was about to say, and walked back into her apartment. "Boys, get your things together."

The boys didn't move from her side but she began to tell the others about her dream anyway.

"It was a nightmare. Dark entities entered my room. I was paralyzed. I could hear my children screaming, and there was nothing I could do. Tears had trailed from the corners of my eyes – I couldn't even wipe them away. Human-like shadows dragged people along the hallway. It was like I was outside my body, watching the shadows remove the people from the lodge and take them into a stormy, dark fog. It was as if they were meat for the slaughter. The screams became silence, and I thought it was over. Then a dark, desolate, muscular angel; naked, with sharp teeth and leathery wings, entered the room. It reeked of death. It offered me its flesh. I closed my eyes and refused to acknowledge it presence. It wanted me to see it, to know it was there. A snake wrapped its way up and around the demon's torso. I couldn't tell where the snake ended, and the angel began – it was as if they were one being. Its eyes were narrowed in a frown, its nostrils flared. The sound of a flute filled my ear. Its black, sharp fingernails touched the side of my face, pressing down until it drew blood. I couldn't speak or scream, only move my eyes, but I shut them tight, and wished for him and the nightmare to go. He pressed down upon me, and the pressure crushed my lungs. I thought I was going to die. The snake's tongue touched my lips. I prayed it would go away, that it was all a nightmare. That's when, in my mind, a voice said, 'I am the king of demons, what humans call a fallen. I am the chief of an army of angels that were once known as the Watchers. The race born from the scorching wind and smokeless fire has been summoned, and they will feast on the souls of your loved ones. I have many names, but you can call me Ashmedai. With the other chiefs of ten, we are preparing the way for our leader, Samyazah. This has been foretold. It is the dawn of the last empire. The union of humanoids and the fallen, and you will prostrate yourselves before us and the army born from scorching wind and smokeless fire that shall no longer remain unseen.'" Rebecca shuddered at the memory.

"Then what?" Kevin asked.

"It disappeared. My son George came running into my room and woke me up from the terrifying nightmare. He was crying. My screams had frightened him." She clutched the boy tighter, until his face was squashed between her body and her hand.

"Mum!"

Rebecca glanced down at her son and ruffled his hair. "He's my little hero. He was a premature baby. Struggled against all the odds. Now look how big and strong he is. He's a fighter, this one."

"Let's get our bags," George said to his younger brother.

They both ran off to their bedroom and quickly returned, George struggling and straining to drag the heavy bag.

"Is there anyone else on this floor?" Logan asked.

"There's the old couple. They're still refusing to leave. They still believe their son will come down from the mountain and rescue them," Rebecca said.

"Maybe we should talk to them?" Kevin suggested.

"You can if you like. The storm is pressing up against the windows, and I don't know how much longer the glass will last. You need to get my boys out of here."

"We spoke about this, Rebecca. You're coming with us, even if I have to carry you," Logan said, sticking out his neck and clenching his jaw; frustrated.

"Logan, get Rebecca and the boys downstairs, we're going to have a quick chat with the elderly couple to see if we can persuade them to follow us. What are their names?" Shaun said.

"John and Tina Smith."

* * *

DOWN THE HALL, Shaun paused, mustering up patients before gently knocking on the door. An old man let them in and mumbled to himself. The woman smiled at Kevin and touched his face. John walked off in a huff. "You didn't have the same dream?" Shaun followed John into the kitchen, leaving Kevin with Tina in the living room.

"What makes you say that?" John turned on the kettle.

"You don't seem as pleased to see Kevin as your wife is."

"The angel warned me of the false prophet." John winced in pain as he reached into the cupboard above the sink for two mugs.

With a cup in his hand, he pushed his arm out in Kevin's direction, as if he was going to throw it at him. "Your friend there, he's nothing but the devil's work. He's the false prophet, and is not to be believed."

"Does he look harmful to you?"

"Show me your hands." John snatched Shaun's hands. "Just like the angel said, you are the devil's protector. You have stolen from the throne of God, and you will be punished. You're all damned. Mark my words. He is coming for you."

Tina offered coffee as she walked into the kitchen with Kevin.

"Or would you boys like some tea? You're not from around here, are you?"

"No, Mrs. Smith," said Kevin.

"We're from Australia, but we've been living with our friends in Northmead in England. There's a small community there. They are all very nice. You could meet them, if you like. We can take you to them," Shaun said.

She covered her mouth slightly and said out of the corner in a whisper, "Don't pay any attention to my husband. He thinks an angel has spoken to him. He's going a little senile," Tina said.

"Stop whispering, woman!" John said.

"Will you please come with us?" Shaun said.

"No! We bloody well will not go with the likes of you and that false prophet. Get out of here! Get out of my apartment!" John's face turned crimson.

The window exploded, and glass showered over the carpet. Tina screamed, and John jumped with fright. Shadow people materialized out of thin air and entered the room.

Shaun was quick to act, and created a hermetic shield around himself and Kevin. He reached out for Tina and pulled her towards him and into the safety of the shield. The shadow people flickered in and out of existence and moved, shifting around the outside. Shaun reached out for John too, but the older man pulled away, refusing any help. Tina didn't want to leave her husband, but there was no choice. They had to get out of there.

The air had quickly thickened as the room filled with smoke. The air darkened and the shadows grew taller. John reached out to Tina, but he couldn't penetrate the shield. Behind him, a demon approached. The fallen angel reached out, grabbed a handful of air, and its clawed hand squeezed tight. John doubled over, clutching at his chest and falling to the kitchen floor.

"Give me the sacred stones, or I'll crush his heart," said the fallen angel, which appeared to be more like a demon than any kind of angel.

"K, can you see…?" Shaun didn't take his eyes off the winged demon.

"Yeah, I see it. It's what Rebecca described. We should get out of here," Kevin said, holding onto Tina.

"John! John. I'm not leaving without him." Tina pulled away from Kevin and pushed through the blue wall of the hermetic shield. She fell to her knees by her husband and cradled his face, begging him not to leave her. "Save him!" she screamed at Kevin.

Quickly, Shaun searched for a way to grab John. With the flow of blue light, he pushed the hermetic sphere outward, trying to encompass Tina and John without giving the fallen angel a chance to access the shield.

The fallen angel laughed. "You humans are stupid. Give me the stones you have stolen from the throne of God. This is my world you live in now, not His, so the stones belong to me. He had His turn and look at what He created. Morons full of greed and anger, which destroy everything they touch. Your kind do not deserve to inhabit such a beautiful world, it shines like a jewel in the expansive cosmos."

It was so self-assured. Shaun and Kevin's presence did not threaten it at all. Shaun made a split decision and retracted the shield, to let out a photon blast. The fallen angel hadn't expected such a bold move, and was momentarily caught off-guard. Its leathery wings closed around its torso, protecting it from the blue laser blast. Kevin dragged John to his feet, and Tina followed him closely down the hallway, to the elevator. Shaun pivoted around and ran from the room, jumping through the elevator doors as they were closing. Before the elevator began its descent, the doors buckled inward. Relief washed over Shaun as the elevator jolted downward.

"What did you do?" John asked, out of breath. "You angered the angel. He promised me eternal life. He promised that Tina and I would be young again and live forever in his kingdom if I gave them you!" John stabbed his finger at Kevin.

What John said made little sense. The fallen angel was asking for the stones, not for Kevin. "It doesn't want him, it wants these." Shaun took his stones out of his pocket. John couldn't see what was inside the pouch, but he reached out for them anyway. But there was no way he would be quicker than Shaun. John was pushing eighty. He was overweight, and his breathing was labored.

"Listen, old man. Just catch your breath and look after your lady, and we'll get you out of here. Then you can meet the man in charge of this operation. You may have heard of him – God. Does that ring any bells?" Shaun was agitated. Feelings of anger and rage, feelings he hadn't felt in a long time, surged up inside him. Kevin touched his arm but Shaun roughly pushed him away. Something was happening to him. He wanted to stop himself from becoming enraged, but he was out of control.

There was a loud thud on the top of the elevator. They all looked up. The elevator stopped and Shaun raised his first, ready to ram it into the fallen angel's face. Kevin got in the way and grabbed Shaun's forearm as the fallen angel tore off the roof of the elevator. The demon that dared to call itself an angel peered down at them.

"Give me the stones." Its voice rolled like thunder.

The doors opened and Kevin pulled Shaun through them, backwards.

When I get to turn around, I'm going to pound Kevin into the ground like a squashed banana, Shaun thought. But suddenly he was floating, the feelings of anger and rage dispelled. It was like he had been under some evil spell. The demonic angel had whispered into his mind, manipulating him, pushing his buttons, willing him to destroy Kevin. But Kevin had opened a portal and whisked him away. They were back at the lodge, back where they had started from.

"Are you alright?" Kevin said, collapsing the portal.

"Sorry. I'm so sorry," Shaun said.

"No harm, no foul. I sensed what was happening. It's okay. It wasn't you. I must go back for Logan and Rebecca," Kevin said.

"You're not going without me. I'm ready for it." Shaun paused and composed himself. He clenched his fists, ready to blast the demonic angel the minute they stepped back into the lobby.

He stepped through the portal with Kevin, straight into an ambush. Shadow creatures surrounded them. The portal collapsed. Glowing like a blue flame, Shaun pushed out the energy with just a thought, and shielded Kevin and himself.

Brenda and Colin were on the floor, their bodies lifeless, blood pooling around their heads, soaking into the carpet. Shadow men pressed into Colin's and Brenda's bodies, sucking up their life force – their essence. The life force was like gold to the shadow creatures. The shadow men were in a frenzy, feeding on the couple.

"I'm going to turn the shield into a wall. I want you to get the others and get them out of here." Shaun fixed his eyes on the dark, evil entities made of smoke.

"What about you?" Kevin said.

"Don't worry about me, just get them out of here." Shaun reduced the hermetic sphere into a wall, from ceiling to floor, and wall to wall. Kevin moved quickly and found Logan, Rebecca and her two boys with John and Tina. He returned to the room, breathless.

"I'm going to open a portal to Olivet. When I tell you to, drop the shield and jump into it."

The air behind him crackled, and the atmosphere became electrifying. It drew the hair on his head towards the portal's energy behind him.

"Now!" Kevin yelled.

But the screams and the crying of children, the pleads for help, swamped him. Kevin's voice echoed in the distance, as if he had already gone without him. Shaun wouldn't blame him if he had. He had been a real asshole to Kevin most of his life. They were all better off without him.

Amongst the glitching shadow men, the demonic angel stood laughing at him. "You're a worthless piece of shit! You cannot defeat me. I am you. You belong in hell with your worthless father," the demonic angel said.

Shaun resisted the suggestions inside his head when the shadows joined the demon, although together they filled his mind with snakes, monsters, and painful memories of demons sucking out his mother's soul as she died of cancer.

It was like a punch to his solar plexus. The shield had gone, the power of the stones had left him. He was all alone, and weak. He was nothing. Just when he thought he had found his purpose to serve God, to find people and help them find their way home to the heavens amongst the stars, his hope abandoned him. His father, stinking of alcohol and cigarettes, smothered every happy memory. "You're good for nothing," the voice of his father said repeatedly. "You're a useless piece of shit!" Shaun had heard those words over and over again, most of his life.

He was falling – toppling backwards. Down into the depths of a cold, dark abyss.

"I've got you," Kevin whispered.

10

DECEPTION: KEVIN. CANADA.

K evin held tight onto Shaun's arm, pulling him through the portal and into the dining room at Olivet. It was mealtime, and families packed the room. Everyone was gawking at the newcomers that had passed through the portal wall. Shaun, confused and dazed, smiled as he recognized Rachel and let her help him to his feet. If she hadn't gotten to Shaun first, Kevin believed Geoff would have picked him up and cradled him.

Geoff was such an emotional person. He had to be hiding most of his feelings. He seemed rock-solid on the outside, but bordered on being an Empath. Kevin smiled at Geoff. *He's got to know,* Kevin thought. Geoff gave him a knowing smile in return and relaxed a little. When things settled down, they would have a chat.

How different life could have been if there were more Empaths in the world. Everyone could benefit from having acute emotional intelligence. Then maybe no one would want to hurt another living creature. Kevin remembered when the bushfires had destroyed the wildlife and the trees in his area. His heart broke with their pain and sorrow, but he also felt the joy of rebirth when the seed pods had fallen, opened, and bloomed weeks later. Nature recovered more quickly than the human psyche.

"Take me back." Logan grabbed the front of his jacket. "Now, goddammit! Take me back!" Logan shouted in his face.

"Calm down!" Abraham said as he and Delilah took charge.

Kevin wasn't surprised by Logan's rage. Geoff pulled Logan off, as if he sensed the fear that built up inside him.

"What gives?" Delilah said.

"My daughter's back there. Take me back. I beg you. Please tell him to take me back! He don't have to stay, but take me back."

Delilah rested her hand on Logan's shoulder, calming him down, "It's up them if they take you back."

Kevin pulled down his shirt. "Where do you suggest we start?"

"Anywhere. Take me back now!"

"I'll go with you," Geoff said.

"I'll go too," Shaun said.

Shaun didn't want to go – Kevin could feel his need to stay with Rachel. Shaun had been shaken up. The demon had gotten inside his head. "You don't have to come," Kevin said, also picking up on Rachel's dread.

"I owe you, man."

"You don't owe me anything."

"Both of you, just go and hurry back." Rachel pushed Shaun forward. Then she pulled him back and held him tight, kissing him hard on the lips. "You better bring him back to me." She gave Kevin and Geoff the evil eye.

"You're so beautiful," Shaun said to Rachel as he gently touched her cheek. "I will always come back to you, no matter what."

Kevin's body felt heavy and he wondered where Jade was,

wishing he could be holding her tight. His heart felt heavy with longing. He had to push his feelings aside, and focus on finding survivors.

"Where to?" he said to Geoff. He tried to hide his longing, and spoke way too loud. He felt like a fool. He wasn't used to jumping between time zones, and he didn't know if it was day or night at Olivet. Jade would know. There was not much she didn't know, except his feelings for her. Kevin tried to distract himself while Geoff and Logan decided where the best location would be to open a portal. Shaun and Rachel embraced again. Kevin looked around at all the people in the restaurant, where there must be nearly a hundred people. Some were wearing military uniforms, some white lab coats; there were people in scrubs, and others in general civilian clothing. It was like a microcosm of the society they had left behind. All survivors. Together with their combined skills, they could build a new world.

There's still hope. Or is there? Kevin wondered.

"I know those hills like the back of my hand," Geoff said. "If she strayed from the lodge, the best place to start is Singing Pass Trailhead, and just hope she didn't go off-trail. The cub was a grizzly, and they're a lot harder to find than black bears."

"You're right on the money. Let's do it. Open the doorway," Logan said to Kevin.

"It's not that easy. I'm exhausted. I need a recharge. Negative energy saturated the mountains. The dark realm smothered nature's life force, and mine." He wasn't going to mention how his thoughts of Jade were problematic.

"You can't go outside. There's a giant snake, and another sandstorm. It's not safe outside," Rachel said.

"There's a shadow army on Whistler Mountain and Blackcomb Mountain, and a demonic angel, that attacked while we tried to help

Logan's sister. She said she had a dream of a fallen angel, and it said its name: Ashmedai," Shaun said.

Delilah raised her eyebrows at the man with a black ponytail next to her; Abraham nodded, as if approving her unspoken question.

"If you can't defeat it, you mustn't let it capture you," Delilah said to Kevin.

"If it catches him," Delilah said, walking over to Shaun and Geoff, pointing at them both, "you must kill him."

The room went quiet.

"What? You want me to kill a fallen angel?" Shaun said.

"No. Him," Delilah tilted her head at Kevin. "You must kill your friend."

Shaun turned his head, looking from Delilah to Rachel, seeking clarification. None came. "I'll die first."

"Then he cannot go," Delilah said.

"What's wrong, Delilah? What will happen if he gets caught?" Rachel asked.

"It wants my stones," Shaun said.

"Yes. But it wants Kevin, too, and if it gets him, it's game over. We will all be doomed and the Kingdom of God, Hashim, our Elohim, will be hauled from his throne and tossed into eternal darkness," Delilah said.

"That's impossible. Absolute nonsense," Geoff said.

"Delilah. A moment, please?" Abraham said.

She stepped aside to speak quietly to Abraham, who was extremely concerned, but was trying to act calm. Kevin didn't think his concerns were for his life. Kevin sat down on a chair and retied his shoelace. Delilah was sure of herself, which bothered Kevin. It made him nauseous to think he could be responsible for the fall of the Kingdom of God. It must be a mistake. He swallowed as if something were stuck in his throat.

"You alright?" Geoff asked.

"Can I get a drink of water?" Kevin asked.

"I'll get you one."

"We're wasting time." Logan paced with his hands on his head. His sister tried to calm him down, and he shrugged her off.

Kevin handed him a glass of water. It tasted different.

"It's desalinated," Geoff said.

"Why did you say that?" Kevin asked.

"The look on your face. It was as if it tasted different to you. You paused after the first sip, and sipped slowly the second time."

"You're an Empath. You read and feel people's emotions," Kevin said.

"Don't know nothing about being an Empath. Who I am is what I am. I am that I am," Geoff said.

"We should talk, if we ever get some downtime," Kevin said.

"As long as you don't cause the fall of the Kingdom of God, I'm willing to chat and hear whatever you have to say about who and what you think I am."

Kevin thought Geoff was wonderfully odd, and that he would make a good friend. He was reliable and caring. "So, do you have an image in your head of where we should start looking for Melody?"

"I'm pretty sure Melody went to find a new mom for the cub. At this time of year, there will be plenty of black bears, but if she's looking for a family for the cub, she'll need to find a grizzly. You want to hope she hasn't found what she's looking for?" Geoff said.

"Shaun, when you ignited the sapphire in your hand, the stones in your pocket released a vibrant white light. It energized me and gave me strength to open the portal, even though I was really, really depleted, and shit-scared. Can you to do it again? So that I can connect to the stones and draw in their power?"

Shaun's eyebrows raised. "Sure. Why not?" He glanced around at the people.

They all knew what Shaun could do. He was their blue angel. Kevin smiled to himself. It was nice to see Shaun a little embarrassed by his ability. His hand glowed, and light trailed around his body like a glove. The energy expanded and the stones illuminated.

Kevin inhaled, as if smelling fresh morning flowers in a meadow. He breathed in the gloriousness of life. Strength filled his veins until he believed he could battle ten men. He'd never known such power. There were many types of power which could fuel a person. A kind word; a positive thought; Love. Anything that made him smile energized him, but this was an even greater power.

"I'm good." Kevin stepped away from Shaun. He reached out for Geoff's temples. But before he touched them, Geoff went flying backwards, as if he had touched a live electrical wire.

Abraham helped Geoff to his feet, and Abraham's hair came alive with static. "Maybe a little less enthusiasm next time. Perhaps taper off that energy flowing through your body," Geoff said.

Kevin wiped his hands on the side of his jacket. Adjusted the knife holster that was buckled around his waist and tied to his thigh. "Right. Take two."

Shaun stood with his arms crossed, smirking and nodding. "Anytime you're ready, K."

"Take care of Brody," Logan said to his sister as he handed his baby boy to her.

"Leave your stones with me," Rachel said.

Shaun took his stones out of his pocket and returned them. "It's best they stay with me. K might need another boost."

Kevin readied himself, moved his hands towards Geoff, and

connected with the image that emotionally fueled Geoff's memory of hiking Singing Pass Trail. Kevin focused on the image of Geoff with his brother. They were hiking along a stone-covered trail, a gondola passing overhead. Within a few seconds, they could hear the crackling of the static of the portal membrane.

Logan pushed forward.

"Wait. We'll go first. Shaun, follow behind and cover the rear. See you on the other side," Kevin said, stepping through the portal with Geoff and out onto a trail. Darkness had blackened the mountain.

"It shouldn't be this dark," Logan said as he stepped through.

They had stepped out and immediately butted up against a turmoil of dark, storming clouds.

"We're going to have to pass, though. Shaun?" Kevin didn't need to say anything else. Shaun was on it, creating a hermetic shield to cover them through the thunderous clouds that rolled on the ground and back within itself.

Kevin thought of Jade, and was grateful that she wasn't with them. Casey and Mingan would protect her. As soon as he thought about Mingan, Kevin felt stupid and inadequate. No matter what he told himself, he shouldn't have left her without saying goodbye, or telling her when he would be back.

"What gives, man?" Geoff said, slapping Kevin on the back. "What are you beating yourself up about?"

Kevin adjusted his jacket. "I'm good."

"Yeah, right," Geoff said.

Kevin hadn't been called out before by another Empath. It was a little unnerving, knowing someone else could sense his feels.

The barreling clouds compressed the blue hermetic shield slightly. The party was walking in a row, and it was comical. He imagined that from behind they might be mistaken for brave – albeit stupid – men, ready to step into a category-five hurricane.

The shield compressed even further, and for a moment Kevin thought they were going to be crushed, but the walls of the shield bounced back into place as they passed beyond the rolling clouds, out of the edge of the dark realm, and into a misty fog which covered what seemed to be an afternoon sky. What had happened to the night? *Was time speeding up?* Kevin zipped up his jacket, and pulled up his hood. The minute Shaun disengaged the hermetic shield, the air was thick with ash. A sudden chill made Kevin shake.

"Melody! Melody?" Logan called.

Everyone called out her name as they searched along the white rocks to the side of the track and headed up Singing Pass Trail. But there was no sign of any living thing. They climbed further up the trail.

"Bear droppings," Geoff said.

"It could mean this is the way Melody went," Logan said.

"That pile is too big for a cub. Let's hope it's a black bear."

"If we want to find a grizzly female, we should go off-track," Logan said.

"No, she would stick to the trail. She knows not to go off it."

"Is your daughter going to think like that? Think like her," Kevin said.

"I suppose you're right. She is headstrong, and if she knows the bears are off-trail, then maybe she will go off-trail. Shit!" Logan said.

They walked for another twenty minutes, regularly calling out Melody's name and pausing, listening vigilantly for a reply until the trail narrowed.

* * *

KEVIN FOCUSED on the energy in the air and knew they were heading in the right direction, he could feel and hear in his mind the softness of Melody's voice as she soothed the cub, talking to it and keeping it calm. The cub was heavy in her arms, but she refused to put it down, worried it would run off into the trees. She was aware of the dangers. "Melody's a very smart girl," Kevin said to Logan.

"She has her mother's brains and good looks. I hope you are what you say you are," Logan said.

"I didn't say I was anything. I only came here to give you a message about the ascension. Everything else is on you." Kevin refused to take the responsibility. Too many times, he had taken on the responsibility of others, making sure they didn't get physically or emotionally hurt.

"Shh!" Shaun put up his hand.

They all stopped and waited. Kevin listened closely to the sounds in the woods.

"The tree," Geoff said.

Between the foliage, a bear stood on its back legs, scratching itself against a tree.

"It's a black bear. They have better hearing than dogs, by tenfold. It would've heard us coming. It isn't threatened by us, so let's keep walking and leave it to its back-rubbing," Geoff said.

Kevin's heart pounded. He started jogging. He couldn't catch his breath. Geoff turned to him and they quickened their pace away from the bear.

"What is it?" Logan said.

"Melody. I think. She's trapped," Kevin said, trying to push Melody's physical response to danger away from his being.

Logan stopped. "Where is she? Melody!"

Kevin slowed down to a trot and listened. He could feel Melody's emotions as if they were his own. His chest heaved with emotional sobs, while holding back the noise, as if she was being stalked. She was trying to be silent. A bear cried out.

"Did you hear that? It sounds like a cub calling to its mother. Could it be the one with Melody?" Geoff said.

"She went that way," Kevin pointed into the brush off-trail.

"Oh, fuck no. Are you sure?" Logan said.

"Yes." Kevin stepped across a stream that was trailing down the mountain from the glaciers. They hopped across the stones, careful not to slip, and entered the bushes off the track. Kevin held back branches to prevent them slapping Logan in the face behind him.

"You okay up there?" Shaun called out.

"I'm good. Look for a small tunnel or something like a wombat's hole."

"What's a wombat's hole?" Logan asked.

"It's brush that is slightly arched because a wombat has burrowed its way into the ground, to hide itself from its hunters and the elements. We used to see them a lot in the bush back home," Shaun said.

"Be careful where you tread. Out here, we don't need any broken bones," Geoff cautioned.

The bear cub cried out.

"This way!" Logan ran off in front of Kevin, pushing the twigs out of the way, but he let them spring back, slapping Kevin in the face.

The cry of the baby bear grew louder and had the distinct sound of coming from a hole. Logan stepped out into a small clearing and there was a grizzly bear toying with a fallen hollow log. The cub was inside. Melody's pink puffy jacket was on the ground.

"Melody?" Logan said.

The grizzly turned to Logan. It stood on its back legs and

roared, before dropping to its feet and running at them. Geoff went left and Logan went straight for the bear. "Wait!" Kevin yelled.

Geoff yelled too, trying to distract the bear. Logan was heading for the log recklessly, putting himself at risk. The bear took off after Geoff, and Shaun followed.

The log was heavy. Logan dropped to his belly and peeked inside.

"Daddy!"

"Oh, baby girl."

"I'm stuck, Daddy."

Kevin peered into the other end of the log. The cub was facing him. It cried at the sight of him. Both cub and girl were stuck in the log.

"How the hell are we going to get her out of there?" Logan quietly spoke to Kevin, trying not to let Melody hear the concern in his voice.

Kevin checked on Geoff and Shaun. The bear was on the ground. It got up again and Shaun pushed it back to the ground with a blue laser beam, channeled from the palm of his hand. The bear got up again, but this time it ran off in the opposite direction.

"You hurt?" Kevin asked Geoff, sensing his racing heart.

Shaun was quite calm. "I think the big fellow scared the grizzly more than the grizzly scared us," Shaun said, looking at Geoff.

"Damn right!" Geoff grinned.

"How are we going to get them out?" Logan repeated.

Kevin got on his knees and assessed Melody's predicament. Kevin's dad was a firefighter, and he had told him many stories about kids getting stuck down drains, and in between stair rails, but he had equipment to get the kids out. Kevin had nothing.

"Reach out your arms to Daddy."

"They're not long enough," Melody said.

"Let me see," Shaun got on the ground next to Logan. "Why don't I trim the log inch by inch, until you can reach her? I'll do it very slowly."

"Okay. Melody, honey, I want you to close your eyes for Daddy. Can you do that?" Logan said.

"Tell her not to open them, even if she sees a pretty blue light against her closed eyes," Shaun said.

Logan counseled his daughter, and when he was sure her eyes were closed, he gave Shaun the go-ahead. Shaun broke out in a sweat, trying to control the energy into a narrow laser beam. It burned through the log to the other side. Logan snapped off the piece, and Shaun went to work again. Slowly, he inched towards Melody.

"Mel, can you open your eyes, honey? Reach for my hands." Logan sighed as he touched her skin. "I've got her. Thank God, I've got her. On the count of three, I want you to suck in your tummy, and push against the inside of the log with your feet."

Kevin counted to three, and Logan tugged his daughter free from the log. Scratches and splinters covered her sides. She cried against Logan.

"What about the bear?" Geoff said.

"It looks wider from this side," Kevin said.

"I can push it towards you," Geoff said.

"Okay, on my count. One, two, three," Kevin said.

The bear popped out, and Kevin reassured it. Melody, with an acute sense of responsibility, checked the cub was okay. "Don't cry, we'll find a new mommy for you," Melody said.

The girl was talking to herself and the bear. They were both without mothers.

"We'll have to go up higher and try to stay out of the edge of the dark realm's storming clouds."

Logan picked up Melody's puffy jacket and put it on the girl. He zipped it up. "It might be springtime, but it gets colder the further up the mountain we go." Logan lifted the hood up onto her head.

The wind picked up and carried the sound of a flute on the tail-end. The view would have been spectacular if the dark realm hadn't covered the village and the valley between the mountains below.

11

DELUSION: SHAUN. CANADA.

From the incline of the trail, Shaun should have been able to see the village in the valley below, but the thick clouds of the dark realm covered it. He wished they could hurry and find a home for the cub, and get out of there. He worried the grizzly they had scared off earlier could be stalking them. He also sensed eyes looking down on them. *Is it the fallen angel or the Jinn? And what are they waiting for?* Shaun wondered.

The remnants of a footbridge brought them to a stop. "We'll have to rock-jump." Shaun slipped, and his foot went into the water. "Shit, that's cold."

The little bear drank the fresh water from the other side of the stream. It didn't seem to have any problem crossing the flowing water.

"Wait here," Kevin said, scaling up the embankment off the track.

"What is it?" Shaun asked.

Kevin lay on his belly and looked over the next rise, then slithered back down. "There's a bear with its cubs, out in the open."

Geoff crawled up and took a peek. "They're grizzlies alright. It must be a female, because there are two cubs. Females keep away from the males, to keep the cubs safe. Pass me the bear."

Melody and Logan crawled up the steep embankment to spy on the grizzlies. "She looks like a nice mommy. And Harmony will have a brother and a sister," Melody said.

"You called the bear Harmony?" Shaun smiled.

Melody screwed her nose up at Shaun and squeezed her lips tight.

"He's not making fun of you. He thinks you're cute," Kevin said.

Melody clenched her teeth and gave a big smile to Shaun. "Come see," she said in a soft voice.

He climbed and lay on his belly alongside the rest of them. They were like a group of hunters, ready to take aim. Geoff pushed the cub away. It cried out and ran back to the safety of the group.

Melody wriggled forward and comforted the cub. "That's your new mommy. You need a family to care for you. Now out you go." Melody pushed the bear forward but, when it didn't go, she was on her feet and stepping out into the open for the bear to follow her. The cub gave chase. The grizzly bears sniffed the air.

"Melody, get back here," Logan chased after her, keeping low.

Kevin went to follow. "Stay here with Geoff!" Shaun said, and ran after Logan and Melody. He pumped his fist with the energy of the sapphire spinning in his palm. He was ready to blast the bear if it made a move to attack either of them. Logan caught up to Melody, scooped her up, and backed away from the bears. The cub joined the two others. They were playfully wrestling. Shaun held his position, until Logan and Melody were behind him.

They all retreated and took their position on the grass next to Geoff and Kevin to view the cubs. With her nose, the mother pushed Harmony away as she moved over to her cubs. They were intent on playing with Harmony, however, and the mother went back to foraging.

The human group watched and waited until Melody was convinced that the cub would be safe and happy. The big grizzly mother sat down, and the cubs sat with her, including Harmony.

"Come on, we should get back," Shaun said.

They all slid down the embankment and back onto the trail.

"I can't believe how fresh this water is," said Kevin.

Geoff joined him, and so did Melody.

"It's glacier water. It's so yummy. Daddy said that we are the luckiest people in the world to have glacier water," Melody said, beaming at her dad.

She put her hands on her hips, as if she had just achieved a mammoth task. Shaun didn't know what to say to her. He just smiled, and she smiled back.

Melody waited for Kevin to finish wiping the water from his mouth. "We can go now," she said.

Kevin didn't have to be told twice. He generated the energy to open the portal. Shaun could feel the static in the air. The colored energy was beautiful.

Suddenly, Kevin collapsed the portal. "Someone else is up here."

"Who? We got everyone out. Now we have Melody. What are you waiting for? Let's go!" Logan said.

"I can't. There's someone out here that needs help."

Geoff searched the surrounding area. "I don't see anyone."

"Me neither," Shaun bit his bottom lip. Kevin was doing the same with his. They had been hanging around each other way too much. But if Kevin thought there was someone who needed their help, that was good enough for Shaun.

"Did you hear that?" Melody said.

"Yes, I heard it," Shaun said. Screams floated on the air. Everyone could hear them, but they couldn't pinpoint the location.

"There's a hut near here. At Flute Summit. The sound could have come from there," Logan said.

"Let's have ourselves a look," said Geoff, heading off.

"It could be the demonic angel getting inside our heads, just a hallucination. If we find nothing, we head straight out of here. I'm not sure this is a good idea." Shaun assessed the distance between them and the edge of the dark realm. It was too close for comfort.

"You won't have to tell me twice," said Kevin.

The area widened, and there were boulders with black mounds on top.

"They're bears. The boulders. They're black bears. They won't hurt you unless you provoke them," Geoff said.

Nervously checking over his shoulder, Shaun walked behind Kevin and Geoff. The two had established a rapport that required few words. The further they went along the trail, paranoia crept in. Shaun glanced over his shoulder and peered out of the corner of his eye, checking behind him. The fog of the dark realm moved closer. The temperature continued to drop. He hugged himself, trying to stay warm.

It frustrated Shaun, being so aware at how much more he perceived. His sensitivity to everything had expanded and it made him agitated, and scared. It was like the stones had given him a heightened sense of consciousness and connection to his environment. Connection between all things. The people, nature, everything somehow connected.

It was something he had thought a lot about recently, the

connections they all had to each other, even though they were from different cultures and different parts of the world. They were all survivors, and they had found each other. What were the odds of that happening? It made it impossible for him to not believe in a grand design, and that he must follow the signs. Right now, his nerves were on fire, his muscles tensed, he broke out in a cold sweat. He was anxious, ready to fire up a shield or shoot a photon blast at any second. They were being hunted; he could feel it. It was the same feeling he'd had when his dad had come home drunk and needed a punching bag. It was best to keep a low profile.

Something flickered off to the side. He did a double take, and the shadow of a man appeared and disappeared.

Shaun whispered to Kevin and Geoff. "We're being followed."

They both had become quiet. The sounds in the air had gone. The breeze, gone. A fog settled around them. Gently, Shaun tapped on Kevin's shoulder.

Then he tripped. He had gone down as he backed away from Kevin and Geoff – their faces were gone. Shaun rubbed his eyes and looked again, but his friends' features were black holes of dense matter. A snake's tongue shot out from the place that once was Geoff's face.

Shaun recoiled. "What the!" He swiftly created a hermetic shield around his body, as quick as the flick of a rubber band, and it felt the same too; the sudden flow of energy through his body from the icosahedron and his nerve endings, fueled by adrenaline, ignited by his fear. What had been his friends walked closer, as if they were going to walk straight through the shield. It scared him. He backed away, dropped the shield, ready to blast them. His eyes watered. He wiped the moisture away and saw it was blood.

"What's happening? Get away from me!" Shaun scurried backwards on his hands and knees, trying to get to his feet. He held his arm out, and aimed it at Geoff first. Geoff and Kevin parted, jumping out of the way. Logan and Melody were gone.

"What are you? Where are my friends?" he yelled at the faceless bodies of Geoff and Kevin as they advanced. Kevin mumbled something; words Shaun couldn't hear. The tongue of a snake kept darting in and out of the darkness.

"It's me! Kevin!"

The voice was right, but what Shaun was seeing didn't look like Kevin or Geoff. Suddenly, his leg elevated into the air, as if a phantom had yanked him skyward. He slid backwards, crunching his abs to stay upright.

His friends were gone, and he was tumbling through the whitewash of a stormy, dark ocean. It went on and on. He needed to breathe. His leg dropped heavily to the ground. Everything had turned to black and gray, like Casey's charcoal sketches. The shadows were black. The dark realm had closed in around him. He couldn't see the others. There was no one with him. He was alone.

The feeling of despair was like a heavy cloak, before the darkness consumed him. He became self-aware and willed the energy of the stones to cocoon him in a hermetic shield. A level of calmness restored his thoughts, and he heard his own voice of reason. The storming clouds were right in front of him. He checked his leg and there was a black burn mark of a hand around his heel. Something had dragged him into the dark realm. Shaun ran at the clouds and entered the storm. He fell out the other side, where Geoff and Kevin were waiting for him. A few yards away, Melody and Logan entered a hut. Shaun reached out for Kevin and pulled him into the sphere, then Geoff.

"What happened to you?" Kevin asked.

"You just went ballistic; like a raving lunatic," Geoff said.

"Something pulled me into the dark realm and took away your

faces." Shaun showed them the mark around his ankle. "You had tongues like snakes. I think one of the demonic entities from the dark realm hijacked my mind, making me hallucinate. I nearly killed you both. I thought you were the shadow men. This is bad."

"Logan and Melody are already inside the hut. Let's take a look, and get the hell out of here," Geoff said.

Someone cried for help, and Kevin rushed up to the hut.

"There's no way to know if what we are seeing and hearing is real. Be careful!" Geoff warned.

They stumbled into the hut, like a group of tired hikers that had used up their last ounce of energy. Geoff threw his arm out to the side, instinctively protecting Shaun. A lanky, undernourished man with a long beard was holding a gun at Logan's head.

Kevin stepped towards the man. "Who are you? Put the gun down."

"We don't want to hurt you," Geoff said.

How do we know he is even real? Shaun thought.

"Yes, you do. This little witch has been screaming inside my head. Telling me to kill myself." The man had his foot on Melody's chest. "Come any close and I'll put a bullet in his head and crush her with my boot."

The tendons in the man's necked strained. His face was red as a beetroot and his veins, full of blood, bulged like rivers trailing down from his bald head, getting soaked up by his beard.

Shaun put his hand behind his back, and closed his eyes. Within two seconds, he had surrounded himself and Geoff in a hermetic shield. The man stood motionless, confused, and he took his foot off Melody. She reached up and bit him on the leg. The gun went off.

Geoff leaped for the man and tackled him to the ground, wrestling the gun from him. The man was shocked and dazed, as if he was snapping out of a trance.

"It wasn't me, it wasn't my fault," the man yelled.

Melody, sobbing, threw herself over her father's body. Kevin lay motionless on the floor. Blood escaped from under his body.

Shaun dropped the shield and knelt beside his friend. He turned Kevin onto his back. "No. No. No." A circle of blood expanded rapidly over the gray and white areas, staining Kevin's jacket. Shaun unzipped Kevin's jacket and pulled up his shirt. The blood was bubbling.

Logan was on his feet, holding Melody in his arms. Geoff handed Logan the gun. "Shoot him if he moves."

Melody slid down her father's hip to the ground. "Is he sleeping?"

Shaun couldn't speak. He moved Kevin's leg and arm across his body to turn him on his side as he searched for an exit wound.

"Find something to help me stop the bleeding," Shaun cried, as he frantically scanned the cabin until his eyes fell upon a case with a green cross on it. "Get the first aid kit! There! On the shelf."

Logan reached up to the top shelf for the box.

"I can help," the man said.

"You shut your mouth," Shaun said.

"My name's Phillip. I'm a medic. I can help."

"I told you to shut up." Shaun lunged at Phillip, punching him in the mouth.

Geoff pulled him off. "Forget about him."

Shaun took the box from Logan. He was helpless – he didn't know what to do.

"Gauze. Stop the bleeding!" the man shouted.

"Maybe we should let him help. He can't die. We'll all die," Logan said.

"You better be telling the truth, or I'll kill you myself," Geoff said.

The man rubbed his sweaty head, and cautiously stepped forward. His face was no longer like a beetroot. His eyes didn't look like dark pits.

"It's a traumatic pneumothorax," Phillip said.

"English," Shaun said.

"He has a punctured lung. Air's leaking into the cavity around it. His lung is filling up with blood. He will drown if you keep him on his back." Phillip turned Kevin onto his side. "Help me lift him up onto the table."

Geoff and Shaun picked up Kevin, and Logan cleared the table.

"I'm going to need a sharp knife, and a tube," Phillip said.

Shaun pulled out Casey's pocketknife.

"Sterilize it," Phillip said.

"With what?" asked Shaun.

"Here, the gas burner. It's always here for hikers that camp overnight. I used it a few days ago; it'll work."

"Let's hope it still has gas," Geoff said.

"It does." Phillip began taping up Kevin's chest wound.

Shaun held the knife under the flame. "What are you going to do?"

"I'm going to make an incision to insert the tube to drain the air that is trapped between his chest cavity and the lungs. We need to get him to a hospital. He is going to need surgery. The lung tissue can repair itself, but it will need time."

Shaun searched Kevin's backpack. Sophia had always said Kevin was often prepared for emergencies. There was a first aid kit there. Two pens and a notepad, a fold-up raincoat, and some protein bars. Everyone searched the hut for tubing. Shaun dropped Kevin's backpack, and rifled through the cupboards Geoff had already searched.

"Anything will do: a hose, or the barrel of a pen," Phillip said.

Shaun rummaged back through Kevin's bag for the pens and handed one to Phillip.

"I need two."

"What for?" Shaun said, handing him the second one.

"To drain the blood."

Shaun tried to ignore the rattle coming from inside Kevin's lungs as he breathed. When the second pen was inserted, it sounded like opening a bottle of soda; rushing gas. Shaun looked at Geoff, alarmed.

Geoff nodded at him, as if the sounds were normal. "What now?" he said to Phillip.

"We wait and see if he wakes up. Unless you know someone with a helicopter that can airlift him to hospital? Oh wait, it's a pandemic, there is no one left but us, there are no hospitals. All you've got is me!" Phillip said sarcastically.

Geoff grabbed him by the collar. "You don't get to be a smartass. If he dies, we all die!"

"Oh God. How long do we have to wait?" Logan said.

"It's hard to tell." Phillip went to go outside.

"Where the hell are you going?" Geoff demanded.

"To clean up." Phillip held up his bloody hands.

From the doorway, Shaun waited while Phillip cleaned his hands with bottled water. "That wasn't me in there," Phillip said.

"Then who was it?" Shaun wondered if Phillip had been hallucinating, also affected by the dark realm.

"I don't know what took hold of me. I had been hiking all winter to get to Whistler before the spring. After that, it would be too late," Phillip said.

"Why would it be too late?" Shaun waited for it. For Phillip to tell him all about the dream that he'd had of Kevin opening the portal, rescuing everyone on Whistler and Blackcomb Mountain. Shaun waited for Phillip to speak. But he just kept staring at him.

"My wife called out to me one night, telling me to walk. Not to take a car, or any form of transport. I had to walk."

"Your wife doesn't concern me. You shot my friend. You held a gun at a man's head. What is wrong with you?" Shaun said.

"My wife is supposed to be here. I followed her voice for months, but I can't find her. She was crying out for me day after day. I've been waiting here for her, for weeks. Two days ago, I used up the last of my rations. I'm hungry and tired. I heard a man's voice. A deep, convincing voice, like the voice of God. It was crystal-clear. It echoed off the mountains. And I believed the voice. It was silent, then suddenly it spoke to me again, warning of your coming. It said the men who have taken my wife, who murderously tortured her, were close, and that's when you and your red-bearded friend arrived. Then I thought I heard my wife's cry for help, again. I was so pleased to hear her, it meant she was alive, there was still hope of finding her; until the voice changed into a little girl's giggle. It wasn't my wife. It was that little witch in there. I saw her face. I saw you all. You killed my wife."

Shaun put his hands out, as if to stop Phillip's train of thought. "We didn't kill anyone! Do you know what has happened to the world?"

"There was a plague that turned people mad. Most folk are dead. I'm not infected. What else is there to know?" Phillip moved back towards the hut. His face reddened. He was changing again. Something had wormed its way into his head, filling it with lies.

Shaun directed blue light to expand from his being and to capture Phillip, too. "You're being mind-fucked by unseen entities from the dark realm." He waited for the color to drain from Phillip's face. "I don't know if your wife was calling you to the mountains to find her, or if the dark realm lured you here. Either way, you have been under the influence of entities from the dark realm. The guy you shot is the only way you will ever see your wife again." Shaun jabbed a finger at the hut where Kevin lay on the table, fighting for life.

"What? How can…?" Phillip said, shaking his head in disbelief.

"He is a wizard in opening and closing portals. He can get you to an ascension portal that will take you to your wife. She has either already ascended in the last ascension, or she is waiting for my friends and me to return for the next ascension, which will be the last before the planet is destroyed."

Phillip searched the outer rim of the hermetic shield. "You did this before, and my head cleared, just like now; how are you doing this?"

Shaun held up his hand, showing him the icosahedron sapphire embedded in his palm.

Phillip's eyes went wide. "Impossible!"

"Nothing is impossible anymore. If I let down the shield, you need to control your mind and push out the negative thoughts, or entities we call the Jinn, made from the fire of scorching wind from within the dark realm, will control and destroy you. If you want to see your wife again, you need to do everything possible to make sure he doesn't die. It's up to him if we get out of here, before the dark storming realm, with all its dark entities, descends."

Shaun looked at the storming clouds as he walked back into the hut and left Phillip in the cold, scorching wind.

12

SWARM OF DEATH: KEVIN. CANADA.

Kevin floated in and out of consciousness and from time to time, in fleeting moments, he smelled chicken noodles. With each breath, his chest hurt. A bat flew over his head. Nervously, he waved it away.

The darkness surrounded him.

Jade wasn't near. He could feel she was far away. She'd left him. The darkness emerged back into his mind, but impressions of Sophia quickly pushed it back. Her soft, pale skin, and rose-colored cheeks. She reached out her hand. He didn't take it at first, but she insisted, and when she pushed her ghostly, angelic hand out again, reluctantly he gently placed his hand in hers. Her hand was surprisingly warm to the touch. With ease, she softly lowered him down onto his back, into a golden stream of light. He gently floated down the stream as Sophia faded into the distance.

* * *

THE SMELL of rot and dry blood made him gag. The pain in his chest exploded throughout his body. He was back in the darkness. Emptiness filled his ears. He wished Sophia would return. Time seemed irrelevant in the darkness. There was no light. He tried to speak. No sound came from his lips. His senses were starved of stimulation. The rhythm of his heartbeat was so fast, if he didn't slow it down, it would explode.

Usually in the astral realm, colors and light triggered positive emotions, filling up his spiritual body, but there were no waves of color from the spectrum of light; they were void in the darkness. The dark provided nothing more than comfort from his physical pain. Shining like a star that grew brighter as it drew near, Sophia's essences preceded her as she returned to his side. He had to turn away until her light dimmed.

"Don't be afraid." Her voice sparkled through the darkness, and the Milky Way erupted from her mouth.

"I'm not afraid. I'm ready to go with you into the light." Kevin didn't feel the movement of his lips.

"It's not your time. Fight, Kevin. Return to your body and heal yourself. I'll see you soon enough."

Then she was gone, leaving him once again in darkness.

He tried to move his body. An arm, a leg. Nothing. He squeezed his eyes and blinked.

Without fear, Kevin patiently waited for his body to heal. He drew on his memories of swimming in the river on a hot summer's day, riding his bike with his arms outstretched, feeling the warmth of the sun filling him up with light. The memories floated by one after the other, timelessly, until the shadows marched out of the darkness and into his mind. The shadows moved closer. Still, fear evaded him. *None of this is real*, he told himself.

Shadows suddenly blasted with a brilliant blue light, and

exploded. He hoped it was Shaun destroying the shadows, leaving sparks of red, and smoke. Shaun was fighting for Kevin's life.

Swarms of the smokey shadow-creatures raced out from the darkness and assaulted Shaun. In his mind's eye, Kevin watched Shaun as he struggled to protect Melody, Logan, Geoff, and – who was that other guy? Kevin couldn't recall.

It's not real, it's just a bad dream.

The darkness lit up with an impressive blue hue as Shaun erected a huge hermetic shield. Kevin counted four men. Where was he in all of this? Melody hid behind her father, inside the shield. Kevin sensed her fear. Sympathy for her plight filled his heart. *It's just a dream, a bad dream.* He tried to breathe, but it was too painful.

A hundred dark shadow entities, hideous with melting faces and hands, which reminded him of old Halloween masks and costumes. Vile, loathing, resentful dark evil energy emanated and fueled the dark realm's allies' attack as they pressed themselves up against the shrinking sphere. Shaun struggled to keep the shield up.

A flash of light cleared the darkness. His chest ached. He drew in another breath, forcing his lungs to work. The strength to will his lungs and heart to work in unison was depleting the little energy he had.

"Wake up! Wake up, K!"

The timbre of Shaun's voice sounded weak. Kevin focused on the painful rise and fall of his chest. He imagined the tiny atoms in his body, and how they all came together to make him what he was. He just needed to sleep. It was, after all, only a dream.

The hermetic shield was pressed out of shape, and it was losing its power when the creatures pulled back. The blue membrane wobbled.

Tall, leathery wings; sharp rows of teeth. Another demonic angel.

It had no body hair, and it appeared to be old and ugly. Fallen or not, it was nothing like he imaged an angel to be. It was just a dream. Kevin studied the creature and wondered how many of them there were. He scanned its being for emotion.

Rage, greater than the shadow men, which Kevin started to think were the Jinn, hit him like a punch in the stomach. He coughed, catching his breath. Pain radiated through his entire being, and he could feel from head to foot. Kevin allowed himself to float away from his failing body, into the cosmos of his dreamscape, moving closer to the creature for a better look. Behind the rage was sorrow. Like a lost, abandoned child, it longed to be reunited with its father.

A giant push of energy sent Kevin flying backwards, tumbling out of control, deep into space. Somersaulting into oblivion, he suddenly jerked to a stop, and began moving in the opposite direction, at an even greater speed. Only in his dreams could he move at the speed of light.

PRESSURE upon his chest made it hard to breath. He opened and closed his fists, moving his stiff fingers. His head dropped to his left shoulder. It was still hard to breath. Slowly, he partially opened one eye. Dozens of shadowed entities, the same creatures with long arms and long fingers, fought for a purchase of his flesh. He tried to thrash his body against them; anything to wake up from this nightmare, but he was too weak to move. They held him tighter, as the demonic angel flew above him.

"We will get our stones, and open the door to the heavens. We will return to our rightful place of birth," the demonic angel intoned, pressing hard onto Kevin's chest.

The pain was unbearable. He needed to wake up from this nightmare. The fallen angel pressed its sharp fingernails down on Kevin's chest.

In the distance, behind the shadow creatures, Shaun stepped into view. "You want the stones? Come and get them."

The creature flew at Shaun, giving Kevin time to free himself from the clutches of the shadowed men in his dream. But no matter how much he thrashed, he couldn't free himself. Sophia's voice rang in his mind. "No doubts. Faith." Kevin willed his hand up, but it was quickly pushed downward.

"Try again! Move!" Melody yelled in the distance.

A black hand, though only a shadow, weighed heavily upon his head. He struggled to lift it up. But the hand and pain forced him back into the darkness.

"You must try harder. It's not your time. If you don't survive, no one will," Sophia said.

Kevin imagined his glowing, golden spiritual essence, and forced it back into his body. Ready for the pain, he pushed through and saw a hut on a snow-covered mountaintop in Canada. His body was in the hut on a table, and his jacket was soaked with blood. It all rushed back into his mind. A stranger holding a gun at Logan's head, and Melody – quickly, he searched for Melody, and sensed her presence by his side, pleading for him to wake up. Her face was streaked with tears and snot.

He fought against the pain, and settled back into his fragile body. Shaun was holding back the dark entities that had enveloped and invaded the hut. The shadowed men dragged Melody, kicking and screaming, away from Kevin.

Wake up! Move, dammit! Kevin willed his limbs to move and

fight against the dark creatures, his energy waning. *Oh God, help me!* Within a flash, he was out of the dream and able to move his body, which was lying on a cold metal table, surrounded by shadow men who were trying their best to hold him down.

It wasn't a dream. The demonic angel was in the hut, with a few of its army of Jinn. The shield had retracted, exposing Geoff. The fallen angel seized the opportunity, reached out its long fingers, and crushed Geoff's face. Kevin could hear Geoff's bones breaking.

As the shield dropped, the Jinn wrestled Shaun. They went for his pocket, trying to get to the sacred platonic gemstones. White light from the combined stones in Shaun's pocket glowed so brightly that Kevin couldn't see Shaun from the waist down. The light pulsed outward, and the creatures exploded, turning into falling ash. Quickly, before more Jinn emerged from the dark realm, Shaun blasted the demonic angel with a solid white laser beam that should have cut the creature in half. The angel folded one set of wings like a shield, protecting its torso, and pushed the beam of light back towards Shaun. He jumped out of the way, and the light beam disintegrated the hut wall. The edges of the wall smoked.

"Shaun!"

Shaun grimaced on the floor.

"I command you to open the portal to the heavens," the demonic angel snarled and clenched his teeth with fury. Hot, foul air from its mouth scorched Kevin's cheek.

Each movement and each breath of his own produced unbearable pain. It was still too hard to catch his breath, as silver dots blinded Kevin's vision. He blacked out again for a few seconds and when his eyes flung open he drew in a deep breath with razor-sharp pain, and clung onto consciousness. His chest and body dangled and stretched, pulled down by gravity as the demonic angel's hand tightened around his throat, holding him five feet off the ground.

"I command you to open a portal to the heavens, or they will die."

Kevin struggled to speak. The fallen angel lowered him to the ground.

His throat constricted. He tried to cough and force his lungs to gulp back the air. Pain shot through his chest. Quickly, to avoid passing out again, he took rapid, tiny breaths.

Six dark, smokey Jinn popped into existence behind the demon – they were hungry for flesh, waiting for a command from the demonic angel. *Why did they obey it? The fallen angel is their puppeteer,* Kevin thought. They didn't harbor the emotion of sorrow and longing like the fallen angel; they embodied rage and revenge.

"I can. I need…" Kevin tried to speak. He swallowed the pain. "I need to look into your mind and see heaven."

"Then look!" The demonic angel picked Kevin up and raised its head to meet his eyes.

Kevin didn't want to see. He braced his arm against his side, unable to lift his arms up to touch the temples of the fallen angel. But it didn't matter. Once their eyes locked, there was no pulling back, as hypnotic spirals filled the fallen angel's eyes.

Images of purity, crystal reflections, joy and hope filled Kevin's body. The beauty was overwhelming. It channeled a power Kevin had only glimpsed. The emotion of the magical place the fallen angel wanted to go to filled Kevin's solar plexus and heart.

Oh God, forgive me for what I am about to do.

It was the strongest, most emotionally charged memory he had ever experienced. He could feel the energy building up inside him. The crackling of static filled the room as the waves of energy searched for grounding. Suddenly, the energy was severed, and it filled him with darkness. The portal shut down, and the fallen angel's eyes pooled with black ink.

Shaun had caught the demonic angel off-guard, while Kevin accessed its memory. He blasted it with a white light that was like a hand grenade exploding in the hut.

The demonic angel dropped Kevin, as the force of the blast punched its body outside. On the floor, Kevin held his head. His ears were ringing. Dizzy and shell-shocked, he squinted through the dust. A chilly breeze, a whistling wind, entered through the scorched hole in the wall, and the roof began to sag from lack of support.

Shaun dropped heavily beside the upturned table. Kevin crawled over to him, and they helped each other to stand. Unbalanced on their feet, they supported each other as Logan dusted himself off and held Melody in his arms.

"Give me a boost," Kevin mumbled, noticing the pens sticking out from between his ribs.

Shaun shook his head. "I can't. I've got nothing left."

"Yes, you can! You have the stones of God; the power is eternal. Draw on them and give me a boost. I'll get us out of here."

"What about Geoff?" Shaun asked, looking at his lifeless body.

"He's gone," said Phillip.

"You shut the fuck up!" Shaun held out his hand to Kevin as the icosahedron turned in his palm, speeding up, generating energy. Grief impaled Shaun, his hurt great. Kevin wished he could take it away and make Geoff whole again.

The velocity of the icosahedron increased. Their power was beyond his understanding. The blue light grew stronger and ignited the power in the rest of the stones in Shaun's pocket. Shaun took the pouch out and gave them to Kevin. They were burning hot, and he had to resist the urge to drop them. Kevin pulled down the sleeve of his bloodied jacket and covered his hand, then put the pouch on top of the material protecting him from the heat.

Kevin thought of Jade, and the light that had ignited between them the day they met. It had almost been like a nuclear reactor, and this was a lot like that. He focused on Olivet. He jolted, the roof totally caved in, and the metal walls collapsed – the Fallen angel had returned.

"You can't defeat me. Enough of this nonsense! You humans are pathetic!" The demonic angel had his fun toying with them, but he now would administer the final blow of punishment.

Shaun pushed the iron sheeting that had landed on his body, and Kevin stood beside him. He shot a blue laser beam at the fallen angel. He advanced forward. The demonic angel pushed back Shaun's energy.

The stranger lifted the metal sheeting up and helped Logan and Melody wriggle free.

Kevin concentrated on the power of the stones. The energy rose and fell. As Shaun advanced with the sapphire, the light from the nine other stones weakened. Staying close behind Shaun, Kevin was ready to open the portal back to Olivet. Shaun stopped the laser beam and stretched out the forcefield, raising a wall of energy to protect them. It held for a few seconds, and that was all the time Kevin needed. First, Logan and Melody entered the portal, then the dumbfounded-looking stranger.

"You can't escape me! This is now my world!" bellowed the demon.

Kevin wanted to reach for Geoff and drag him through. But he had been dead too long to be revived. Even if he dragged him through the portal membrane, he wouldn't heal and rejuvenate. Kevin could only hope that Geoff was now with Sophia.

The portal doorway was the size of an average door. Worried the fallen angel could follow them, Kevin grabbed Shaun from behind and together they fell backwards into the portal, Kevin closing it as they went.

Lying on the floor of Olivet's main dining room were the two pens that had been sticking out of his body. His skin had fused, healed, when he jumped into the portal.

Shaun rolled to the side and got to his feet.

Kevin drew in a breath – no pain. Shaun held out a hand to help him up.

Phillip, mesmerized, turned around, orientating himself to his new surroundings, and the people in the restaurant. "What is this? Where are we?"

Logan wasted no time reuniting with his sister and Brody. They had mixed feelings about Phillip.

A woman pushed through the crowd. "Phillip! Phillip!"

She had short blond hair, and a pale face. She ran into Phillip's arms. He pushed her away and then pulled her back into them, speechless, unable to believe she was real.

The room fell silent as the remaining sparkle of energy in the air from the portal went out.

"WHERE'S GEOFF?" Rachel asked, holding Shaun's face.

Shaun couldn't hide the pain and Kevin felt that he wanted to push Rachel away, but he rested his head on hers. "He's gone. The demonic angel killed him. Geoff saved our lives."

Phillip moved back into the crowd, ashamed. If he hadn't been sorry for what he had done, Kevin would've decked him; he wanted Phillip to feel the pain Shaun was feeling. It was because of him that Geoff had died. He had caused the chain of events.

Abraham came over and patted Kevin on the shoulder. "You did well, son."

"They will not stop looking for you both," Delilah said.

"Let's get these men something to eat," Abraham called out.

It was clear they had been in the middle of planning something. "What's going on?" Kevin asked, noticing the serious atmosphere of the room. He scanned Rachel.

"Oy," Rachel said.

"Sorry, it's a bad habit." Kevin blushed.

"Don't you worry. You've done enough," Delilah said.

"What's wrong, Rachel?" Shaun also had picked up on the strange vibe.

"It's the people at the Sphinx. We're not sure if they're still alive. You've been gone for three days," Rachel said.

Puzzled, Kevin searched Shaun's face for verification.

"You were in and out of consciousness for seventy-two hours. It was a miracle you pulled through," Shaun said.

"What happened?" Rachel was looking at the blood on his jacket.

"I could do with some clean clothes," Kevin said, avoiding her question.

"Sure thing. Let's head to our quarters," Rachel suggested. "You both can get cleaned up there."

13

KNOW THY ENEMY: SHAUN. EGYPT.

While Kevin cleaned up, Shaun took the penthouse's private elevator up to the helipad. He stood shielding his eyes, trying to see the helicopters, but thanks to the thick sandstorm it was impossible. He couldn't see two feet away from the exit. Was it a sandstorm, or was it the Jinn? He didn't know what he was looking at anymore.

He couldn't believe Geoff was gone. Shaun turned his face up to where the sky should have been. "I'll see you soon, big guy."

He turned away from the storm and headed back down into the underground city, to see if Kevin was ready to open the next portal in search of survivors. He was glad Kevin was alive, but it was hard to show this when someone else that he cared for was gone.

Shaun knocked on the bathroom door and listened.

"I'll be right out," Kevin said, and turned off the shower.

Shaun returned to the kitchen, where Rachel had replaced her clothes with clean, dark special-ops gear. Shaun grabbed a bottle of water.

"Throw me one? Ta." When he did, Rachel put the bottle on the carpet and fastened up her boots.

"I went up. I couldn't see beyond – the sandstorm?"

"Be careful, you shouldn't go outside on your own. Dark entities could be hiding inside the storm, waiting for you," Rachel said.

Steam drifted out of the bathroom as Kevin emerged, hair slicked back. He was also wearing clean black-ops cargo pants, and a black t-shirt. Most of the time, Kevin let his hair trail over the left side of his face, trying to hide his emotions; only his right eye would be visible. All through school, Kevin had hidden behind his fringe. However, today was different and with his hair pulled back, he looked like a badass. He just needed black steel toe-cap boots to complete the getup, but he wore his old gym shoes – the ones he had worn for as long as Shaun could remember. Blue Converse All-Star boots. Kevin looked drained; his face pale. He needed a recharge. Shaun was quick to grow angry at Jade; she should be here with him. Kevin was trying to hide his feelings. Saying he was fine all the time. Soon, he was going to snap.

SHAUN TURNED and looked through the elevator's glass wall as they descended towards the atrium. The clean-up crew were doing a great job after the destruction of the Leviathan's attempt to harvest human organs. Shaun rubbed his side, where his kidney should have been.

"I still can't believe you and the icosahedron sapphire generated the energy to do this much damage," Kevin said.

The elevator doors opened, and they walked across the grass and stood outside the worship hall that was used for all religious groups. The Muslim community were in the middle of their evening prayers. "Why are we waiting here?" Shaun asked.

"We're waiting for Ali Ben Her. He's a professor from Oxford University, and he did a study on the Jinn decades ago. We need to know more about what we're up against. The Quran warns of the Jinn. We need to combine our knowledge and teachings to defeat them," Rachel said.

"I don't think we are supposed to defeat anything. We need to just prepare for ascension," Kevin said.

"But how can we ascend, if we cannot get to the Sphinx?" Rachel asked.

"I don't know. I'm not a fortune teller – I'm an Empath."

Shaun scratched the side of his face, and rubbed the back of his neck. "I went to a fortune teller once; nothing she said rang true. Nothing she said came true."

"How old were you?" Rachel said.

"About fifteen?" Shaun leaned against the side of the worship hall doorway, where the clean-up crew had installed new glass.

"Why did you go?"

"You know. The usual. I wanted to know if my mom was in Heaven." Shaun crossed his arms over his chest. He was uncomfortable discussing his foolish behavior.

"What did the fortune teller say?" Kevin asked.

"That Mom was in Heaven waiting for me, and that she was very pleased I was doing well at school."

"What? That's a lie," Kevin said.

"Don't hold back, K."

"What else did she say?" Rachel said.

"That my dad would take good care of me, and we would have many adventures together, and not to worry about my mom, because she was in Heaven."

"Seriously?" Kevin said.

"Yep. My mom is in Heaven, but that's a no-brainer. The rest of the stuff was false. K, you know what my dad was like?"

"Yes, I do."

"You shouldn't go to fortune tellers you don't know," Rachel said.

"Why?" Kevin asked.

"No matter how certain they are, it doesn't mean that they're right. There are entities, beside the Jinn, floating around beyond our sight, ready to tell us all sorts of crap. All they want to do is create havoc, and for us to doubt our own intuition. The negative spirits are just waiting to feed half-truths to an egotistical fortune teller who has no real protection, and knows no better. I'm not saying fortune tellers are bad people, just that some don't really know what they're connecting to. The astral realm isn't only for angelic beings," Rachel said.

"But what about Casey and Sophia?" Kevin asked.

"Casey sees the past, and occasionally draws pictures of the future. But he doesn't believe in what he sees. Sophia was a prophet nurtured by God. Their egos don't govern. These are not ordinary days. We are living at the end of our current conscious reality. Casey and Sophia are warriors of Hashim," Rachel said.

Shaun propped his leg up against the wall behind him. He thought about what Rachel had said. Before he became friends with Kevin, he didn't have any faith in fortune tellers. He didn't even have faith in God, until he met Sophia and Casey.

Rumbling movements came from inside the hall, and Shaun peeked inside. People were neatly stacking their mats before leaving the prayer room. Respectfully, he stood off to the side and waited for the worshippers to leave.

Rachel took off her shoes, and Kevin waited with Shaun at the entrance. Calm, peaceful energy floated inside the hall, and light sparkled, as if caught in sunrays. As a child, Kevin would have imagined the flickering lights were thousands of tiny, good angels that blessed those that had prayed. He bowed his head slightly, in awe of the light in the room. It reminded Shaun of the Supreme Master's dark energy, when the Leviathan was in human form. Shaun's body shivered.

"What are you doing?" Kevin asked.

"Nothing." Shaun averted his eyes.

"Yes, you are. Don't give me that crap," Kevin said.

"No, I'm not."

Kevin turned his head and faced Shaun. "Yes. You. Are. You can see the light in the room, and the goodness I feel. Love and blessing filled the room."

Shaun thought about it for a few seconds and Kevin was right. He didn't think to articulate it. He bowed his head as a sign of respect. "Would you say it's like being in the presence of a good angel?" Shaun had spoken the words before he could change them.

"Maybe?" Kevin fell silent, and he too bowed his head in respect.

"This is Professor Ali Ben Her," Rachel said.

Shaun and Kevin shook hands with Ali and they walked together into the restaurant. Abraham and Delilah were seated at a large dinner table with a group of men. Kevin wondered why they were meeting in the restaurant. There were hundreds of places they could meet. But then he supposed if they had been in the resistance tunnels under the compound for eighteen months, they would be comfortable anywhere.

"Do you mind?" Kevin said, grabbing a plate.

"No. Go ahead," Ali said.

Shaun joined Kevin. They looked at the trays of food. They

were going to need a lot to sustain their energy levels for the coming hours.

"What do you feel like eating?" the woman behind the counter asked.

"Scrambled eggs, and toast with strawberry jam," Kevin said.

"I'll have the same," said Shaun.

"I'll make you both a fresh batch," the woman said, going into the kitchen.

* * *

SHAUN PEEKED OVER HIS SHOULDER. Ali, Rachel, Delilah and Etain nodded in agreement with three soldiers he didn't recognize. Delilah gazed around the cafe suspiciously. Then the others did the same.

Shaun half-expected Geoff to walk out of the kitchen with the dish of scrambled eggs, and instantly his stomach spasmed, seeing the woman coming instead. He took the serving spoon after Kevin, and stared at the fresh eggs on his plate. They sat separately from the others.

Kevin just stared at the food, not picking anything, lost in thought.

"You alright?" Shaun nudged him. "What gives?"

Kevin shook his head as if coming out of a trance.

"You're thinking of Jade, aren't you?

"Sometimes I can feel her, as if she is reaching out for me."

"You miss Geoff?" Kevin said, not making eye contract.

"Yeah."

They ate the rest of their meal, slowly, pushing the food around, taking small bites, looking grim.

Etain came over as Shaun picked up a slice of unbuttered, cold toast, spreading it with strawberry jam, then taking a bite, washing it down with a warm cup of coffee.

"Meet us upstairs, in the war room," said Etain.

Shaun took another sip of coffee. "I don't know where that is," he said, after swallowing the last piece of jam toast.

"I'll show them the way," Gil said, entering the restaurant.

"Roger that, I'll see you in fifteen," Etain said, exiting the doors.

"Gil, Kevin… Kevin, Gil," Shaun said.

"The portal master," Gil said, grinning. "I hope we get to meet your other friends too. I've heard a lot about you guys."

Kevin put down his fork and shook Gil's hand. "Nice to meet you, Gil."

"How's Theo doing?" Shaun said.

"He's a tough cookie. Speak of the little devil…" Gil said, seeing Theo run between the open glass doors.

"Daddy!" Theo wore a blue t-shirt and brown shorts. He stopped in front of Shaun before reaching Gil. "Are you going to help us fight the Jinn?"

"How do you know about the Jinn? Have you been eavesdropping again, Theo?" Gil said in a scolding tone.

"No. Yes. Sorry. But Daddy, is the blue angel going to help us?"

Shaun interrupted. "I'm not an angel, Theo. I'm just a man. My name is Shaun. Please call me Shaun, Theo."

Kevin stood quietly, chewing the inside of his mouth, and pushed his cuticles down with a slight impatience. Shaun could tell he was sensing something that was eluding the rest of them.

"We must go. You go back and help the clean-up crew get this place in order." Gil crouched down to Theo's height, and gave him a hug and a pat on the bottom to send him on his way.

Shaun recognized love; the love he never had from his father. "Lead the way."

"The place is totally amazing," Kevin said as Gil rattled off the specs of the underground two towers, the rest of the city, and its ability to sustain life for a decade if needed.

"Don't you two geek out on me," Shaun said.

Guarding the door to the war room was a soldier, and an old woman they called Mama Bina, who was resting in a chair, her eyes squinted, concentrating as if scrutinizing, assessing, and approving each person as they entered the room. Rachel and Shaun bent down and gave her a kiss and a hug.

"This is Kevin, my friend."

Mama Bina took Kevin's hand and patted it.

The energy inside the war room was heavy; nothing like the atmosphere he had sensed in the worship hall. Shaun didn't know what to do with the information his receptors were picking up on an energetic level. Military men sat around a conference table.

Mama Bina closed the door before sitting in the chair next to Shaun. Kevin moved, as if cramped, awkward – even nervous – sitting between him and Rachel; he knew what was coming. When Shaun first met Mama Bina, she had presented herself as an old lady brushing off invisible crumbs while she cared for the resistance's children. Shaun had wondered why she was at a briefing.

Shaun watched Kevin as he took a sip of water; he looked hot and flustered, as if hiding something.

At the front of the room was a giant, transparent screen.

"Now that everyone is here, we will put forward a strategy to defeat the Jinn and get the people to the portals for ascension." Abraham sat down at the head of the table.

Ali took the floor and walked in front of the screen. "We are in the final days of our civilization. We are up against a revengeful, supernatural race that existed before our time. We cannot see the Jinn in their natural state, which makes them even more dangerous. As you may already know, they are a race born from the fire of scorching wind. They can take on the form of any one of us. The Jinn are determined, strategically structured. They are stronger and more cunning than any human."

Ali waited for the information to filter through the room before continuing. "Seeing that no one objects to my description of the Jinn, I will continue. They have families and beliefs, but don't mistake them as good. For every Jinn you believe to be good, a thousand will be evil. They will form themselves into an army. Their one aim is to destroy humankind. Enoch forewarned us of these days, in the Quran and all the other scriptures, before the book of Enoch was removed from their sacred text. The Jinn are a very devious species. Though rare, they can possess the human body. Mostly they will assume the human form, like the Leviathan that took on the form of the human it consumed, calling itself the Supreme Master." He nodded at Shaun. "Thank you for freeing us all from the Supreme Master and his mind-controlling eldritch pendants."

Everyone at the table stood and applauded Shaun. He could feel his face burning up with embarrassment.

When all were seated once more, Ali continued. "We are seeing more and more human possessions as they grow stronger. Do not be fooled by them, for they can take on the appearance of your brother, your mother, your superior, or your beloved pet."

Shaun was listening, but didn't understand how this was going to help them defeat the Jinn. He was never one to sit still, and found it difficult to remain seated. Rachel caught his eye, and everything slowed down. He breathed in, as if he had sniffed back the most delicious fragrance in the world. She motioned for him to look ahead at Ali. Shaun smiled, and returned his attention to the speaker.

"What you see outside, the dark storms, is nothing more than the cover for an army of tricksters that hunt each and every one of us, leading us into the dark realm. Every day they are growing stronger," Ali said.

"We have been seeing the Jinn as smoky gray apparitions. So, the sandstorm is not good Jinn here to protect us," Shaun said dryly.

"That is correct. There is only one way to arm ourselves, and that is with the faith of Allah – God."

"So, there is nothing we can do to defeat it?" Kevin asked.

"I'm surprised that God has blessed you. You must pray he does not take those blessings away," Ali said, bluntly.

"Excuse my ignorance," Rachel said, standing.

Shaun wasn't sure if that was a good idea. In a room of fifteen, only three were woman. And he was sure Ali had just said he didn't think Kevin deserved his powers.

"We're here to form a strategy. It is good to know our enemy, but what is the plan to get to the Sphinx for ascension in the coming weeks?" Rachel said and looked to Abraham.

"First, we must rescue those camped at the Sphinx and bring them back here," Delilah said.

Kevin moved in his seat uncomfortably; he knew what she was going to say next, and Shaun did too. She was going to propose to use him to open a portal to the Sphinx, so they could send in a team to rescue the pilgrims waiting for the ascension.

"Thank you, Ali," Abraham said, taking the floor.

Delilah and Rachel sat back down.

"Because of your wisdom, Ali, we will not send any more soldiers to travel across the desert to the Sphinx, because they will need to pass through the storm which we know is the merging dark realm, and the Jinn are hiding behind its walls, preparing to attack. We are forearmed," Abraham eyed Kevin.

"We thank Hashim our Elohim for sending you to help us," Abraham said.

Here we go, and why can't they all just say God, for Christ's sake? Shaun thought. "What is it you need us to do?" Shaun said, cutting to the chase.

Gil reached for a laptop computer that sat on a walnut credenza against the wall behind him. Mama Bina smiled at Shaun, and he lovingly smiled back. The transparent screen behind Abraham filled with light and schematic lines on a map mirroring Gil's laptop.

"This is where the tents are, and the buses used as accommodation are here. The storm has expanded to these surrounding areas."

Gil moved a cursor across the large screen towards Olivet, showing the six-hundred-mile expansiveness of the dark realm.

"We can no longer send out helicopters to rescue the people, and the choppers at the Sphinx cannot take off," Gil said.

Get to the point, Shaun thought.

Abraham spoke directly to Kevin. "Can you open a portal and hold it open long enough for my men to marshal the pilgrims and get them back here?"

Kevin moved forward and leaned his elbows on the table, clasping his hands together as if in prayer. "I can hold it open for fifteen minutes, tops."

"That might not be enough time," Etain said.

"If that's all the time you have, then that's all the time you need," Abraham said.

"If he can." Shaun studied Kevin, then turned back to Abraham and Etain. "And how do you propose to protect the soldiers marshalling the people?"

"The pilgrims could already be dead, or possessed by Jinn," Ali said.

"You, Shaun. You will protect them with the hermetic shield," Abraham said.

Shaun made strong eye contact with Abraham. Tilting his head slightly, he lowered his voice and said, "I can't be in two places at once. I need to protect Kevin from the fallen angels and the Jinn."

Ali pushed back his chair and abruptly stood up and turned his body to face Shaun. "You speak of fallen angels. They do not exist in the Quran; only the Jinn. In the Quran, angels cannot disobey Allah. Only Christians and Jewish mystics believe angels can disobey Allah. You must protect your friend from the Jinn. He is our key to survival. When you are out there, beware of negative thoughts and emotions. The Jinn will whisper in your ears and implant negative thoughts in your mind," Ali said, praying quickly before taking a sip of water.

"The fallen angels are real. It doesn't matter what we call them, but they're different from the Jinn. We have more than one adversary," Shaun said to Ali.

Kevin stayed in his seat and in a quiet voice said to Shaun, "I'll be okay."

"Etain, get the team ready. You go in ten minutes. The longer we delay acting, the more likely we won't find any survivors alive," Abraham said.

"Abraham," Rachel said, as everyone rose from their seats to leave. "If we don't remove the Jinn from the portal, how will we ascend?"

"One thing at a time, soldier, let's get those people out there safely back here," Abraham said, pointing up to the ground above.

"It's all right. God will show us the way," Mama Bina said.

The room went silent, and everyone stilled themselves while Abraham said a prayer.

14

ARMY OF TRICKSTERS: KEVIN. THE SPHINX.

The soldiers put on their enhanced night-vision binoculars to see through the sandstorm. They gave Shaun and Kevin identical equipment. Rachel led one of the two teams and Etain the other. There were nine people. The men readied themselves as Kevin recalled his last emotional memory of the campsite. He visualized all the people he had seen, took in a deep breath, and let it out.

They could all be dead.

Kevin's thoughts strayed to the spacecraft, and he wondered what it would be like to fly. It was exhilarating to think it might still have the potential. He loved to fly. It would be great if he could return later with Casey and, hopefully, Jade, if she was willing to leave Mingan. An image of Mingan embracing Jade entered his mind, putting him off-balance, causing him to disconnect from the emotions he had of the camp at the Sphinx.

"What's wrong?" Shaun asked.

Kevin turned away, looked up at the ceiling, and took a deep breath.

"You've got this."

Kevin harnessed the thrilling memory of boarding the chopper, but he could still feel the sadness he felt imagining Jade in Mingan's arms. The sparks he had managed to create went out.

"What the hell are you thinking about?" Shaun said.

"Clear your mind, and use my memory," Rachel said, taking Kevin's hands and putting them up to her temple.

It was a good idea. Adrenaline raced through his veins as he hooked into her image of her launching a hand-to-air missile. Static energy filled the air and the portal membrane, waves of color crackled and sparked with light. With the emotions and memory flowing through him, he stretched out his arms, making the portal wide enough for them to step through in two groups.

The membrane of the portal was as wonderful as it always was, and the soldiers were not immune to the bliss. Kevin, Shaun, and Rachel helped the others to advance beyond the energy.

Kevin stepped out into a raging sandstorm. He coughed, choking on the sand that blinded him. It whipped up into his face. He held his eyes shut tight, and lost his sense of direction.

Someone pulled down his protective night-vision goggles. Instantly, he had vision into the storm. Shaun had wasted no time erecting a hermetic shield around the group. They pushed forward into the storm, leaving him behind.

Kevin watched them fade away. He didn't know how long he was going to be able to hold a portal open on the edge of the dark realm. If they didn't return in fifteen minutes, the plan was for him to return to Olivet and regenerate another portal after ten minutes. A gale-force wind whipped sand against him as he tried to see. Everything was

shades of gold and brown. Occasionally, he would see dark shapes –
moving silhouettes, flickering in and out of existence as they moved
towards him. He just hoped they were the returning soldiers.

"Who's there?" Kevin shouted into the storm. The dark mass
moved closer. Maybe he should collapse the portal, just in case, but
he didn't need to worry, because evil couldn't penetrate the walls.
Which was why it made no sense that the fallen angel would want
Kevin to open a portal to Heaven. It wouldn't be able to pass
through the membrane.

The sand whipped against his body like sandpaper, chafing
against his clothes. It would've ripped his bandana off his head if it
hadn't been for the tight-fitting goggles. They could not last long in
such a storm. He couldn't imagine how anyone could survive.

Come on, guys, hurry.

Kevin changed his stance, ready to step back into the
membrane, when he saw a group of figures headed his way. A
silhouette of a female stepped into view. *Rachel?* He saw the defini-
tion of the other shapes too – human. But he couldn't tell if Shaun
was with her. He couldn't imagine Shaun leaving Rachel on her
own unless something had happened to him.

With their heads bowed, they clutched the ends of the blankets
that covered them from head to toe and snapped violently in the
wind. It reminded him of summer houses closed for winter, when
people covered the furniture with dusty sheets. "Rachel, is that
you?" Kevin yelled into the storm. He strained to hear.

The ground beneath him trembled. He took a few steps to the
side. "Rachel!"

She couldn't hear him. Maybe she didn't see him. Her head
tilted downward, protecting her face from the rough sand as dirt and
pebbles thrashed into their bodies. Kevin peered deep into the storm
with the night-vision goggles, as if it would make it easier to see

Rachel's features. He reached out emotionally, searching for Rachel's energy signature, as well as trying to gauge the state of those around her. He came up empty. *Come on, Rachel, answer me,* he thought. He stuck his hand under his armpits to protect them, and nervously waited for them to get closer.

Not much further now. They pushed and struggled against the wind. Kevin stepped aside for Rachel and her group of survivors to pass by and enter the portal's healing membrane.

Just as she was about to step into the portal membrane, Rachel fixed eyes with his. Hers seemed black. Suddenly, the membrane flung her backwards, like she had hit an electric fence, and the portal collapsed. The first row of people went to her aid. Rachel, unaffected by the sandstorm, removed her blanket, revealing her head. He didn't need to see her whole body — it was all in the eyes. They were black with rage and fury, and he was the target. Evil surrounded him. Its appearance resembled Rachel but, unlike her, it was devoid of positive emotions and intentions. Kevin quickly glanced at the rest of the group, then ran into the storm, as fast as he could. He remembered his radio and plucked it off his hip. "Shaun. Come in. Shaun, do you copy?" Kevin said into his radio.

The radio crackled. Nothing but static crackled back at him. The dense black entity that had disguised itself as Rachel went flying into the storm. Kevin couldn't tell where it went. He turned to see if the group was still there, but they too had disappeared. The ground trembled again. He just prayed it wasn't the giant cobra. He had never had a fear of snakes – just a healthy sense of caution – but he could feel his nerves stretched.

The absence of the sun was the worst. He was going to need to create a portal and get himself out of here. Kevin tripped over a rock, and came down hard on his knee. His kneecap popped out of place. "Shit! Dammit!" He held his leg as the sand covered him.

Soon he would become part of the desert. Trying not to think too much about what he needed to do, he popped his knee back into place and screamed into the storm. If he could dig down to get away from the Jinn and the storm, he would. He placed his hands on the ground, and imagined a hole to fall into. Before he realized what he was doing, Kevin opened a portal and fell into a chamber, landing on his stomach. His knee healed, but his neck ached from whiplash. Air returned to his lungs as he sucked in a deep breath, feeling the material of the balaclava enter his mouth at the same time.

Kevin dusted himself off as he examined the carvings on the chamber walls. There was a set of steps that led upward. He thought of using them but realized he could see into the dark chamber, and fear washed over him. *How can I see when there's no light?* Kevin thought. Panic pounded at his chest.

"Idiot!" he spat, remembering the goggles on his face.

The drawings on the walls were of people; animals; people with animal heads; lines, and circles. Egyptian hieroglyphics. None of it made any sense to him. He walked into the center of the room. Maybe this was where Rachel and Etain had transported to the stars.

Despite everything, he found the ancient chamber fascinating. It must be the portal that everyone would travel through on the day of ascension. He placed his hand on the wall and tuned in to the energy. Love… joy… fear… so many emotions throughout time were soaked into the walls, and he could sense a lot that he didn't have words to describe. He wondered if it only went to one place, or if it could take them to other worlds across the universe, or even beyond the universe.

There was a circle in the middle of the room, and in the circle was another, and another, and another, like an unconnected spiral. Circles within circles, like a bull's-eye target. Kevin walked the parameter of the outer circle, then stepped into the next circle, and the next, until he was at the center. He waited for something to happen, but nothing did. He went to step out, to head up the stairs, when light began traveling around the circles towards him. It followed the same pathway he took, until it was under his feet, and a magnificent blinding white light illuminated the circle which rose up around him.

Kevin pushed the goggles off his eyes. The portal was activated, and Kevin was afraid of what might happen next. Quickly, he stepped out of the circles, and the light traveled back the way it came, like water.

"Kevin!"

The word exploded into his head with a flash of blue light.

"Kevin!"

It was too loud to register who was calling him.

"Kevin!"

He dropped to the ground with the pain and squeezed his head.

"Kevin!"

This time, the voice was external. It was coming from the top of the stairs. With the light gone, Kevin pulled his goggles back down, and approached the stone steps with caution. His body was heavy with fatigue. He just wanted to sleep. To rest a while. His body was out of balance, and it was hard to walk straight.

Shaun and Rachel came down the stairs. He felt them before they came into view. Kevin stopped at the bottom of the stairs and waited.

"What's wrong? How did you get in here without passing us?" Rachel said.

"I've been searching the storm for you, calling out your name. I thought you must have left to recharge," Shaun said.

"A Jinn, disguised as Rachel, tried to pass through the portal. But the portal collapsed and repelled her. I ran, fell, and ended up down here." Kevin tuned into Rachel's energy, just to make sure it was really her this time. He recognized her fiery emotions.

"Hey, I can feel that," Rachel said.

"Me too, K. You're getting stronger," Shaun said.

"Or you're more sensitive," Kevin smiled.

"How did you know it wasn't her?" Shaun asked.

Kevin could hear a commotion coming from up the stairs. "I didn't. I let it pass. The portal stopped her like she had hit an electrical fence. It wouldn't let her in. What's up there? What's all the commotion?"

"We found most of the survivors taking shelter inside the Sphinx. They're short on space, and people are getting agitated," Shaun said.

"What about Etain's group? Are they up there too?" Kevin asked.

"No. We lost contact," said Rachel.

"Is this where you were you transported to the heavens?" Kevin asked.

"Yeah, why?" Rachel asked.

"Just checking."

"We need to energize you, and get these people to Olivet. Now," Shaun said, encapsulating Kevin and giving him a boost. A fight broke out above them.

Shaun ran up the stairs in a shroud of blue and broke up the fight. The power of the stones pumping through his muscles was exhilarating. He felt superhuman. He took two steps at a time as he followed Shaun and Rachel up the stone steps. His intuition heightened, the toxic energy in the upper chamber came flooding into his solar plexus, as if he was an opened book. He resisted the urge to hold his breath, and pushed back the energy with this super strength – a temporary gift from Shaun he wasn't going to let go to waste. Something was wrong with these people. Rachel's team was trying to help Shaun with the escalating violence. Kevin scanned the faces for black irises when, suddenly, a man with a blade charged at him. A blue laser beam blasted the man, and he turned to smoke. The soldiers corralled as many people as they could in Kevin's direction, while others ran in a wild panic out into the storm. Shaun turned his shield into a wall between them and the chaos.

"Open a portal and get us out of here," Shaun said.

Waving his hands in the air, collecting the energy from Shaun's shield, Kevin constructed the portal, people rushed forward to enter. The soldiers intervened, controlling the crowd, while Rachel led the way through the portal back at Olivet.

The portal repelled dozens of people, who were Jinn in disguise. The soldiers swiftly took care of the imposters, while Kevin created new portals back to Olivet. Etain's crew, with more survivors, appeared close to the Sphinx paws, just as Kevin was about to leave. He held the portal open, urging them to hurry. He could feel that the superhuman strength the stones had bestowed upon him was running out, fast.

The group raced towards him. Fear spread through Kevin's body. Emerging from the apocalyptic sandstorm was the thirst for revenge dripping off the souls – they weren't all human. All at once, they became a black mass. One out of every three people turned out to be a Jinn in disguise. Shaun stepped back through the portal from Olivet, and it was near impossible to hear what he was trying to say. It was nearly as impossible to see, even with the goggles on. Kevin pointed to the mass getting closer. A foul odor, like rotting garbage, exited the storm, entered the chamber, seeped through his mask, and made him gag. The portal collapsed. Shaun erected the hermetic shield and Kevin welcomed the blue haze arched above them.

"Why did you come back? We must get of out here," Kevin said.

He had only taken two steps, but Shaun was already out of sight.

It was a mistake that he couldn't put right. The black mass was upon him.

"Get off me!" Kevin struggled to pull his knife out of its sheath. The creatures clawed at Kevin's face and ripped off the goggles and balaclava. Kevin's feet left the ground as they carried him outside. The Jinn lifted him higher, but a blue bolt of lightning penetrated the storm, and divided the dark mass.

They dropped Kevin, but the wind picked him up and he tumbled through the air. "Shaun!" he yelled, knowing his cries were hollow. Like he was an autumn leaf, the wind pushed him into the outside stone wall of the Sphinx. He couldn't breathe; he didn't want to breathe – he didn't want to gulp the air, but he couldn't stop himself. Sand entered his mouth and scratched his throat until he heaved and coughed. He climbed across the Sphinx's paw and fell backward down the steps. Battered, he crashed into another wall that stopped him. In the dark, he froze, listening. A solid figure crashed into him.

"Who's that?"

"It's me. Etain."

"You went into the portal," Kevin said.

"I followed Shaun and stepped out just before the portal closed. I'm missing two men."

Etain moved closer and reached for Kevin's head. He had brought another pair of night-vision goggles. Kevin sighed in relief. Through the storm, he searched for the Jinn, and for Shaun. Three dark figures headed down the steps towards them.

"There's a fifty-fifty chance that the shadows heading our way are Shaun and my soldiers."

"It's not Shaun."

"How can you be so sure?" Etain asked.

"I sense a powerful state of bliss. The closer they get, the taller they seem. Shaun's hermetic shield would be glowing. I don't see any blue hue."

Etain readied himself for a physical battle. Kevin got out his knife, and together they stood in the shadows.

At least seven feet above the ground, piercing red eyes stared down at him. *It's a demonic angel.* Where the hell was Shaun? Kevin hoped nothing this bad had happened to him. "Let's get out of here."

He pulled Etain down the next set of stairs, into the portal chamber, and summoned the energy to open a portal. A blue explosion erupted, and light shone down the stairs. Kevin turned and hooded his eyes. *He does look like a blue angel.* Kevin smiled.

"What are you grinning at? I just saved your ass," Shaun said, walking down the last few steps.

"Nothing. Nothing at all."

"Then why don't you get us the heck out of here, before those things come back?"

Kevin opened a portal back to the war room at Olivet and quickly closed it behind him.

Delilah and a few others were helping the survivors. They had handed out clean blankets and water. Theo helped Mama Bina, who was still checking each person entering the room. Theo stared in amazement, his mouth hanging open.

"Is he an angel, too?" Theo said to Shaun.

"No. We're not angels, buddy," Shaun said.

"Can I go inside?" Theo asked.

"Not now, but maybe one day," Kevin said.

An air of relief washed over the room. Most of the people were being seen to by doctors. Some sat with their heads between their legs and others were hyperventilating.

"What's wrong with them?" Kevin asked Rachel. They had passed through the portal. Whatever ailed them should be gone.

"They're in shock. So much has happened to them, passing through the portal. They believed the hand of God had touched them, and they became overwhelmed," Rachel said.

"The Jinn are getting stronger," Kevin told her.

"The merger of the realms might give the evil entities strength. But what about the fallen angels? How many have risen, and how many more will rise?" Rachel asked.

"Can't we talk to the Jinn? Maybe we could coexist, and defeat the fallen angels together?" Kevin said.

"If God had wanted us to co-exist, we would co-exist. It was God who chose for the Jinn to be separated from humans," Rachel said.

"So why is he letting the two realms merge?"

"It is written in the Quran," Ali said, entering the room again.

Delilah stood up and winked at Shaun and Kevin. "If the rest of you would like to follow me, I'll show you where you can get clean clothes and have a shower, and if you would like to say a prayer or two, there are a couple of worship halls downstairs. You will be welcomed in any one of them. We all pray to the same God. Please come with me," she said to the survivors, leaving the room to them and the soldiers.

"Good job, men," Abraham said.

"Get some rest before you head off to gather my men from

around the world, with, I hope, hundreds of survivors. Recharge your batteries," Etain said.

"I will, but I'm going to check on Logan and Melody and make sure everyone that got off Whistler is okay. Then I'm good to go," Kevin said.

"Like hell you are," said Shaun.

15

―――――

INFERNO: SHAUN. MT FUJI, JAPAN.

"You guys ready?" Etain said to his men then turned to Shaun and Kevin. "Are you sure you don't need more rest?" he asked Kevin.

"I'll be fine."

"Then hurry back with my men."

Kevin moved his arm in a swirl and opened the portal. From the moment they stepped into it, they were bathed in glory. For a second, they hesitated. Shaun followed Rachel through and stepped out under a Japanese Torii. Ash drifted down from the sky like snowflakes. Neither of them had accompanied Kevin when he'd dropped off the soldiers. Kevin had described the area as beautiful, with pink and white cherry blossoms.

The scene was nothing like he had described. Ash covered the trees, and plumes of smoke rose up from the collapsed peak of Mount Fuji. Shaun searched between the dying trees for a sign of the soldiers.

"What's that smell? Where are they?" Rachel shouted, covering her mouth with a balaclava from around her neck.

"Sulphur! They're supposed to be here. I told them to make sure someone was waiting," Kevin said, covering his mouth.

"Maybe they had to evacuate the National Park at the base of the mountain. It looks like it's going to blow. I didn't think Mount Fuji was a live volcano," Shaun said.

"It's always been an active volcano, but it hasn't erupted for centuries. It doesn't look like we have much time before it explodes," Kevin said.

Rachel pulled out her binoculars and searched the landscape for human heat signatures. "How long do you think we've got?"

"I don't know. But it can't be long," said Kevin.

"Can I see?" Shaun reached out for the binoculars.

"I'm going to search the shrine. Come find me if I'm not back in a couple of minutes."

"You be careful. It doesn't look stable. If anything happens to you, we're stuck here," Rachel said.

Kevin climbed over the rubble to get into the part of the shrine that was still standing. The ground was torn apart. Shaun turned back and searched the area, using the binoculars. "If there's people down there at the base of the mountain, they might not make it up here before she blows."

"Let's get Kevin. We shouldn't let him out of our sight. We need to find a way down there and hope we meet survivors en route," Rachel said.

Shaun jumped over fissures as the earth quaked. He landed on the edge and slipped back as the ground fell away. Rachel grabbed him and hauled him to safety as the terrain continued to move like water. Kevin emerged from the shrine as it collapsed, yelling, "Earthquake!"

Together, they stood waiting for the land to stop moving. The ground buckled and cracked between their feet. The fractures snaked under the torii into the landscape beyond. Trees toppled over and disappeared into the fissure as it grew.

Someone touched Shaun on the shoulder from behind. "You scared the shit out of me!" Shaun yelled over the grinding earth as it settled.

"Sorry! I'm glad to see you guys. The earthquakes started the moment we got here. Mount Fuji is about to blow," the soldier said.

"Are there any survivors? Where's the rest of your team?" Rachel asked.

"The team is fine, and we've found plenty of survivors, but they're all down there at Pica Fuji campsite. The survivors had a prophecy dream. I lost radio contact about thirty minutes ago. I think it's the ash."

The mountain exploded, sending rocks and lava into the sky. The dark cloud rolled outward, and the burning rock succumbed to gravity.

"We've got to move. This way!" the soldier called out, protecting his head as burning embers and molten rock fell around them. The rubble and trees combusted into flames.

Before they moved, a burning rock the size of a baseball hit the soldier in the back. He screamed. Kevin quickly took hold of the man's temples.

"What do you see?" Rachel asked.

"People, a couple of hundred people. Tents, vans. Cabins and glam tents."

"What's a glam tent?" Shaun asked. Kevin didn't answer him. There was no time. Shaun protected Rachel as Kevin created a portal.

It was chaos at Pica Fuji campsite. People running scared passed them by as the cabins, dome tents, and trees burned. Total destruction was imminent. It was so crazy, Shaun didn't know where to start. The soldier that had gone through the portal with them had healed, and sprang into action. He grabbed a few people fleeing into the burning forest. Pulling them aside, he ordered Kevin to keep the portal open and Rachel to take them through, but Kevin began to close it.

"What are you doing? We must get everyone out of here, now," the soldier yelled.

The scared people rushed Kevin before the portal closed.

"That portal just goes back to where we came from. We need to go back to Olivet," Kevin said.

The soldier yelled for order, but nobody paid any attention, intent on fleeing, running scared into the woods, trying to get to higher ground.

One Japanese man ran up to Shaun and grabbed him by the arms, chattering in broken English, "The fire god is very angry. Ymi soon be God, of all things. The underworld and earth, soon be one. Ymi comes for us."

"It will be okay," Shaun said.

"Darkness, earthquakes, storms. World much chaos." The man, petrified, still tried to get them to understand that they must run, too. But when Shaun went to speak to him, the frightened man pushed himself away, and ran into the burning woods.

"Where are the other soldiers?" Shaun shouted.

"I don't know!"

"Okay, okay, just let me think. Let me think." Shaun stretched out his arms and hands. He turned his back on the mountain and faced the forest where the people had fled away from the erupting volcano. The light of the sapphire projected outward and upward, to create the largest hermetic orb he had ever generated. In the final push of energy, a wave of electric blue surged and arched over the treetops, around the fleeing survivors. "Bring the survivors and wounded here," Shaun said as Rachel ran into the burning forest in search of survivors. "I don't know how long I can maintain this level of power. Kevin, open a portal to Olivet."

"Shaun, you're shaking. You can't maintain this level of energy. It could kill you."

"Just get ready to open the portal when Rachel gets back. She can take them through. At least she'll be safe."

"Dammit, Shaun, this is too risky."

"I know what I'm doing, and I know what it feels like to go atomic. I've survived it before, and I'm not even close."

People slowed down when they realized that they were protected by the shield and were no longer being bombed by volcanic rocks. They turned back to Mount Fuji. The show had begun. Boulders of molten lava, cooled by the upper atmosphere, crashed down upon the hermetic shield.

"Shaun, you know I can't open a portal inside the hermetic shield," Kevin said.

Two soldiers jogged towards him, each with a group of people. Shaun kept the shield in place. He was becoming one with the shield. The people became orderly, forming three lines in front of Shaun. His arms remained stretched out. If someone touched him, it would be as if lightning struck them.

"You must reduce the size of the shield and let me out to create a portal," said Kevin. "I can't open the portal inside the hermetic shield."

The people moved in closer. "I know, I know, give me a minute." Shaun tried to reel in the energy.

Kevin and Rachel's faces changed as he reduced the size of the shield.

"Shaun, behind you," Kevin said.

He glanced back over his shoulder. The rivers of lava pooled at the base of the mountain, and flowed in their direction.

"This has to be quick," Kevin said.

"We're all good to go," said Rachel.

The Japanese people and the tourists from across the world, who had taken refuge under Mount Fuji, showed great strength and faith in Shaun.

"Behind you, the lava is backing up against the shield," Rachel said.

Shaun reduced the shield until it wrapped around them like a glove, but that also meant the lava was closer, too. He opened one side of the dome for Kevin while keeping the others protected. Kevin wasted no time and opened a portal back to Olivet. Shaun hoped Etain was on the other side and ready for a surge of people, otherwise they would trample over each other. "I'll widen the portal. Rachel, take the people through."

Shaun could hear Kevin yelling and the people hustling as the lava flowed closer. Dehydrated and light-headed, Shaun knew he was going to have to pull back the energy. Gradually, as the people left, he brought the walls closer and closer, until it was just him and Kevin inside the three-sided hermetic shield. The lava was at the height of his knees, and he was ready to drop the shield when Rachel stepped back through the portal.

"What are you doing? Get the hell out of here!" Shaun yelled.

"I'm not leaving without you," Rachel said.

It was the first time Shaun had seen fear in her eyes.

"I've got him, Rachel. Trust me. Go!" Kevin said.

"You better!" Rachel said, stepping back into the membrane of the portal.

Kevin focused on Shaun. "You ready for this? Pull your energy in quick, just like we did on Mount Whistler, and I'll pull you backwards into the portal."

Shaun trusted Kevin, but he couldn't see how they both could get out. "If I reduce the shield, we'll both burn alive. Go, K. Leave me."

"I'm not leaving you. I can do this. Now turn around and face the lava," Kevin yelled.

Shaun turned and faced the lava. It was higher than he imagined. Not good. The blue wall had a tinge of orange as it heated.

Kevin wrapped his hands tightly around Shaun's waist, grabbing the edges of his jeans. He wouldn't leave without him, no matter what he said. He shouted over his shoulder. "This better be quick, K. On a count of three. One, two…"

Shaun lowered the shield, and the lava spilled over the edge as he backed into Kevin. The heat was unreal.

"Three!" Kevin yanked him from behind, lifting his feet up off the ground, and they flew backwards. Shaun reeled in the energy in a millisecond, and the hermetic wall was gone. Lava dropped to the ground, like the gates of a dam had opened. It flowed towards him as he sailed backwards. The heat was unbearable, until he floated in the safety of the portal.

Together, they fell onto the floor of the atrium at Olivet. Disheveled people from Mount Fuji clapped and cheered. Smoke trailed off their clothing. Emotions surged into Shaun's throat, and tears pooled in his eyes. He was so grateful to be alive, he wanted to burst into laughter, and tears. He really thought he had seen Rachel for the last time. His muscles felt like jelly.

Kevin got to his feet and offered Shaun a hand, but Rachel was there just as quick.

"Hell, K!"

"I know, right?"

The Japanese people stopped clapping as Etain asked Maria, Reis's wife, and Leah to escort the new arrivals and see them settled. As they passed Shaun and Kevin, they nodded, giving thanks for Shaun had saved them, freeing them from the Supreme Master. Rachel smiled and threw an arm around Kevin's and Shaun's waists, and hugged them at the same time.

"You probably need to rehydrate," Rachel said, looking at Shaun.

"I won't mind having another look at that spacecraft you've got up there." Kevin grinned.

They were waited for the elevator to return when Maria suggested they use it for the penthouse suite.

"No rush," Shaun said.

The elevator stunk of smoke. The trio got out on the civilian living-quarters level, leaving a bunch of mesmerized people.

"You know what they're missing?" Shaun said.

"No, what?" Rachel asked.

"Cameras."

Rachel slapped his arm. "That joke sucks."

In the corridor, Josh rode out of his apartment on his tricycle and ran into Shaun's leg, just like he had a week ago, when the underground city was fighting for freedom.

"Ouch!" Shaun said, pretending to be hurt.

Josh got off his trike and rubbed Shaun's leg.

"All better." Josh was only three, and 'all better' sounded more like 'ball better'.

"All better," Shaun agreed.

Josh rode ahead of them. Before Shaun walked into the apartment, Josh turned around. His head was down, looking at his feet, turning the pedals and trying to drive them hard.

"Slow down, buddy," Shaun said.

At the sound of Shaun's voice, Josh snapped out of his trance, raised his head, and did as he was told.

"You take the first shower," Rachel said to Kevin.

Shaun headed straight for the refrigerator and drank a bottle of water.

"Don't have too much. You might make yourself sick," Rachel said. She was biting her bottom lip.

"What's troubling you?"

"I don't know if this planet is going to survive another nine days," Rachel said and let out a big breath.

"It's the end. It's going to get worse, babe."

"We need to get back to Peru and Russia."

"I agree. Do you have any more clean clothes?" Kevin asked, walking out of the bathroom.

"Yeah, sure," Rachel said, getting up.

"I'll get in the shower now," Shaun said.

The dark cargo fatigues and black t-shirts made them look like a badass black-ops team.

"All we need is baseball caps," Kevin said.

But Shaun was too weary to be amused.

* * *

HE WAS glad he chose not to eat anything. His stomach was unsettled. Mount Fuji had drained him. Ready to go, they left the atrium, and headed back up to the command center. Kevin hadn't eaten more than a couple of mouthfuls, but he filled up on caffeine. "You're not hungry either?"

"Nah."

"Good job out there. My men told me what you all did," Etain said, leaning against a console, looking at a radar.

"Here, sir," an operator pointed to a mass on the radar.

"What is it?" Rachel said.

"It's a new storm cell covering the entire Asian continent. We think it's the rise of the dark realm," Etain explained.

"What about Australia?" Kevin asked.

"It's spreading in all directions. It might be something worse than a storm cell – the resurgence of the Jinn. The Australian skies look clear," Etain said.

"From what we witnessed in Japan, I don't think the planet will last until the 8th day of Leo," said Rachel.

"We're thinking of a contingency plan." Gil spoke up from the other end of the console. "We've contacted several bunkers across the world, including China and Mt. Cheyenne, and delivered the ascension message."

"What about Australia?" Kevin asked.

"Sorry. There has been no contact."

"We better get Abraham and Delilah. They want to be here for this conversation," Etain said.

"We're going back to Peru to extract the team, and hope they've found survivors," Kevin said. "We'll bring them all back here. Is there still enough room at Olivet?"

"Don't you worry about that. This place is big enough to hold ten thousand people," Etain said.

"I hope we'll only be gone an hour, tops. We can discuss Plan B then," said Rachel.

"When you come back, can you open the portal into the atrium again?" Etain said.

"Sure, easy," Kevin said.

Kevin didn't waste any time to form a portal back to Peru, to the beachside village where he had left Etain's men.

The tiny fishing village was quiet, and the water had receded from the beach. Stranded boats on sandy banks sat idle, while fish on their last breaths flapped on the waterless shoreline. Shaun stood next to him as he stared out at the receding oceans.

"Hey! Over here! Hey," a voice cried out.

The air tasted metallic, and the birds were flying away from the beach. A familiar, urgent voice cried out to them from the trees. They turned and searched the area behind them. Shaun hooded his eyes. Kevin turned back to the ocean.

"What's wrong?" Shaun asked.

"I feel a pull in my solar plexus, as if the moon was trying to drag me into the sea. Shit! It's a tsunami!" Kevin said with wide eyes.

Way in the distance was a tower of water, two hundred feet high and heading straight for them. Back at Olivet, before he defeated the Supreme Master, Shaun had dreamed of this wave. Frozen to the spot, he gazed up, straining his neck as the wave swallowed up a cargo ship. "Give us a break! Goddammit!"

"We have to get out of here," Kevin said.

They turned away from the ocean, and searched the trees and the mountains for the person who cried out.

"Over here… run!"

"Up there. It's Reis," Rachel said as a soldier climbed down from the tree and ran towards them.

Rachel grabbed Shaun's hand.

"Run. Move it!" Reis yelled.

Kevin got to Reis first, and took his head in his hands.

"Where are the survivors? Think of the survivors… now!" Kevin said.

Kevin opened the portal as the towering wave arched above their heads, blocking out the sun. Time had run out. Shaun's arm jerked as Rachel pulled him through the portal.

Pain shot up his back as he rolled heavily down stone steps. He tried to grab hold of anything to stop his descent, which seemed to go on and on, until he quickly focused and activated the icosahedron sapphire, which seemed to take forever, but the hermetic sphere pulsed, protecting him from each impact. He did not know where the others were until they slammed up against the wall of the shield.

"Oh my God, I think I've broken my cheek," Rachel said, trying to stand up. Reis picked himself up, then he helped Kevin.

"Thanks. Where are we?" Kevin asked.

Kevin was out of breath. His energy was draining quicker with each portal opening and closing. Shaun should have insisted Kevin take time to recharge.

Shaun regained his sense of direction and reeled in the blue light of the icosahedron energy as he looked down the giant stairs. They were standing in the middle of a block of at least a hundred stairs. At the bottom, people gaped up at them, as if they were aliens. Shaun dusted himself off. "They're leaving?"

"Where are they going? Anyone speak their language?" Rachel asked.

"Some speak Spanish, and some Peruvian," Reis said. "I speak Spanish."

"How far away are we from the ocean?" Kevin asked.

"We're safe, for now. We're high up in the Andes Mountains. This is an Inca citadel. A gateway to the gods, and other worlds. Their ancestral priest passed down the knowledge of a secret portal that would one day reveal itself at the dawn of a new era, and that's now. They have the ancient crystal skulls, and it is their time to return to the stars. They must have activated the skulls to a doorway to the other world. They must be ready to leave," Reis said.

An old local man, wearing a colorful holiday beach shirt, climbed up the gigantic steps.

"How is he able to run up these steps?" Shaun said.

Kevin took a step up, to be on the same level as Reis. "They can activate an ascension portal?"

"I don't know if it will be to the same destination, where Rachel and Etain went, but it's their idea of heaven. It's a doorway to a world beyond earth. This old man can tell you more. He is the last keeper of the skulls," said Reis.

"Maybe we should head down to meet the old guy, before he keels over."

They descended the stone steps and met the old man a quarter of the way up.

"Come quick. We've been waiting for you. Now is time for the awakening," the old man said, pulling Kevin down the stairs.

A radio on Reis's shoulder squawked into life, but Shaun couldn't understand the muffled voice. He searched the crowd of moving people below until he spotted a soldier speaking into his shoulder.

"They're leaving," Reis said, repeating the message from below.

"What was that?" Rachel asked as the ground trembled. She tried to keep up with Shaun as they moved even quicker down the stairs. She looked back up the stairs and touched her sore, swollen cheek.

"If they're leaving, maybe we should, too. We've got to keep moving," Shaun insisted.

"We have to make sure they will be okay, and only you truly know the final destination, Rachel..." Kevin stopped mid-sentence.

The ground rumbled again, and a dark, massive cloud formation traveled at great speed across the sky, blocking out the sun.

"That's not right," said Reis.

"Quickly. We are children of the sun. It is time to return. Now is the dawn of darkness," the old man said, out of breath. He pointed up, and on the top of the steps was a fallen angel.

It stretched out its strong, haunting wings. Shaun held onto Rachel as the ground shook for a third time, and the step under his feet crumbled. Reis caught them both.

"K! We have to get out of here, now!" Shaun shouted.

"What the hell is that thing?" Reis said.

"It's a fallen. We know because one attacked us on Whistler Mountain and killed Geoff. It wants Kevin and the platonic stones."

Reis glanced at Kevin. Faceless, streaming gray clouds headed towards them. "It's the Jinn!"

"What the hell! The Jinn? We won't make it down the stairs," Reis said.

The old man reached for Kevin's hands and placed them on the side of his temples. "I dreamed of this day."

Kevin searched for a memory as the fallen angel took flight. The dark, streaking smoke landed around them, and formed into faceless human shapes.

Kevin opened the portal.

"Go! I'll hold it back," Reis said.

"With what? Your knife? I doubt you'll get that close. I'm not going back to Maria with bad news. You're coming with us," Shaun said, pulling him into the portal.

Kevin closed the portal behind them.

Shaun could hear the old man breathing next to him and taste his stale breath in the air. Up ahead in the dark cave, something glowed. He stood up on his toes to see over the crowd of people they had joined. A short man but who was still a head above the crowd of other Peruvians held a crystal skull above his head.

"What's he doing?" Kevin asked.

"He's going to open the portal," Reis said.

The old Peruvian squeezed against the tunnel walls and the rushing crowd, pulling Kevin along.

"Wait up, K," Shaun said.

Rachel pushed ahead of Shaun, to catch up with Kevin. At the sight of the old man and Kevin, the crowd calmed down and moved aside to let them pass.

Light glowed upon the sea of faces. A tremor moved through the cave. Dust and pebbles fell from the ceiling. Shaun thought Kevin glowed on cue, as if connected to the skull.

"Maybe we should just open our own portal back to Olivet, and get everyone out of here before we're all buried alive in this tunnel," Shaun said to Rachel.

The man holding up the skull gave it to the old man with Kevin. He turned to the wall at his side where twelve crystal skulls were embedded in the wall, arranged in a circle. The old man placed the last skull in the middle of the circle, and took Kevin's hand.

"Kevin, be careful!" Rachel yelled.

Holding tight to Kevin's hand, the old man forced the skull on the top of the center crystal. Instantly, all the crystal skulls illuminated, connected by waves of electric light that surged from the center crystal. Together, the skulls radiated and changed color – first red, then orange, yellow, green, blue, indigo, violet, magenta, then finally a brilliant, blinding flash of white light. A rectangular stone in the wall slid back and disappeared, revealing a narrow opening. The man let go of Kevin's hand, bent down, and entered the tight space. One by one, the people followed, bowing their heads in thanks.

"There has to be a chamber on the other side," Rachel said.

"Or they've entered a portal," Reis said, ducking his head and entering the passage. His soldiers followed.

"K, wait. We don't know where it leads," Shaun said as the last few people entered the nook, shrouded in light.

"Come on, we're the only ones left. It's our responsibility to find out where they went," Rachel said.

"I'll go first," said Shaun as the demonic angel entered the tunnels.

For a few seconds there was nothing, until he stepped out into a room that seemed like the inside of a crystal beehive, with streams of color and light reflected in all directions. Two apparitions stood at the far end, welcoming people. They didn't look solid. All of Shaun's platonic gemstones shone, drawing the attention of the two ghostly figures in white.

"This is the place; this is where I saw my mother. Those two are the elders. The celestial beings I spoke of," Rachel said behind him.

Kevin walked past Shaun, headed for the elders.

"K, stop," Shaun said. He searched for his mother, wondering if she was aware of his presence. Voices inside his head welcomed him, and Shaun was sure it was two voices combined as one. Their lips never moved. If they didn't leave now, he didn't think they ever would. "We have to go, K," Shaun urged.

Kevin turned and faced him. Shaun could see in his eyes that Kevin knew he was right. He guessed this was a test. They could stay, or go back and continue to risk their lives to save the other survivors. The two celestial beings parted the crowd and glided towards them. The silence was awkward. Kevin handed the crystal skull to one celestial being. Shaun wondered why Kevin had taken it in the first place.

"Well done. The fallen angels cannot follow our ancestors' pathway, because you intuitively knew to bring us the crystal skull, sealing the pathway forever. You are wisdom. Through you, the creator's unfailing wisdom takes form, through your thoughts and words. In you, all of you, we see the expression of divine beauty. Do as you will," said the non-binary voice inside his head.

Kevin, Rachel and Reis all looked at Shaun as they listened to the celestials.

Kevin hesitated, as if he wasn't sure he was going to be able to open a portal under the watchful eyes of the celestial beings, but energy flowed quicker than usual and they smoothly passed through the portal, stepping out in front of a roofless Saint Basil's Cathedral, in Russia.

16

____

FORKED TONGUE: KEVIN. RUSSIA.

This time, Kevin was ready for Mother Nature and all her surprises. They were prepared for a natural disaster to unfold on their arrival, but in fact everything was almost perfect. The walls of the cathedral were barely standing, the roof completely gone, but the other buildings were undamaged. The streets were peaceful. Empty; too quiet. Kevin stared down at his feet, daring the earth to crack open, when suddenly the church door was flung open and Etain's team walked out, with a group of about fifty people of all ages.

"We're ready to go when you are," the leading soldier said.

Shaun and Kevin glanced at each other, picking up a weird vibe.

"Should I open a portal straight back to Olivet, for us?" Kevin said suspiciously. His eyes darted between Rachel, Shaun, and Reis.

"We can't just leave them here!" Reis said.

"Wait here," Rachel said, and walked up to the commanding officer.

She walked back, shouting, "They're all good to go. The

survivors were waiting in the church when the extraction team arrived. They've been waiting for you. But first we should have a quick scout around for other survivors before we leave for Olivet." She winked at them.

"What? And what do you mean, waiting for me? Waiting for extraction, or waiting for me?" Kevin asked, taking a step back as the crowd of people moved purposefully closer.

Rachel turned back to the men and spoke in Hebrew. She turned back to Kevin and the look on her face spoke louder than her words. "You. They're waiting for you. The portal master and the blue angel," Rachel said.

"Tell your soldiers to take the people back into the church while we scout around and check a few places before we open a portal and head back," Kevin said to Reis.

"Why don't we take these people to Olivet first, then you can come back? They're hungry and cold," the team leader from inside the church said.

"Take everyone back into the church and keep them safe. That's an order," Reis said.

Standing three rows behind was a soldier. Close behind him was a gypsy woman, with long, unkempt hair held back by a rainbow-colored hairband. Her tongue darted forward, like the forked tongue of a snake, flicking against the soldier's neck, and as if hypnotized, the soldier didn't move, not even a blink.

Kevin turned to Shaun. "Did you see that?" he whispered.

Shaun gave a slight nod.

"We must go. We'll be back," Reis told the survivors.

Rachel and Reis started jogging away from Red Square, as if they had a predetermined destination. Shaun and Kevin followed and ran away from Saint Basil's Cathedral, rounded the corner, and headed into a misty fog.

"This way," Reis said, running across the road.

Kevin followed into the fog and up a few steps into a dark corridor, where Reis and Rachel were waiting. He didn't like the fog; it was a bad omen.

Shaun ignited the sapphire in his hand, illuminating the walkway.

"What's going on? There's something you're not telling me," Reis said.

"Some of the people back there were possessed by the Jinn, or were the Jinn in disguise. I felt the lust for the power of the portal and their vengeful emotions. I sensed malice," Shaun said.

"So did I. Where are we, Reis?" Rachel said.

"Looks like I missed those signals. We're in the passageway to the underground train station."

Something felt terribly wrong inside the train station; worse than the Jinn at the church, and they knew they shouldn't go any further into the darkness.

"This leads to the subway. We can walk along the tracks to the next station while we sort out what we are doing, to weed out the imposters. I was here with Maria, visiting the gravesites of our relatives before the rest of the world ostracized Russia," Reis said as he began to walk down into the subway.

Shaun lit the way.

"Tell me what you saw back there," Rachel said to Shaun and Kevin

Kevin studied the hue surrounding Shaun. It didn't just shine from the icosahedron in his hand, the light came out of every pore. They came to a silent understanding between them, that he would be the one to speak. "A woman, dressed like a gypsy from an old carnival, had a forked tongue, and she was licking the back of a soldier's neck; controlling, maybe possessing, him. I don't know for sure, but it wasn't right, whatever she was doing." Kevin explained feeling the jitters: back or forward, neither way had good vibes. He had to move, before he became paralyzed with fear.

The lights of the tunnel suddenly pulsed on. People swamped around them; rushing commuters filled the tunnel. *What the hell is going on?* Kevin thought as the rushing crowd jostled him along. He tried to keep sight of Shaun, who was taller than most in the crowd. Rachel was nowhere to be seen. "Shaun!" Kevin ran forward to catch up, but it seemed useless. The harder he tried to go against the flow, the more difficult it became. He gave up, and allowed himself to be pushed out onto the platform, where a train waited. Kevin tried to move back away from the train, but he was swept up to the front of the crowd and the doors opened.

A very tall man stared at him. He wore a long cape, which hid the magnificence of his size. He was taller than everyone on the train, at least seven feet even without his hat. His head touched the ceiling. There was something familiar about him, but Kevin couldn't hold onto that thought.

The man's facial features darkened with shadows, but his teeth were prominent, pointy, and yellow. His eyes glowed red. Hands pressed against Kevin's back, pushing him forward. There was nothing he could do to stop the swell of the surging commuters from behind, carrying him forward like a strong undertow, onto the train. Kevin raised his right leg, to step through the open carriage doors.

"Kevin! Stop. Don't move!"

Behind him, Shaun's voice sounded distant and lost in the crowd. Kevin couldn't stop himself from being pushed and pulled towards the tall figure that sent shivers up his spine.

From behind, a hand slapped down hard onto his shoulder, grabbing him. Another hand clamped on the other shoulder, then arms wrapped around his waist. He was afraid to look. Afraid the people would not let him go. With a hard yank, someone pulled him backwards, and off his feet. He fell onto the cement platform, away from the train, covering his face with his arms, protecting himself from the crowd.

"Kevin!"

The sound of the rushing crowd dissipated. Slowly, he opened his eyes. A blue, pulsating light enveloped him from behind. Shaun held him tight, legs wrapped around Kevin's lower body. Beyond the hermetic shield, a bottomless sinkhole was revealed, exactly where the train should've been. There were no crowds, and the platform was in ruins. Kevin studied the air where the train had been, and saw two red eyes disappearing into the darkness.

"What the hell were you thinking, K?" Shaun said.

Kevin looked around, confused. "Where's the train, and people? I saw people rushing, and a train. What happened?"

"You ran off into the dark," Rachel said, searching his eyes. "What were you thinking?"

"I was swept down the tunnel and onto the platform, by rushing commuters. A train was at the station. The doors opened, and there was a tall, strange, hypnotic man with piercing eyes, wearing a leather trench coat. Beckoning me, luring me to board the train. I couldn't resist. That's then you guys pulled me away."

Shaun lifted Rachel down onto the tracks. Reis followed.

"What are you guys doing? We need to go back. We shouldn't be down here."

They weren't listening. Curiosity had gotten the better of them. Kevin hesitated, looking back along the eerie empty platform. *What the heck!* He jumped down after them. He, too, peered into the sinkhole, which was covered with moving shades of black. A foul odor;

a breeze, like an exhale, exited the pit, sending the substance to the ceiling like steam, before it settled back down again, into the hole.

He covered his solar plexus as something pulled at him. "There's something down there!"

Reis pointed his flashlight down into the pit. "I can't see anything!" The light bounced off the opening, unable to penetrate its depths.

"Come on, this place gives me the creeps," Rachel said.

"Let's search for survivors within a one-hour radius of Red Square, and then create a portal between a doorway. That way, we can take out the Jinn one at a time," Shaun said.

"If your men are being controlled, the portal membrane will cast them aside, and how will you take out the Jinn?" Kevin said.

"We can slit their throats when they're in human or animal form," Rachel reminded him.

There was a screech, like that of a wild animal, deep inside the train tunnel. Kevin stepped over the metal train track and caught up with the others. No trains were running, but he didn't want to take the risk of being fried. Another screech echoed in the depths of the tunnel. The sound resembled a human copying the cry of a large, predatory bird. It came again. It sounded as if there was more than one creature, and he didn't believe for a minute that it was a bird.

"Maybe we should head back," Shaun said.

"We're halfway there," Reis said, pulling his knife out of its sheath.

Kevin took out his own bowie knife, and held it down by his side. The screeching stopped. The beam of the flashlight bobbed up and down the curved walls as they continued down the tunnel to the next station, but there was no visible light at the end.

"Stop!" Reis said, and swung his light to the left.

"What did you see?" Rachel asked.

"I thought I saw…" Reis said, and froze.

There were two red dots in the dark. When Reis turned his light back towards the red dots, they had disappeared. The flashlight moved across the walls, leaving the red eyes in Kevin's peripheral vision.

"What are they?" Rachel whispered, touching Shaun on the forearm.

"Maybe we should go back. I'm not so sure we're alone," Reis said in a low voice.

Shaun illuminated the icosahedron light down into the tunnel, until it splayed off the walls, revealing a mass of opaque eggs five feet high. Reis zeroed in on one egg and navigated his flashlight over its surface. Its shell stretched like elasticized skin as the shape of a curled up, gaunt human stretched upwards, trying to breach the surface of the egg from the inside. The egg broke, the head popped out, and the creature spilled free, like a newborn baby, covered in the creamy white fluid that had nourished it in the confines of the egg. Kevin thought of purulent abscess. The creature's eyes opened and glowed red. Its mouth stretched open, revealing its pointy yellow teeth.

Kevin quickly counted three more creatures breaking free through the top of the egg's membrane. There were maybe a hundred eggs or more. The creature stretched out its bony limbs.

Suddenly, something scurried across Kevin's shirt. He pulled his eyes away from the creature and frantically slapped at his chest, brushing his shirt down. His eyes widened. Cockroaches covered his feet, and climbed up his boots. He slapped at them and stomped his feet. "Get them off me!" he cried, moving away from the others, and closer to the eggs.

Shaun yanked him back. "K, there's nothing on you. You're hallucinating."

"Get them fucking off me!" They crawled up his neck and into his hair. He couldn't pull them off fast enough. Why weren't the others helping him? They just laughed. A cockroach ran over his face and covered his eyes. The point of the cockroach's leg touched his eyeball. Kevin held his mouth closed tight. His heart raced. His chest heaved up and down. Cockroaches ran over his body. A hard slap to the face stung his cheek.

"Open your eyes." Shaun pulled at his hands.

Separating his fingers a fraction, Kevin peeked out. The feeling of the cockroaches had gone.

He glanced at the ground, and the railroad tracks at his feet. "It was that thing. It got into my head," Kevin said, and heaved as if he had swallowed a fly.

"Hell no!" Shaun said.

More of the creatures had wriggled their way out of the eggs. The first abomination to free itself was on all fours, trying to flap the wings on its back, but they were held down by a sticky substance. It reminded Kevin of a fowl trying to stand on its feet after being birthed. The wings rose above its head and began to flap, expanding behind. Air moved up the tunnel. The abomination lifted itself from the ground, rising towards the roof of the tunnel, and its piercing red eyes stared down on them. It wasn't as big as the others they'd seen, but it was still an abomination.

"All the eggs are the rebirth of the demonic fallen angels!" Kevin whispered in horror.

It screeched, gargled, and creamy liquid oozed from its mouth, clearing its throat. It screeched again. Another joined it. Other fallen angels birthed and screeched as they tried to get control of their forms. More and more heads broke free of the skin-like shells.

"Fuck me!" Shaun said.

"I don't want to go into hand-to-hand combat with those things," Rachel said.

"These don't look as powerful as the other ones we've seen, maybe they're the offspring of the two hundred?" Kevin suggested.

"It was powerful enough to manipulate your mind before it had even had a chance to gain its strength," Reis pointed out.

Shaun concentrated the light of the icosahedron into one solid laser beam and fired at the eggs, blasting them and their contents to pieces. Goo and body parts burst and splattered across the walls and ceiling. The birthed fallen angels took flight. Kevin couldn't help thinking how hungry they would be.

"Go! Get out of here! What are we waiting for?" Shaun shouted.

Shaun fired up the energy again. The sounds of the screeches were unbearable. He covered his ears and cringed.

"Get out of here!" Shaun said again, pushing out his energy with one hand and shoving Kevin with the other.

Kevin closed his eyes, focused on the church door in Red Square, and opened a portal. "Red Square," Kevin said to Rachel as she entered the portal with Reis.

"All right, Shaun. Back up." Kevin had hold of the back belt loop of Shaun's trousers.

"This is becoming a habit," Shaun said, stepping backwards and allowing Kevin to pull him back into the portal. Dozens of red eyes blinked. Light dispelled, and they left the creatures to die.

* * *

"Where's Reis?" Kevin asked, shutting down the portal.

Rachel tilted her head toward the church. "He's gone in there."

Reis walked out with everyone in a line.

Kevin sighed. "I'll open a portal to Olivet. Get ready, Shaun.

Rachel, you lead them through." Kevin put up his hand for Reis to stop. "That's close enough." He waved his hand for the first person to move beyond Reis. But Reis touched the woman on the shoulder, and stopped her. He walked up to Kevin. "I want my men to pass through the portal first," Reis said.

"Okay, send them up."

Reis's men entered the membrane of the portal with ease. The gypsy woman was next. She touched the membrane and pushed. It moved like jelly. She glanced at Kevin and, avoiding further eye contact, she pushed again.

"Stand aside and let someone else try," Kevin said.

"No."

Kevin stole a glance at Reis, and from behind, Reis grabbed the gypsy and sliced her throat. Instead of blood, smoke poured out. The next survivor turned and fled. Others followed, dropping their clothing, turning into dense, black smoke.

"We've got to go!" Reis shouted towards Shaun.

But there was one more person hiding at the back of the church. Shaun ran deep inside and bent over a pew, coaching a survivor to stand.

"Reis, something is wrong," Kevin said, and he collapsed the portal. His shoes on the asphalt were hollow. Each step seemed to make little difference to his progress. Shaun held out his hand. A young boy reached out for Shaun's hand and that's when Kevin saw blood dripping from it.

Reis moved around the pew to come up behind the boy. Kevin stopped in the aisle. The boy's long, pointy fingernail dug at the edges of the stone embedded in Shaun's palm. Shaun didn't flinch. He was frozen to the spot, letting the boy dig away at his palm. Reis grabbed the boy and pulled the knife quickly across the boy's neck. As with the gypsy woman, smoke swirled from the wound instead of blood. *Another Jinn*, Kevin thought.

Shaun dropped to his knees, holding his hand, suddenly aware of the pain. It bled heavily.

"Where are your other stones?" Kevin asked.

Shaun reached across his hips to the pocket on his right side, feeling for the sacred stones.

"Where are they?" Kevin demanded.

Shaun locked eyes with Kevin. "Rachel! I gave them to Rachel. Get me out of here, K."

Kevin checked his surroundings before manipulating the atmosphere, and suddenly light shining through the roofless church disappeared. A fallen angel hovered above, its eyes burning like fire. How long had it waited to be free, to bring darkness to the world? He wanted to tell Shaun to blast it. To blast it out of the air, so it never got a chance to step one foot in Heaven. Instead, Kevin focused all his energy on opening the portal.

He kept eye contact with the creature as Shaun and Reis passed through safely. The demonic angel flew down with lightning speed and, for a split second, Kevin thought he had made a huge mistake. He fell backwards into the portal, twisting his ankle. He could feel the demonic angel grappling at his foot, clawing off his shoe and skin, his foot twisted and snapped, as Kevin dragged his leg into the membrane, closing the portal behind him.

He landed on the concrete floor of the command center at Olivet. Kevin examined his foot. It had scarred, with claw marks where the demonic angel had grabbed and torn his shoe off. He wiggled his toes, then flexed his foot back and forth. He touched the scars. It was the first time that he hadn't healed to perfection.

Shaun helped him up. "What happened to your foot?"

"The demonic angel," Kevin said, putting weight on his foot.

Gil stood by, ready to assist, while Abraham talked to Reis and Rachel.

"What are they talking about?" Kevin said, putting his foot on the cold floor.

"A bunch of eggs."

The cluster of eggs the fallen angels used as incubators. Kevin didn't have to imagine what they would want to do next. Probably go back and make sure they were all dead. *They must have been the army of fallen angels that reported to the Chief of Ten, the ones Ashmedai had spoken of,* Kevin thought.

"I'm not going back to kill them. We're supposed to find survivors and get them to ascension," Kevin said.

"You don't need to do anything. We can nuke them," Abraham said.

"Don't do it!" Kevin said.

"Why not? Give me one bloody good reason why we shouldn't?" Abraham said.

"There could be survivors we don't know about in Russia, waiting to ascend at a sacred portal. If you do it, you're no better than the Fallen and the Jinn. Rachel, tell him. Tell him again the message from the celestials. It's a test, Abraham. It's a test for us all. You don't want a heavy heart at ascension," Kevin said.

"He's right, we need to focus on keeping the people at Olivet safe," said Delilah, entering the area.

"Can I get another pair of shoes?" Kevin asked, taking off his old favorite Converse.

* * *

KEVIN DIDN'T WAIT to find out what Abraham and his men would do. He imagined an elder at Uluru showing him and other tourists how to use a woomera to propel spears while hunting kangaroos. It had been some years since he thought about that birthday trip. His family had flown to the Northern Territory and, on their first day, had rented bicycles, and ridden around the red desert.

Now he could open portals to anywhere in the world. Looking back on that day, he could never in a million years have guessed where he would be now. Kevin walked off.

"Where are you going?" Shaun asked.

"Home. Want to come?"

IT STARTED with shades of pink, then orange and gold, before giving way to a crystal-clear, fresh morning sky, as if untouched by the destruction of the world. Kevin didn't have the words to describe the glory of his homeland. The peace of life emanated from the red earth as a new day dawned, filling every cell and organ, revitalizing his body. Everything about Uluru and the land rejuvenated his being.

It was perfection.

On the golden horizon, the rising sun, as if peeking out from a cave on the left of Uluru, emerged and ascended the side of the giant rock, chasing the shadows away. In the past, he had thought the sun was like a marble rolling up the side, to the top of Uluru, traveling across the plateau then rolling over the edge, to settle on the right-hand side as it set, as if it had fallen off the face of the earth.

"I thought you were going to take us back to our hometown, to see if there were any survivors. Why are we here, in the middle of nowhere?" Shaun asked.

Kevin didn't want to answer; he didn't want to break the

connection with the spirit of the land. "This is the heart of the world, and this is where many people would be called to come," Kevin said.

He stepped onto the red path with his bare feet, and headed for the middle of the base of Uluru.

"Did you ever climb it?" Shaun asked, walking quietly beside him.

Kevin sensed Shaun was feeling the scintillating essence of life around them. "No. When I was here, I was nine. This is a sacred place and, out of respect, we didn't climb."

They walked in silence for half an hour, but there were no signs of people. They went into the tourist center and found it empty, too.

"No one is here, K. We have to get back," Shaun urged.

Kevin listened with his heart. He was there for a reason. "Just a little longer."

"What are you looking for?"

"I don't know," Kevin said, and walked amongst the boulders at the base of Uluru. He touched the red rock.

It was like putting his hand on the heart of a sleeping dragon. There was so much life and strength.

"K, over there!" Shaun called.

Kevin pulled his hand away, and went to see what Shaun had found. Two women were sitting on the ground. One was singing, and the other was painting spirals. The woman who was painting raised her bushy head and smiled.

"We've been waiting for you. Sit," she said.

Kevin nodded at Shaun and they both sat down to join the women. She put down her paint stick and picked up a bowl of plants and leaves. First, she went to Shaun, and gave it to him to hold, while she lit the contents with a lighter and blew the smoke into Shaun's face. Shaun coughed violently, and Kevin worried he was choking. He went to touch Shaun, to smack him on the back, but the woman reached out and took his hand, stopping him.

She placed in Kevin's hands a different bowl, with a new blend of leaves. Shaun's blend smelled different, but both blends burned black smoke that turned white. The woman continued to sing. She spoke to his soul, waiting for them to stop coughing. Shaun turned away and threw up. Emotions bubbled inside Kevin, his face red-hot, and his throat dry and sore. He swallowed obsessively, but it was useless. It was like grief blocked his esophagus. The flood gates opened, and he wept.

"Let your tears flow like the rivers through the land. The grief of the land weeps through you," the woman crooned, and continued to paint a spiraling sea of stars. Kevin wiped his damp cheeks, getting his emotions under control. Shaun shifted his sitting position, crossing and uncrossing his legs.

"What's wrong with him? What did you do?" Shaun asked, trying to keep his voice calm.

"Little Pebble speaks to him of great sadness. Smoking Ceremony cleanses and purifies him because we must go back to country. The spirits of our ancestors know we are here, and they are happy you've arrived. Wandijina calls all his people home."

"Who is Wandijina?" Shaun asked.

The woman pointed to the sky. "Wandijina in the Dreamtime gave us the land, the birds, and the water for us to watch over. We are the custodians of the land. Now we must go back to Eagle's Nest. We come here to wait for you. Eagle's Nest is in the land of my ancestors. The Wiranga Manda. We must go back to the home of Yugarilya, the seven sisters."

Kevin didn't understand what she meant. His chest expanded as he breathed deeply with a blocked nose.

"You ready now, boy?" the woman asked.

The marble sun had moved up the edge of Uluru to the top. Time had disappeared. It was already early afternoon. Shaun drew his eyebrows and squinted, silently questioning him. Kevin knew he wanted to go back to Rachel. Deep in Shaun's eyes, there was something he had never seen before; in his right pupil, Kevin would've sworn he saw a sparkling night sky. It disappeared when he blinked.

"I'm ready," Kevin said.

The woman singing took his hands and placed them on the side of her head. *How does she know what to do?* he wondered. He thought she would show him an image inside a cave at the base of Uluru, but it was an ocean of sadness surrounded by tall cliffs. Deep blue waves and foaming white caps crashed against the rocks below. Like a fast time-lapse video in which the sun set and the stars appeared. Kevin opened a portal, and the woman took them by the hand. Together, they stepped forward, and through the membrane.

The smell and taste of the sea-salt cleared his nose. The sounds and vibrations of the didgeridoo were haunting. A man sat on the ground in between two boulders, playing the instrument. The woman led Kevin past the man and beyond the boulders that stood like a doorway, open to the vastness of the great land. Kevin's heart skipped a beat. Thousands of people were sitting in prayer, waiting for the ascension.

The woman who had been painting handed him the picture, as if it were a gift. She gestured between the painting and the sky, connecting them as she told them the story of the hunter, Orion, and the Pleiadeans – the seven sisters. She tapped his heart, then waved her hand, as if to encompass all the people that were there. They all stood and vanished. He wasn't sure if he was seeing things in real time, or if he was witnessing a past event.

"This is our connection to Yugarilya, the beautiful sisters. Many people have traveled cross-country to go home, not many more to come," she said.

"This is Tgilbi, the hunter," she said, pointing to Orion. "Tgilbi, he chased the Yugarilya," she said.

Kevin understood what she was saying because Orion always followed the Pleiades in the night sky.

"What happened to the people?" Shaun asked.

So, he had seen them too, Kevin thought, listening to the timbre of the didgeridoo echo through the rocks. Kevin's stomach stirred.

"Them people gone. They're up there now," she said, pointing to the sky.

He frowned, trying to understand what was happening. "Were you left behind?" Shaun asked.

"No. Not left behind, and you will not be left behind," she said, tapping Shaun on the chest with her painted finger. "We stayed here, to give message from Wandijina. We tell you the story so you understand where you must go," she said, and tapped Kevin's heart again.

Kevin pushed his hair back off his forehead, confused.

"You go there now. Listen to your heart. Your friend's life, in your hands. No more waiting, you go now?" the woman said.

"Go where?" Shaun asked.

Together, the women pointed to the sky, and walked away, toward the man playing the didgeridoo. They vanished in a blinding, golden light. When the light settled, Shaun and Kevin could see the ocean again, and they could see that the man was gone, too. The only sound was the crashing of the waves below.

From the moment they had arrived at sunrise, time had been unpredictable, slowing down and speeding up, forever changing.

"What was that all about?" Shaun asked.

"I'm not sure I know," Kevin said, leaning the painting against the rock. He walked to where the man had sat, and the women had disappeared.

"Wait!"

Kevin waited for Shaun before walking between the boulders.

"I don't want to be left here on my own," Shaun said.

Together, they passed between the rocks towards the edge of the cliff. Nothing happened.

"If it's not a portal, they have to be here somewhere," Shaun said.

Kevin gazed toward the west, at the blue sky and the resting sun on the horizon.

"It could have been the sun," Shaun said.

"What could have been the sun?"

"The golden light."

"They're not here, but they are here. They're all around us, in everything," Kevin said.

"Why did you bring us here? Did you find what you were looking for?"

"Maybe. I'm not sure." Kevin was looking over the cliff. It was a long way down, and he would hate to fall.

"Do you think we should quickly check the different states for survivors while we're here?" Shaun said.

"Yeah… no. I don't think there will be anyone. I think the country is clean. There's no dark clouds of Jinn, and we haven't spotted a fallen angel. It's different here – don't you feel it?" Kevin said.

"Yeah, I just don't know what the feeling means. Maybe the Jinn and the fallen angels are going to get here eventually," Shaun said.

"I think everyone has already ascended, and the women were

trying to show us. There was no waiting for the 8th day of Leo for them. They just up and left." Kevin studied the sky.

"I know! Maybe they all had made the first ascension last year, when we returned the Emerald Tablet," Shaun suggested.

"Maybe, but something tells me the original custodians of the land had a much stronger connection with the heavens. Those women waited for us, you and me, then they disappeared. Why?"

"If you think there isn't anything we can do down here, we should go," Shaun said.

Confused, Kevin searched around, touching the rocks, picking up the essence that lived within everything, hunting for clues. He was still missing something. Like he had listened to their message, but he didn't really hear it. He scratched his head and pushed his hair off his face, frustrated. Things were getting stranger by the minute. He just hoped that when he got back to Olivet they would all still be there, and had decided not to fire off any nuclear missiles.

"Can we go back to Olivet and get Rachel now?"

"Yeah, sure," Kevin said as he scanned the area one last time, feeling grateful for Shaun's friendship.

17

SEVEN SISTERS: SHAUN. EGYPT.

The walls groaned. At first, he thought his ears were playing tricks on him, but then he heard it again. He leaned over the rail and observed the people in the atrium gardens. He couldn't recall seeing so many at Olivet. *The city must be close to its maximum capacity,* Shaun thought. It was an incredible compound, but he questioned its structural integrity, hearing the walls straining.

After being in Russia and witnessing the beginning of the fallen angels' army re-birth, there was no doubt in his mind that the Jinn and the fallen angels were different species, but in collaboration. The peace at Uluru and Eagle's Nest was a vast difference from Olivet and Russia. Shaun hoped Kevin would work out the meaning of the message from the women. Kevin had brought along the painting, and if Shaun hadn't forced him off the couch and out of the apartment, Kevin would have sat staring at it all day and night.

Shaun promised that once he had Rachel they could head to the States, to Black Mountain, for Jade and Casey, before returning to Casey's estate and their families. He wondered why Kevin didn't mention Jade; she must have done something that hurt him deeply. He also wondered how all the portals were going to open on the 8th day of Leo. Would it be one by one, or simultaneously?

He took the elevator down to the atrium. Why would they bother restoring the facility if they were all leaving? Through the atrium, he found Rachel. She was standing next to the restored waterfall, with Abraham, Delilah and Etain.

"Where did you go?" Rachel asked.

"You've been gone for eighteen hours," Etain said, looking at his watch.

"What's happened?" Shaun asked, digging his hands into his pockets.

"Come with us." Abraham jerked his head, leaving the congregated people under the guidance of Etain's team.

If it's not one thing, it's another.

They headed back up to the military zone. "You didn't do it, did you?" Kevin asked, rubbing his eyebrows.

From the sound of Kevin's voice, it seemed he had almost convinced himself that Abraham would have given the order to fire the nuclear missiles. Rachel would have stopped them.

"No. We didn't," Delilah told him.

The command area was a hive of activity. "Abraham! Tell us what's going on?" Shaun demanded.

"The Jinn have infiltrated the city."

"What, the bunker? Olivet?" Kevin asked, looking around at the faces.

"Yes. We're no longer safe here. We don't know who is human, and who is a Jinn," Abraham told them.

"Mama Bina has locked herself in her room," Rachel said.

Theo sat at his dad's feet under the console, afraid to come out.

"What? Why?" Shaun asked.

"She can see the Jinn and was pointing them out for us to destroy, but now she's afraid, because they know she sees them in their natural form."

That's why she was in the war room, Shaun thought.

"There's only one way to know who is human and who's not," Abraham said.

"Kevin, you're our guy," Delilah said, pulling out the chair at the control panel next to Gil. "We need you to open a portal for all of us to get out of here. That's the only way to know for sure."

"That's close to ten thousand people," Shaun said. *It could kill Kevin,* he added in his mind.

Kevin wasn't speaking. He was tired. Shaun could see the energy draining from him.

"We just brought those people here from the Sphinx, and now you want him to take them all back? It's suicide," Shaun said.

"I'm not sure I can do it," Kevin said, looking at his feet before meeting Abraham's eyes.

Suddenly, they felt Olivet rock.

"It's Apep, trying to find a way in," Rachel explained.

"Of course, it is!" They had built the place to withstand earthquakes and nuclear explosions, so Kevin doubted a giant snake could destroy the place, but that didn't make him less uncomfortable.

"You have to try, or more people will die," Delilah said to Kevin.

Shaun fixed his gaze on Rachel. They weren't telling him everything. "What happened to our ten weeks? We still have eight to go. What happened while we were gone?"

Gil stood up. "We found hundreds of people... dead. Two of the residential zones and a floor in the military quarters; it seems they all died in their sleep." Theo reached for his dad and held tight to his leg.

"SUNDS. Sudden unexplained nocturnal death syndrome," Delilah said.

"Everyone is afraid to sleep," Rachel added.

"But eventually we need to sleep. We have eight weeks to go," Shaun said.

Kevin was looking up at the ceiling, thinking. Shaun knew that look. Kevin needed time to think to come up with a plan. It was as if someone had dropped a seed into his mind and he was waiting to see it bloom. Shaun studied Kevin's eye movements, and it was almost as if he was chasing the idea around his head. Everyone waited impatiently.

"There might be another way," Kevin said with his head tilted to the side, as if listening to his own thoughts.

It would be so much better if Jade was here. Kevin would share the idea with her and together they would toss it around until they had reached a conclusion. Shaun had first thought it was annoying, especially when Jade, deep in concentration, twirled her hair, and Kevin pushed down his cuticles. He did that now.

"Out with it, K," Shaun said.

"I can't guarantee it will work. This could be a big mistake."

"What is it?" Abraham said a little too fast.

Kevin searched Shaun's eyes. "You said the sandstorm has passed, right? Then how long will it take to move everyone at Olivet to the Sphinx?"

"Why?" Delilah said.

Kevin shuffled his feet as if stalling.

"We can't go back there. You need to reveal what you're thinking, K," Shaun said.

Kevin always kept his ideas close to his chest, afraid he was wrong, or that someone would get hurt. He was too sensitive and took on the responsibility for others way too much. It hurt him when he couldn't help. Jade often dragged his ideas out of him, bringing them into the light, and together they all made his ideas work.

"Don't hold me to it, but I think I can open the portal at the Sphinx. It's the message from Wandijina."

"Not to wait. Go back to country, go back to the Yugarilya. Yes, of course," Shaun said, and suddenly realized the thrill Kevin and Jade must get when they came to an intellectual conclusion. For him, it had always been the completing of an action that gave him a thrill, but this time he had a great connection with Kevin and everything around him. Something was shifting inside him.

"What are you two talking about?" Rachel said.

"Heaven is amongst the stars. You went to the stars, right? The Sphinx, on the 8th day of Leo, will face the stars of Orion and the Pleiades. It's what the women at Uluru were talking about," Shaun said.

"Yes, yes, of course – the hunter – Orion and the seven sisters," Kevin said.

"Exactly!" Shaun said, holding his head as if it would explode.

"Go now. Don't wait. I can't hold a portal open for this many people, but I think I can activate the one at the Sphinx," Kevin said.

Rachel put her hands on her hips, as she did whenever she was confused and wanted clarification. "I have so many questions right now. We have the buses."

"And the trucks," Abraham added.

"What about the Jinn?" Delilah asked.

"If we can get Mama Bina to point them out while loading people onto the vehicles, we could separate the Jinn. Then we can drop them off somewhere in the desert," Etain said.

"What about the fallen angels?" Gil said.

They all gawked at each other. "We'll cross that bridge if we come to it," Delilah said.

"What about these planes?" Kevin asked.

"We can't use them," Etain said.

"Why not?"

"If the Jinn whip up another sandstorm, the engines will stop."

"But the flight is under two hours," Rachel said.

"Maybe the Jinn won't attack while other Jinn are on board." Abraham looked at Etain.

"For our last voyage from this planet, we should use everything we've got. If we make sure only the Jinn are on the plane, it should be smooth flying," Etain said.

"Then what?" asked Rachel.

"I'll crash the plane," Kevin said.

"He's done it before; crashed." Shaun smiled at Kevin.

Kevin smiled back, as if it had been fun crashing his grandfather's Cherokee on the front lawn of Casey's estate. It had been terrifying, and Shaun was lucky to have survived; they were all lucky that day.

"Of course – back at Casey's estate, the plane on the lawn," Rachel said, nodding her head.

"Anyway, in all seriousness, I can't fly a C-17. But the Jinn won't question being on the same plane as me. I'll open a portal in the cockpit before the plane crashes, for the pilot and me to escape," said Kevin.

"I'll come with you," Shaun offered.

"If we're going to do this, we'll need you for added protection, just in case," Delilah said.

"It's risky, but it just might work. Our lives are in your hands," Abraham said to Kevin.

"We can do this. I'll go with Kevin," said Rachel.

"First, we need to know how many Jinn there are."

"Logically, it might not be possible," Gil said, moving toward a transparent screen. He picked up a marker and wrote a number that represented the number of people.

"We have six thousand, eight hundred and two souls to transport. A C-17 carries freight, not people, and at best we could fit six, maybe seven, hundred people in one haul. We would have to make ten trips. We can't crash the plane until the last trip. Either way, it's going to take over eight hours to get everyone to the Sphinx," Gil calculated.

"How long would Kevin have to open a portal to transport six thousand eight hundred and two people?"

Gil started writing numbers, then dividing and multiplying. Shaun tried to keep up, but he would need a calculator. Gil did all the math in his head and on the board.

"If each person takes three seconds to walk through the portal, that will take approximately five and a half hours, if it's in single file, and that's not including the time it will take to segregate the Jinn from the humans. So, if we go two or three at a time, we could get it down to just under two hours."

"My max is twenty minutes," Kevin said.

"Then we better get started loading up the trucks and planes," Abraham said.

Kevin looked up, and his eyes went from left to right, and back to left again. Then he studied the ground and his feet, thinking. Shaun bit the inside of his lip, waiting. If Kevin had an idea, he shouldn't rush him. It may be their last chance. Abraham took a step back, and Gil held his son against his waist.

Rachel couldn't wait. "What is that fabulous brain of your concocting now?"

Shaun squinted and jerked his head forward. "Really!"

"We don't have the time."

"It'll be risky. Like Shaun said, I have crashed a plane before, and I should do it the same way."

Shaun was the only person who understood what he meant. He hadn't been conscious for the entire flight. He was on the brink of death, and the only reason he didn't die was because Kevin had opened a portal in mid-flight. "You want to take the plane through a portal?"

"Yeah. That's what I'm thinking. I'll have to be on board for each flight."

"I like your thinking, but I may have an even better idea," Gil said.

"Okay, let's have it," Abraham said, frustrated.

"You're forgetting the Jinn can't pass through a portal. So, we load up all the trucks and buses, and any cars we can find. Kevin opens a portal for twenty minutes, tops, for the motor vehicles, while we load up the plane with the Jinn. We'll let them think they're the special chosen ones, to get on the plane with the portal master. Kevin shuts down the portal and boards the plane. When it's confirmed all vehicles are safe at the Sphinx, Kevin can get on board and do what's necessary to crash the plane," Gil said.

Everyone moved about, waiting for objections.

"It could work." Abraham felt a tinge of excitement that he quickly wrangled.

Shaun smiled at Kevin.

"What are you smiling about? Get to work," Abraham said to Shaun.

"Delilah, you talk to Mama Bina. Reis, get all the men you need to prepare the transport. Etain, prepare the plane," Abraham said.

"What about me?" Kevin asked.

"You rest; meditate; whatever you need to do to recharge. You're going to need everything you've got to pull this off."

"Swim. I don't suppose you have a swimming pool?" Kevin said, half-joking.

"There is. There's a whole leisure center," Rachel said.

"Rachel, take a couple of soldiers for protection, and stay close to Kevin. We'll radio you when we're ready for him," Abraham said.

"And get him some shoes!" Delilah said.

"Awesome. A pool. The ocean would be better, but a pool is good."

MAMA BINA SAT IN A CHAIR, with Shaun standing guard. If anyone even looked at her strangely, he was going to blast them. His job was to keep her alive. Gil had given her a two-way radio, and all she had to do was push the side button each time she spotted a Jinn in human form. Etain's men randomly picked out people and placed them in different groups, so it didn't look obvious they were separating the Jinn. Shaun couldn't tell how many Jinn there were, but there were at least five hundred, so far. All even-numbered groups headed up and out of the bunker from the west tower, and the odd numbers headed up the penthouse elevator. Yehuda escorted Mama Bina up the penthouse elevator with the last group.

"Okay," Etain said, rubbing his hands together. Shaun hoped the Jinn didn't pick up on his nervousness. He stepped forward to the group of Jinn in the likeness of humans. He couldn't see the difference.

"You're the lucky chosen people, who will come with me and the rest of my men. We will fly out of here on a C-17. We'll be the first to arrive, and we will need to prepare the area for the others. As you know, we believe we can trigger the portal at the Sphinx, and open it ahead of the ascension date. You will be the first to ascend."

Shaun helped the Jinn onto the plane. At first, they were a tad cautious, but as soon as the word got out that Kevin would join them, they let down their guard and boarded the plane without question.

"You look refreshed. You both do. New shoes too? You couldn't pick a different pair?" Shaun said to Kevin.

"I'm feeling good. It's incredible what water can do. I could've sworn he was doing a Mikvah, the number of times he bobbed up and down under the water," Rachel said.

"What's a Mikvah?" Shaun said, giving the signal that meant all the Jinn were on board and the back tailgate of the plane was to be closed.

"It's a cleansing," Rachel said.

"Escort Kevin topside. Get the portal opened and the trucks through, and hurry back before the plane passengers get suspicious. Take the jeep," Delilah said.

"Godspeed," said Gil.

KEVIN EXPANDED the portal for Etain and his men to drive the convoy of trucks through to the Sphinx. The colors of the membrane blended, expanded, and contracted as each vehicle passed through the portal easily. Kevin and Shaun sighed, relieved it all went off without a hitch. Now for the finale; getting a huge cargo plane might be a little trickier for K.

Kevin pulled the edges of the portal together, folding it within itself until it was just a vanishing spark of light. It took twelve minutes to get them all through, and three seconds to close.

Shaun drove the jeep as fast as he dared down the spiraling driveway, the tires screeching as he rounded the winding bends down to the first level, the military level, where the cargo plane was loaded with Jinn.

* * *

"ALL ROAD TRANSPORT vehicles are accounted for," Reis reported.

"Roger that. It's time for take-off," Etain said.

"Shaun, come in. Confirmed all… souls are on board and the back sealed?" Abraham said.

"All souls on board. Tailgate is closed." Shaun entered the cockpit.

Kevin took the seat next to Etain, who was flicking switches and starting up the engines.

Rachel sat across from Shaun and prepared for take-off.

"I'll take her up to twenty thousand feet, level her off, then nosedive," Etain said.

"Roger that," Kevin put on his headphones.

An exit door to the compound for aircraft opened, revealing the ocean. Etain made a sharp right turn, and the heavy bunker doors automatically closed behind them, sealing the bunker empty of human souls. Shaun doubted they would ever see Olivet again. The aircraft bounced and jostled, as Etain turned it away from the water and headed along a road he was going to use as a runway.

"We're supposed to be flying," Shaun said as wings passed within an inch of a resort building. He cringed, waiting for impact. Kevin was taking in deep breaths. "You need a boost?"

"I think I'm good. I'll let you know."

"We just need to get clear of the buildings, then the road will straighten out, and we'll be able to take off. It's going to be fast and steep, so be ready," Etain warned.

The plane shook, and suddenly the force of the acceleration pushed Shaun back into his seat. The aircraft shuddered, as if it was going to come apart. He kept focused on Rachel's fearless eyes and prayed they would have more time together.

If Kevin activated the Sphinx portal, he wondered if Rachel would go or stay with him. Shaun had promised Kevin he would go with him to get Jade and Casey before heading for their family at Stonehenge. He couldn't leave. He wanted to see it through to the end. So much had happened in the past week, he was finding it hard to catch his breath.

Stars filled Shaun's vision. He couldn't imagine what life would be like, somewhere other than earth. There was so much he had wanted to see and do. If only things had been different. He was taking short breaths. Silver spots danced in front of him.

"Breathe," Rachel was saying.

He couldn't catch his breath.

"Breathe from your belly. Long, deep breaths."

Her voice was calm and reassuring, but he still couldn't manage it. A flash lit up the cockpit. It was his stones in his pocket, joining forces with the sapphire in his palm. He was having a panic attack. Soon, life on earth would all be over. He wanted the adventure to go on. No matter how ugly the world had become, it was his home. The platonic stones shielded him from the others until his breathing returned to normal. The blue haze around him dimmed and disappeared.

"Was that really necessary?" Etain said.

Kevin pursed his lips. He had his hands stretched out and had been soaking up Shaun's energy. "You ready? I'm going to open the portal," Kevin said, smirking at him.

"You were leeching off my energy?" Shaun asked, trying to sound confident and unbuckling his seatbelt.

"You sure you're okay? You had a panic attack," Rachel said, moving closer.

"I'm good, already. K, let it rip."

The energy in the atmosphere crackled as Kevin created a portal, but this time there was something different, the colored waves of light were more vibrant, and the membrane wasn't as dense; it was more fluid, and he reckoned it was because of the stones.

"I thought you were going to nosedive the plane through the portal?" Shaun said.

"The portal is just for us. Etain, get ready to nosedive the plane. You two go first. I've opened a portal to the chamber in the Sphinx."

"Got it," Rachel said.

"We all go together. I'm not leaving without you, K."

"As soon as the plane dives, we have to move quick," Etain said.

But Kevin had thought of that too, and as the plane tilted down, the momentum tossed them all into the portal.

SHAUN DIDN'T SEE the plane crash, but he felt his wrist snap as he landed on the stone floor of the chamber at the Sphinx. It was empty, but the area had been prepared for extraction. Lights stood tall around the edge of the chamber circling the ancient portal. From the chamber above, which led to the exit of the Sphinx,

Shaun heard sounds of slamming doors as the people unloaded the trucks.

"Let everyone know we're here, Etain. There's no point in wasting time. People can start entering the chamber. I'll activate the portal now."

"Roger that," Etain said, climbing the stairs.

"What do you want us to do?" Shaun said, favoring his wrist.

"Light me up," Kevin said.

Shaun did as he asked, and channeled the energy to Kevin until he glowed. Kevin stepped on the outer circle and walked in a clockwise direction. With each step, the pathway lit up behind him. He stepped into the next circle, and then the next, until all the twelve rings were ablaze with pulsating light that rose from the floor to ceiling, circling Kevin. The Sphinx portal opened.

Kevin appeared to be talking to someone. Shaun turned and faced the stairs, where people had entered the chamber. Rachel encouraged them all to step forward into the rings of light. As they did, they vanished. Some people were a little timid. They paused, afraid of the light.

"It's all you've dreamed of and more. It's time. Go, be with your loved ones," Rachel said, encouraging them to step forward.

It was a magnificent sight. Their faces lit up in awe as they stepped into the energy of the portal. There were tears of joy, laughter, gratitude, and so much more as they stepped into the ancient portal and disappeared as one. Melody, Logan, and his sister with her boys waved, and gave thanks to Kevin and Shaun before disappearing.

Reis and Maria were up next. Maria carried Ari, Etain's baby nephew. They hugged and kissed Shaun and Rachel. Maria handed Ari to Shaun for cuddles. Time was waning; the end was near. Shaun loved Ari. He didn't want to let go. He didn't want to say goodbye. But Ari looked happy. It was only two weeks ago that Rachel and Shaun had found him on the highway in a car outside of Jerusalem, dehydrated, crying in the back seat.

As he and Rachel said their goodbyes to everyone, Shaun was excited for his friends, yet afraid of the unknown as they disappeared into the light of the ancient portal.

He stretched out his arms, putting Rachel at the edge of the portal. He willed himself to speak. He needed to let her go with the others. He was torn. "It's not my time, and I'm sure I will be heavily judged for the terrible things I have done in my life, but I want you to go," he finally said, pulling Rachel back into his arms.

"I'm not leaving without you." Rachel kissed him.

The light diminished. The portal closed. Darkness engulfed them.

"K?" Shaun said, feeling Rachel's heart against his chest.

"K?"

18

POWERLESS: KEVIN. BLACK MOUNTAIN, USA

Kevin tilted his head toward the absolute darkness of the cave's ceiling. The portal chamber moved under his feet. It shook, and blocks of stones crashed around him, his heart pounding throughout his whole body, as the floor dropped away. The Sphinx was sinking, the portal destroyed.

"Kevin!" Shaun cried out.

The energy in the air merged under Kevin's command as he created his own portal. Tired and nervous, he concentrated on Jade. His hands were shaky. A rock hit him on the head.

"Shaun! Rachel!" he yelled.

"We're here!" Shaun slapped his hand down on Kevin's shoulder.

Kevin's eyes stung. He blinked, trying to clear the sand that felt like rocks. With his elbow, he wiped away the warm blood from his temple. Together, they stepped into the portal and, once again, all their ailments and all their fears disappeared. Now was the time he thought it would be better to stay anxious and keep the adrenaline

225

pumping, but he couldn't fight the healing energy. With great effort, he struggled to exit the portal at the Black Mountain campground. If it wasn't for his love for Jade and Casey, he would have stayed in the portal.

From the treetops, a wendigo jumped down, knocking them to the ground the moment they stepped out. They had no time to defend themselves.

The wendigo pinned Kevin to the ground. He raised his arm up and pressed it against the wendigo's neck, stopping it from biting his face – saliva dripped onto his cheek. Kevin reached down the side of his body, grabbed the knife strapped to his thigh, and plunged it upward into the wendigo's belly. The creature turned to black smoke.

Rachel instinctively drew her knife and sliced off two heads in one motion. Each wendigo turned into smoke. With rapid balls of explosive energy, Shaun blasted the hideous creatures off their feet. The wendigos turned to ghost-like smoke, but reformed into solid killing machines, crazy for human flesh.

From behind, a wendigo hit Kevin at the base of the neck. He fell to the ground. Tingling pain radiated down his spine, arms, and legs. With a foot between his shoulders, the wendigo pushed Kevin back to the ground, ready to suck out his life force. The blue haze of Shaun's hermetic shield touched the side of his face as he struggled to stay conscious. Rachel must have jumped the creature from behind. Her cursing matched each blow she delivered to the wendigo's head, until the creature turned to smoke, and Rachel fell down on top of Kevin.

His ribs cracked. Shaun dragged them both into the safety of the sphere. Foggy and dazed, he almost forgot where he was, and why he was there. Kevin's thoughts gravitated back to Jade. The shield reverberated as the wendigo launched another attack.

"Just start walking," Shaun said.

"What are they? Ghosts? Demons?" Rachel asked.

"They're wendigo. They were once people, until they ate human flesh, and then they were possessed by the supernatural spirit of the wendigo," Kevin explained as they walked out of the forest, under the glowing blue light of the shield, and into the opening in the trees. "Head for the main building over there." He pointed to the community lodge.

"So, all these wendigos were once survivors? Why did they eat each other?"

"They were probably tricked. The doctor called the psychosis 'wendigo fever'. But I saw one of them, Bob, morph into the wendigo. I saw Jade and the others battling against a group of wendigos when I accidentally opened a portal back to here. In a session with her memory stones, Jade foresaw what looked like a preacher wearing a derby hat with a cobra sitting on top, and inside the silhouette of the preacher were snakes, filling him up and reveling in his form. I think the preacher could be a fallen angel, or a Jinn disguised as a preacher man wearing a derby hat. He fed the survivors human flesh for communion."

"The wendigo might be the Jinn," Rachel said.

"Anything is possible." Kevin searched between the wendigo, looking for campfires and cabin lights. They were all dark. A fox screamed. A wolf cried from deep inside the woods behind them.

"Are you sure we're at the right place, K?"

"There was a large community. Sixty, maybe seventy, people. Maybe they headed for the Devil's Towers. The portal. I didn't say when I would be back. I didn't even say goodbye to Jade. I left like a jealous idiot."

"Let's hope Jade and Casey went with them," Rachel said.

"So that's what's been bothering you? We'll find them," Shaun reassured him.

"How?" Wendigos trolled around the shield, waiting for a pound of flesh and a taste of their souls.

Kevin, Shaun, and Rachel jogged across the open field to the community lodge. "In Canada, I went back to Olivet for you, and accidentally opened a portal to here. There was a battle. They must've lost. Jade fought off the wendigo with a staff. The preacher was there, a cabin was on fire. Jade had entered the woods with a group of people. I thought she would be safe. What if I was wrong? What if they all died that night and I could've saved them?"

"Stop. You wouldn't have left if you thought they were still in danger. And besides, you had the people at Whistler counting on you," Shaun said.

The community lodge was in darkness. Kevin led them across the veranda, and into the community hall. It was empty. Tables and chairs were spilled on the floor. He went into the kitchen.

"They're not here," Rachel said.

"What are you doing? We need to leave," said Shaun.

"I don't know!" The wendigo were on the ground floor. Kevin broke free of the shield and ran upstairs. He searched the rooms and infirmary.

"Wait a minute." Rachel stopped him in the hallway, pushing him against the wall. "Listen to me. I think they were planning to leave. But maybe before they could, the wendigo attacked, so they left in a hurry. In the kitchen there was a sack of food." Rachel looked up at the ceiling as the wendigo jumped from the trees onto the roof. A window smashed.

"We've got to go, K. They're in the building."

He studied her face and searched her emotions, hoping she really believed that Jade and Casey had escaped and she was not just trying to pacify him. "They went this way." Kevin headed for the stairs.

"Wait, Kevin, just wait a second. We can't just run out into the woods with those things out there," Shaun said.

"Why not? You've got the hermetic shield. You can keep us safe." Kevin shook his arm free from Shaun's grip.

"We don't know where they went," Rachel said.

"They must've headed to the Devil's Tower."

"Which direction?" Shaun looked up at the ceiling. The building groaned under the weight of the wendigo. It sounded as if they were peeling off the metal roof. "How can I save survivors when I can't save the ones I love?"

"We must think this through," Rachel said, chasing him. "We can't just go running into the woods. And what about this preacher you spoke of? You said it can mess with our heads, making us see things that aren't real, like the Jinn can mess with your head and make you see things that aren't there. Maybe the preacher is nearby? What if the entire community is here but we just can't see them because the preacher is messing with us? Maybe he wants you to run into the woods, and this is all a trap."

"Fuck, Rachel, enough already."

"Okay, okay, I get it!" Kevin said.

"Why don't we head back to Casey's estate, and we can check on the campsite daily to see if Jade or Casey return?" Shaun suggested.

"Shaun, what about when you sent me an image of the Sphinx? How did you do it? Maybe I can reverse the process to find Jade?"

Shaun's hands glowed. Blue light surrounded his body.

"If Jade was in trouble, don't you think she would've tried to do what Shaun did? Don't you think she would meditate and send you a message?"

"I feel like she's been sending me messages since I left."

"Are you serious, K?"

Kevin turned, stopping abruptly. "I was angry and jealous. I had to push away all thoughts of her if I wanted to be able to open portals. The jealousy was depleting. She wanted to be with Mingan. She's chosen him over me, so whenever I thought of her, I ignored it. I don't know what's real. I can't tell what's my emotion or someone else's anymore. It's all jumbled."

"Other people's emotions are easy to understand but our own never are, are they?" Rachel said, rubbing the sides of her arms.

"Let's go to a place where it's safe, so we can meditate and reach out for Jade and Casey. Put aside your feelings for Jade. Forget what you think she may or may not be feeling for Mingan. Find our friends. Connect to them, K. You can do this."

Kevin touched the back of his head where he had been clawed by bats, and Chief Thundercloud had used ant mandibles to seal the wound on his head. He would have died from rabies if it wasn't for Chief Thundercloud. "I know a place."

The wendigo came through the window and smashed through the door, just as Kevin opened the portal to the cave where Jade had traveled to the Realm of Lost Souls while Thundercloud saved his life.

* * *

THE AIR WAS alive with energy. They all took in a deep breath. The scent of sage had settled into the cave walls. The fire-pit was cold to the touch. Kevin placed his hand on the wall and bathed in the residual sacred emotional energy. The recent occupants had shed beauty, love, magic, fear, awe, and sorrow.

Casey's emotions were abundant. Then Jade took up residence

in his soul. He saw a flash of people sitting cross-legged in a circle, meditating around the fire-pit. Casey was remorseful. He had killed Emma after she had turned into a wendigo. Casey, with lightning speed, had sketched images of the spiritual journeys the others sought in meditation.

Kevin sat down on the spot where he had seen Jade. The visual images were strong and something he wasn't used to experiencing; normally, he was a clairsentient and felt the past and present emotions of people, ghosts and animals. He placed his hands on his knees. Shaun and Rachel sat opposite him, forming a triangle.

As he drew in a deep breath and filled his lungs, the lingering scent of incense rushed into him. He closed his eyes and opened his heart and mind. Kevin reached out to the cave for a time frame – *how long ago were they here*? A gold number five flashed into his head.

For the first time, Kevin was having trouble entering the astral realm. He had done this many times before. He had even found Sophia's life essence when she had fragmented in the astral realm, searching for clues to the whereabouts of the Emerald Tablet.

Tim's words echoed in his mind – "You've got this, K." Kevin missed Tim – he made him laugh, and he always had a positive word of reassurance; he had more faith in Kevin than Kevin had in himself. Kevin smiled. The thought of Tim filled him with optimism, confidence, and the strength to move beyond his doubts. *Separated, we're all vulnerable,* Kevin thought. He now understood the value of unity, and being connected. They all needed to get back together. He opened his eyes, shifted his backside, and closed his eyes again. The energy tingled. Atoms, like soda pop, fizzed throughout his body. His ethereal layer of aura expanded. Kevin stepped out of his physical body, into the astral realm.

Golden lights sparkled all around him as he tethered his life essence to his body. He called out to Shaun and Rachel, drawing them into the astral realm with him. He focused on the sensation of holding their hands as they sat in a pyramid of light. The energy flowed, connecting them all. With a blue hue, Shaun appeared in the astral realm, followed by a ghostly Rachel.

"Image a golden rope anchored to your physical body like an astronaut tethered to a spacecraft while on a spacewalk," Kevin said.

Shrouded in sparkling gold and silver light, their energies adjusted to the infinite void of the astral realm. In their spiritual bodies, Shaun and Rachel turned around with amazement, absorbing their new surroundings.

"I've never done this before," Rachel said.

"Crazy, hey?" Shaun said to Rachel.

"Now what? Are our bodies safe in the cave?"

"I hope so." Kevin waited for Rachel to relax in her new environment.

"Let's reach out to Jade and Casey, and see if we can make a connection."

Whispers came from afar. Emotions drifted on waves of energy through the cosmos. A deer stood glittering before them.

"Can you see that?" Rachel said.

"It's a deer. We've seen it before," Shaun said.

"It's one of Jade's totem animals. It protects and guides her when she's lost or in danger," Kevin said.

The deer turned and faced the northwest, deep into the cosmos, away from their bodies.

"I'm going to follow her. I'll anchor to you both and my body. That way I can draw from your energies if I need to."

"We'll be right here waiting. Holler or yank the tether, and I'll send you as much energy as you need," Shaun said.

Kevin wasn't sure if it would be that simple to send energy into the astral realm or not. But there was no time to debate. He needed to follow the deer.

The animal floated in the air, waiting for Kevin. As he followed, he left a golden trail behind him. An image of Jade smiling and thinking filled his mind and heart. Joy, glory, and gentleness resonated through the glittering light of the deer. Abundant universal power flitted into Kevin, and in that moment it was as if all the power that ever was or would be was right there, and his for the taking. Everything he could ever want, need, or imagine waited for him to manifest.

Then an image of a violent, clashing storm exploded his mind. He moved faster. The cloud formation was the dark realm, heavy with despair and hopelessness. It covered a towering mountain of hexagonal columns, which stretched up to the heavens.

At the top was a cluster of seven stars, the Pleiadeans, one step ahead of Orion. Ordinarily, it would have been a beautiful sight. Kevin focused in on the summit, where the Preacher battled the spirit of a wolf and the spirit of a bear, which fought alongside Jade.

Kevin tried to slow things down. Malicious wendigo tossed climbers off the face of the tower. At the bottom was Casey, nailed to a cross. The images cycled so quickly it was making Kevin dizzy. He was back on the summit and the Preacher dropped his façade. He stretched out his arms and they expanded into wings. He grew in stature, towering over the humans; a fallen angel.

The image disappeared.

"Kevin, what happened? Where did the image go? How did it end?" Shaun demanded.

"How do we know what you're seeing is real?" Rachel said.

"That had to be Devil's Tower," Shaun said.

Kevin, dumbfounded at how Shaun and Rachel were seeing

everything he saw, as if they were seeing through his eyes, sped forward, catching up to the deer. *They must be alive. They must be.*

Thick, evil, suffocating energy drained him as he saw Jade and Casey inside the dark realm, powerless. There was magnetic force that rendered Casey's power of telekinesis ineffective. The image suddenly disappeared.

"No!"

Just as quickly as flicking through TV channels, the images retuned. Kevin, relieved, tried to control his own exasperation, which clawed through his body. Birds, passing over a series of twisting mounds that looked like a giant green snake, fell out of the sky.

"Can you see the vision of the birds dropping from the sky? They've lost their magnetic compass. Where are we?" Rachel said.

"I see the birds, and mounds that look like one long, giant serpent, and I don't think it's a memory. I think it's happening right now! They're still alive. In the pit of my stomach, I feel Casey. We're too late."

"Kevin?" Rachel's words inside his head were clear.

"Hurry back," Shaun said.

"They're still alive. It's not too late," Rachel said.

"Shit!" Anguish built up inside Kevin, his vision clouding. *Calm down*, he told himself. Eliminate the negative emotions. The deer flickered in and out of existence. "Where the hell is Mingan? He should be protecting Jade!"

"Stop, K. Focus!"

Kevin concentrated on sucking in unconditional universal love. An elder came into view, sitting next to Jade, helping her control her breathing. The elder tapped Jade's elbow, like Jade's mother and grandmother had done to get her to open and center her energies, and connect with the essence of nature. The elder trailed two fingers over Jade's body, covering all her chakras from the top to toe. As she did, the muscles in Jade's body relaxed, and her breathing slowed.

She's still alive. Kevin took a long breath and synchronized with Jade's breathing. His heart beat in time with hers. Jade's timeline sparkled below him. He moved over it like a breath of air. The timeline passed under him like a fast-forward movie as the deer moved forward and disappeared. The rhythm of Jade's beating heart went with the deer.

"No. No. No!" All the feelings and sounds of the image disappeared. *Were they dead?* Kevin kept moving toward a horizon, in the direction of Jade's presence. The horizon got closer as the distant light sparkled like a shining star. The beating of her heart filled his being. It was her. It was Jade. It had to be Jade. He could feel it in every fiber of his being. He didn't need to see her face, or hear her voice. It was the light shining from within that touched him, time and time again.

The dark realm had not yet descended upon the twisting green hills – the snaking line of hills around which thousands of people had made camp. At the top of the first hill, Jade and Casey stood facing a fallen angel and its followers. Spirit animals stood beside Jade and Casey, a giant bear and a wolf, ready to attack. Kevin tuned into the emotional essence of the spirit animals, surprised to discover they were Crazy Bear and Mingan. Green and yellow lightning lit up the sky behind them as the biggest storm cell of Jinn from the dark realm descended towards the mound.

The fallen angel raised its arms, ready to command the army of vengeful Jinn as whispers of clouds broke off and flew downwards. Hundreds of survivors were gathered and lined up. Their mouths were forced open, and the Jinn sucked out their souls and entered the human bodies.

Suddenly, the golden anchor that kept Kevin connected to the astral realm retracted, pulling him backwards. Everything blurred. He rejoined Shaun and Rachel and said telepathically, "We have a problem."

"We saw everything," Rachel told him.

"We have little time," Kevin said.

"It could be a trap."

"I've got no doubts about that," Shaun put in.

"*Now* you have no doubts," Kevin said drily.

Together, they entered the cave and returned to their bodies.

Kevin forced his stiff body to move. His head was groggy from the astral traveling, but he would not waste any time. He opened a portal to Jade at the Serpent Mound.

Rachel slightly raised her hand. "Wait, why didn't Casey attack? He could have easily thrown the fallen angel off the mound, and cast him into the nearest river. There's something unusual about the energy at the mounds." She slowly got up off the cave floor, as if her body was heavy.

"I felt it too," Shaun said.

Kevin stopped what he was doing and paced the width of the cave. The images of the birds came to mind. "What about the birds? Do you think a magnetic field confused their senses? Would that affect Casey, too?" Kevin rubbed his head, searching for a connection. Time was running out. Jade didn't have the time for them to work out all the possibilities. He needed to act and open a portal to her, right now!

19

SERPENT MOUND: SHAUN. OHIO, USA.

With the mound in sight, the images they had seen in the astral realm were unfolding before them. The dark realm had not completely descended. "Let's open a portal, grab Casey and Jade, and get out of there before the dark realm descends."

Shaun held his breath as Kevin opened another portal up onto the head of the snake mound.

The moment they stepped out of the portal, the sky above blackened so that they were in twilight. The dark realm was descending faster than Kevin had realized; it was going to be close. Shaun stepped out as a bolt of yellowy-green lightning tore apart the sky. Hundreds of Jinn filled the air above. Casey and Jade, along with thousands of survivors, were about to be shrouded by the evil darkness. Those that could prepared themselves for battle.

The storm descended. A shadow of the dark realm crept over the head of the serpent mound. As Casey laid his hand on his dagger, ready to launch an attack, Shaun reached out, grabbing him and pulling him backwards through the portal before it collapsed. The dark realm claimed the head of the serpent mound. Everything happened so fast. Kevin and Jade stared at each other as the portal collapsed, leaving them to the mercy of the fallen angel.

"What the fuck, Shaun? Hell, no! We have to get back up there." Casey turned red as he screamed in Shaun's face.

Shaun had never heard Casey swear, or seen him so angry. He almost didn't recognize his friend. "I can't. Something is wrong with you," Shaun said.

"You're affected by the energy field around the mound," said Rachel.

"I could feel the strength of the magnetic energy as soon as I stepped out of the portal. You're powerless on the mound," Shaun said.

Casey pushed his hair back and grabbed his own hips, as if trying to occupy his hands so he didn't physically lash out.

"I still have the dagger! I'm heading back up there, and I'll stab that evil son of a bitch in the heart. When did you become such a pussy?" Casey ran towards the serpent mound.

"Wait!" Shaun grabbed his arm.

With a flash of anger, Casey mentally pushed Shaun backward, sending him flying into the trees.

"Casey, what are you doing?" Rachel went to help Shaun. "If Shaun hadn't had his shield up, that impact would have broken his back. You don't know what you're up against. It's a fallen angel!" Rachel shouted at Casey.

"I know, and I don't care. I've already taken down one, only one hundred and ninety-eight to go. Are you coming?" Casey ran off and disappeared into the churning dark clouds that marked the boundary of the dark realm.

"We've killed over a hundred!" Rachel shouted.

"He's not in his right mind." Shaun reached into his pocket and took out the stones. "Take these. Keep them safe." He placed them in her hands.

"No. Not this time. I'm going too!" Rachel pushed his hand back against his chest.

"Stay here, Rachel. Please. Protect yourself, and the stones. We can't let the fallen angels get them. Stay hidden. Don't enter the dark realm." Shaun studied her eyes for any sign that she might run after him and join the fight. They were as green and as beautiful as the day they first met. They were just kids. He was seven, sitting on a boulder, staring out at the Judean desert. She had worn a lilac floral dress and boots. He'd spotted her sliding under a truck, as if onto home plate.

"Okay, I'll wait for your signal, and then I'll come in."

She grabbed his face and kissed him hard. He wanted to say something to her, anything meaningful, so she understood how much he loved her. But he couldn't find the words.

THE EDGE of the dark realm's rolling, tumultuous clouds depressed Shaun's physical energy the moment he stepped inside the shield. Even there, it was like gravity had increased by a hundredfold. It dragged him down. He scanned all the people, as he joined the battle.

How can I tell who is a Jinn? Shaun studied the people running, screaming, and fighting. The others formed a straight line, watching and waiting. He caught up with Casey. "How do I know who to attack?" Shaun asked him.

"You should've stayed with Rachel. I see their auras. They're different. The Jinn have a heavy, black aura. Blacker than any darkness you could ever imagine," Casey said.

"All I can see is people attacking people."

"Find the evil haze that surrounds them. When you're close, you'll feel it." Casey didn't wait.

With his dagger drawn, Casey ran at the nearest person, and pierced the woman's heart with his blade, while chanting the final prayer to trap the Jinn in human form. The Jinn couldn't be destroyed, but Casey's ancient dagger set the human souls free. Casey moved from person to person, so quickly that Shaun tripped over their bodies.

A man with a slight haze ran at him. Shaun held up his hand and vaporized the man. A ghostly black fog of smoke covered the remains. He worried he had not freed the human soul, condemning it to the dark realm. But then the tiniest spark of light shot up into the air and joined the other rising stars, leaving the dark realm.

Mingan was the giant, supernatural wolf. Crazy Bear was bigger than a grizzly. Together, Mingan and Crazy Bear launched themselves at the Jinn, tearing them apart, destroying them in mid-air like wild animals. Shaun didn't know who these people were, or if he could trust them to save Jade and Kevin. But together, the spirit animals destroyed dozens of Jinn before they could feed on human souls.

Behind him, a powerful evil lurked. It crept up his spine. The fallen angel scrutinized him and Casey as they battled the Jinn, which stretched out across the serpent mound like an army of pawns protecting their weak king.

With military precision, Casey advanced up to the head of the serpent, killing everything in his way. It wouldn't be long before he reached the fallen angel. Shaun ran after Casey, killing those that tried to kill him. The fallen angel stepped back and repositioned itself as more Jinn emerged from the dark realm. *How many are there?*

Shaun stopped in his tracks. The fallen angel, as if with an invisible arm, raised Kevin and Jade into the air by their throats. They grappled and slapped at their necks, trying to free themselves from the unseen hand. Jade reached around to her back pocket and pulled out her glowing wand. She stabbed and stabbed at the invisible hand.

Shaun expanded his hermetic shield and bowled over everything in his way. The impact against the shield sounded like hail pelting on a car hood. The fallen angel commanded all the Jinn to attack Shaun but nothing that they did could infiltrate the sapphire shield. Jade's body trembled. Kevin struggled against the invisible hold and kicked out at the fallen angel's head.

"You can't defeat me!" The fallen angel laughed, amused by Kevin's petty actions. "You cannot stop the marriage of hell and earth. You cannot stop the dark realm. Soon all this will be ours. Your God has abandoned you. It is our right to rule."

Kevin's body moved closer to the fallen angel, as if he was flying. The fallen angel studied Kevin. "I am Asmodeus, King of the Jinn. You are so insignificant, but God has given great power to a pathetic human. With you, portal master, and the sacred stones, my brethren, led by the Great Samyazah, will ascend into your heaven, the heaven of mortals, and destroy all that is. Then we will rise to the heavens of the angels and end the war of all the angels. We shall conquer the heaven of the gods and all the heavens — the home of your god. Samyazah will claim the throne of our creator." The fallen angel released his hold on Kevin's throat, just enough for him to talk.

"You're insane. I will never help you."

"Silence," Asmodeus said.

The demon was a fool. It did not understand that evil could not pass through Kevin's portals. Shaun pretended to be listening to its posturing rantings. *Unless... what if, with the help of his tones, they were able to open a portal from within the dark realm?* Shaun shivered, and refused to entertain the idea any further.

Kevin coughed but refused to remain silent. "Where is your precious army of fallen angels? Where are they? They're not coming. You want to know why? Because we destroyed them! Where is this ruler you speak of? Leader of the darkness, and all the ugliness from every negative realm? Your vessel is not worthy of the Light of God. You can never go back!" Kevin moved his arms in the air, pulling the atoms together. He produced a rock, and threw it at the fallen angel.

"Keep it distracted," Casey whispered to Shaun.

"What are you going to do?" Shaun felt helpless, watching Kevin struggle as the fallen angel tightened its invisible grip to shut him up.

"Trust me." Casey ran off.

Oh God, help us. Asmodeus squeezed Jade's throat. Deprived of oxygen, her face darkened. Asmodeus dropped her limp body.

"Noooo!" Shaun screamed. Enough was enough. Shaun stopped a few yards away. "Let them go. It's me you want!" he shouted.

"Samyazah is the true ruler, and he will not bother to appear in the likeness of a man." Asmodeus pushed Jade in the abdomen with his hooved foot.

Kevin squirmed in pain. The survivors that weren't being attacked by the Jinn stood silent, petrified by fear, then suddenly, as if they were all connected to Jade, they bent forward in pain, all clutching their abdomens.

"See my power. You too can have such power. Join us, and you can be king of the slaves!"

Kevin groaned and the tension in his body relaxed. Shaun tried not to react, or show he cared. Snakes wormed their way from under the ground and slithered over Kevin's and Jade's bodies. The Jinn, in human form, stood their ground like sentinels. Snake heads darted with lightning speed, striking Jade and Kevin again and again.

Shaun's jaw tightened. His fists clenched and unclenched as he fought the urge to attack. It was difficult to continue to show lack of concern for his friends. Even though, at one point in time, it had been easy not to care. Without the shield, the gravity weighed him down. Shaun dragged his body between the Jinn and stood a foot away from the snakes that marked the boundary between him and Asmodeus. Jinn struck down survivors that dared to seek freedom beyond the dark realm. Shaun wanted to grab the fallen angel by the throat and squeeze the life out of it.

Where the fuck is Casey? He couldn't see him anywhere. Jinn lustfully sucked out the souls of the dying. Agitation, nearly beyond control, welled up inside Shaun. He wanted to explode with fury. Breathe. Breathe. He closed his eyes, trying to control his emotions. A plan of attack was needed. He breathed in through his nose, avoiding the soot. How the hell he was going to get Kevin and Jade out of the dark realm?

An inner strength, greater than any power he had known, grew inside him, fueled by fury and anguish from seeing his friends squirm in excruciating pain. All the surrounding survivors were screaming in agony. He prayed to God that Rachel stayed where she was, and didn't make it her mission to save them all.

Kevin's body flinched. Snakes slithered out from under him. He gave a weak cough — he was alive, but dying. For the past week, Kevin had opened portal after portal, to save countless people he had never met. Thousands of souls had ascended to Heaven because of him. If he could just touch Kevin, and give him a jolt of energy, he could get himself out of there. The warmth of the sun fueled Kevin, but it couldn't penetrate the dark realm.

"Join us! You have the sacred stones. I will let you be the keeper of the stones. United, the power of the stones can defeat any enemy — in Heaven and in Hell. You have the power of God. You can destroy or create worlds."

The Jinn surged from behind, circling Shaun.

Shaun glanced at his glowing hand, thinking about its power. *How could the stones create worlds?* he wondered. When he had gazed into one of the crystal spheres he had left with Rachel, it looked like it contained a colorful, expansive galaxy, inside the crystal, not much bigger than a marble.

Suddenly, the images and feelings of a universe expanding inside him disappeared, and a haunting, disgusting, indescribable sensation slithered into his mind and body.

Asmodeus' voice bellowed. "You think you can trick me? I see you and hear your foolish thoughts. I know who and what you are. You're a murderer, the cause of your mother's and father's deaths. You will never enter Heaven. We controlled the fires that burn your cities. Watching your city burn was pleasurable for you. You know not love."

The words pierced Shaun's armor. The evil within the dark realm weighed heavily on his heart and soul. *Casey, where are you?*

"Those in the light are weak. In the dark realm, our believers are strong."

Dead bodies lay where they fell, forever chained to the dark realm. Shaun drew comfort from the flickering blue light in his hand, but as he listened to the booming voice of Asmodeus, reminding him of every nasty thing he had done in his brief life, the light grew pale, and so did the light inside Shaun's soul. As the power of the light faded, so too did the hope for ascension and a better world.

Maybe this is all there is. Maybe there's no ascension for me.

Asmodeus stretched out his arms and wings, welcoming Shaun. "That's right. Now you see. Come to me. You belong with us in the dark realm. Give me the sacred stones."

Casey yelled, "Put up your shield! Attack, dammit!"

The light inside him was diminishing, and Casey's voice was getting further and further away. Shaun dropped to his knees, curled into a ball, and cried for forgiveness. Suddenly, lifted off the gray wasteland, he moved towards Asmodeus, whose arms and wings were outstretched in welcome. Shaun floated closer and closer.

The softest, calmest voice filled his ears, and her words warmed his heart. Tears rolled down his face as he listened to Sophia. "Heaven is within you. In your heart, the light is always within you. Forgive yourself. Rachel loves you. Kevin loves you, and God loves you," she whispered.

He didn't deserve their love. But the power of her belief filled Shaun's being. The icosahedron pulsed in his hand. Light radiated like a glove around him and pushed back the dark thoughts of despair. The fallen angel dropped him to the ground.

"Where are the sacred stones?" It expanded and flapped its great wings. The air was stale and lifeless. Shaun stood up. The wings flapped hypnotically. A flash of light in the darkness, from the other side of the mound behind Asmodeus, caught his eye.

Casey.

Sparks of light rose into the sky. Casey charged Asmodeus from behind. Jade, like a snake goddess, rose with lightning speed from the bed of snakes, her arms raised. Her wand clasped firmly between her hands, she plunged it down like a dagger, stabbing

Asmodeus in the thigh. The fallen angel batted Jade to the ground. She reached for Kevin and touched him with her wand.

A giant, supernatural wolf leapt over Jade and attacked Asmodeus. Mingan. Asmodeus knocked the giant wolf to the ground with one swipe. Concussed, Mingan shook his head as he transformed back into a human. His bracelet glowed as he reached for Jade, igniting the power in her bracelet. Together, the bracelets illuminated blinding light.

"Kill them!" Asmodeus commanded Shaun. Snakes moved in a frenzy across every inch of the ground. Jade's and Mingan's bracelets created a band of light, joining them. Mingan and Jade jumped to their feet and ran as fast as they could in the opposite direction, stretching out the light and circling Asmodeus, who laughed at their petty efforts.

"What is this trickery?" it asked, amused. In its distraction, the demon allowed Casey to charge from behind.

Shaun pushed out the laser beam from his palm, cutting down the Jinn that tried to penetrate the circle of light Jade and Mingan created. Nothing could enter or exit. Jade and Mingan moved faster and closer to Asmodeus. Behind, Casey dropped to his knees, and slid on the grass between the fallen angel's legs. He sprung to his feet, as if gravity didn't exist, and pierced Asmodeus in the heart with his ancient dagger.

"With the power of the Almighty, unclean demon and spirit, I pierce you with the blade of judgement, and you shall be no more, and it is done, in the name of the Holy Spirit. Amen." Casey recited the prayer while dragging the dagger down the body of the surprised fallen angel.

Shaun's ear drums popped as Asmodeus howled in pain. Its scream exploded through the Jinn, destroying them and their followers. The ground trembled, as if a volcano had erupted deep inside the belly of the earth. Shaun expanded his hermetic shield to encompass Kevin and Casey, Jade, and Crazy Bear. Mingan lay motionless on the other side of the mound, and seemed so small compared to the spirit of the wolf. Jade quickly pressed her wand against Kevin's heart, to heal his body. She made an incision above his solar plexus, and sucked out the venom.

The fallen angel's heart combusted into flames and spread out through its leathery torso and wings. It blazed before them until it turned to a hot black stone on the ground. Shaun willed Kevin to move, as Jade ran from the shield to Mingan. Kevin, groggy, sat up and crawled onto his knees, while Shaun reached down and helped him stand. Groggy and unsure of his footing, Kevin wobbled, as if intoxicated. Crazy Bear dropped to his knees next to Mingan, and Kevin was right behind him. Mingan didn't move. Jade trailed her crystal wand over his body, but still he didn't stir.

"I can open the portal and heal him."

"You can't open a portal to save yourself." Shaun's words sounded harsh. He reduced the shield until it fit him like a glove. "Let me give you a boost so you can open a portal."

Jade held her wand against Mingan's heart as a huge butterfly landed near Mingan's head. Jade left her wand lying across his body, raised her hands into the air, and gathered the wind that whirled around them under her command. She swept up the remaining Jinn and, like a tornado, pushed the dark realm back from the mound, revealing the light of the sun. The greenness of the serpent mound was dazzling. The snakes sizzled in the sun's rays, and combusted into flames.

"How come the snake's venom didn't affect you?" Shaun asked.

"Snake is one of my medicine totem animals. Venom only strengthens me."

The warmth of the light on his face was like a loving hand. Five hundred yards away, the dark realm churned. Lightning filled the skies. Jade had only pushed the dark realm aside for now. Soon, it would push back, and another fallen angel would gather the reins of the Jinn.

The butterfly woman wept as Kevin reached out and touched Shaun's sapphire. He bathed his face in the sunlight before compressing the energy in the air to generate a portal. "Wait, Rachel!" Shaun said.

Crazy Bear picked up Mingan and stepped through the portal behind Kevin to heal Mingan. Kevin and Crazy Bear stepped out from the portal with Mingan and laid him beside Rachel. The butterfly woman ran down the mound.

Crazy Bear knelt by Mingan. "It was his time."

"I'm so sorry," Jade said, letting the tears flow. The butterfly woman pushed her hard, out of the way, and Jade toppled over backwards.

Jade rubbed her wrist, where her bracelet had been. She looked back at the mound, then touched Mingan's wrist, where it paled from wearing a bracelet long-term.

"Don't you touch him!" the butterfly woman snapped at Jade.

Jade pulled her hand away and, looking lost, held her own wrist.

"Are you alright?" Shaun asked.

"My great-grandmother's bracelet is gone. I can't feel her spirit, and I can't feel Mingan's spirit, they're both gone. It's like a link in a chain has broken."

Jade wiped away her tears and pulled out of her pocket a black onyx stone with a maze drawn on it. There was an image of a person nearing the center of the maze.

"What's that?" Shaun asked.

"A memory stone left to me by my great-grandmother, Great Turtle. It's me, or us. We're close to the end of our journey."

Shaun put his arm around Rachel, grateful for the simple touch. He let her aura cover his. Hundreds of survivors, confused and riddled with grief and anguish, combed the mound for loved ones. Kevin was slouched over, as if trying to catch his breath, but Shaun felt he was avoiding eye contact with Jade. He wondered what or whose emotions Kevin was feeling. "K, when you're ready, let me give you another boost, so these folks can end their journey and ascend to the heavens."

Rachel handed Shaun his gemstone pouch, and he pocketed the stones.

It didn't take Kevin long to draw on the energy of the stones and open a portal for the survivors. The butterfly woman, Crazy Bear, a man Jade called Chief Thundercloud, and a girl named Ruby thanked Jade and Kevin. An old woman gave Jade her drum and a wooden box before disappearing into the portal. Crazy Bear picked up Mingan, and the butterfly woman followed as they ascended together. Many carried their dead into the portal. The energy between Kevin and Jade was disjointed and if Shaun could feel it so could everyone else.

Suddenly, Jade slapped Kevin on the shoulder. "Don't you ever leave me like that again!" she said.

"Ready to head back to the estate and deal with those asshole giants?" Shaun asked Casey, worried Jade and Kevin were about to have a major argument.

Casey had changed. Shaun could see that now. Everyone was different. Casey wiped the brown blood off his dagger, then wiped his dagger against his thigh, and peered into the sky. "We will not make it to the 8th day of Leo."

20

ASSEMBLY OF WARRIORS: KEVIN.
UNITED KINGDOM.

Kevin wanted to touch Jade. To feel the warmth of her hand, and take away her pain. Mingan was gone, and her heart was heavy. Once they were all light-hearted, except for Shaun, who had carried a heavy heart filled with guilt and shame for the death of his mother, and carried the sins of his father for over a decade. Now his heart was light with love, while Jade, Casey and Kevin walked with the weight of the world.

Kevin wished it would all end soon. To carry his pain and the pain of all those he loved was excruciating. He was an old man in a young man's body. Casey's unshed tears were choking him. Jade had expected deep philosophical learnings from her shamanic teacher. She had expected him to be old and wise, but he was young and handsome, with a wise old soul, and now he was gone, and she felt lost.

Kevin waited as they all stepped out of the portal at Casey's estate in the United Kingdom. Once the bliss and the healing granted inside the membrane of the portal was left behind and forgotten, they picked up their emotional baggage like treasured heirlooms.

It was hard to know if it was day or night. The sky was bare; a blanket of darkness. There were no silver-lined clouds hinting at a vibrant, glowing moon. No one spoke; no one wanted to speak. They were all lost in their own thoughts.

The end was near, and Kevin didn't know what to expect. It had only been a few days ago when the borders of the two realms were tumultuous with black, churning clouds, like breaking waves at the shoreline. Casey walked past him, over to the shed where his adopted dad, Terry, kept his cars and motorcycle. They were gone, and so was Tim and Seth's campervan. Thirty people, and not one remained.

Kevin stopped in the middle of the curved driveway, next to the wreckage of the plane he had attempted to land nearly a year ago. They had been lucky that day. Luck was the only thing that they had left, and they were going to need a lot more of it if they believed Casey's prediction, that there was no reaching the 8th day of Leo.

Shaun and Rachel retrieved a blanket from the rubble and covered a body.

"Who is it?" Kevin knew, but he just needed confirmation. He was there the night the giants destroyed the estate. The giant had stomped on Seth's father while Billie saved their brother's life. Earnest had still been weak from the exorcism in London that had killed Sophia.

There was never any time for anyone to rest. To grieve. The memories were exhausting. He could only imagine what they had gone through in London. He had been on the other side of the world, dying in a cave with rabbis after attacked by a colony of bats, while Jade had searched for her father in the realm of lost souls. So much had happened in such a short time, it was no wonder they were overwhelmed and fatigued. The day God would white-wash the earth of all evil could not come fast enough.

In Casey's book of Enoch, it said it would be worse than the days of Noah. It didn't matter if he lived or died. Once they were all safe, he was ready to check out.

"K, you okay?" Shaun asked.

"Yeah. I'm good."

"I can't be sure who it is. It's been a couple of weeks. The body is flat as a baby chock, but I think it's Seth's dad."

Kevin wondered what Shaun meant by *flat as a baby chock*. He didn't like the images that popped into his mind. Jade sat on the ground with her wand and started gently beating on her shamanic drum. The sound was lifeless, there was no resonance, so she stopped.

"It's the dark realm. There's no life in the dark realm," she said, and walked off to the shed where Casey was.

She was still angry with him. Kevin turned his back on her anger and walked down the gravel driveway, past the birch trees, to the main road. He was cold, and dug his hands into his pockets, hunched his shoulders up to his ears, wondering why she was angry with him. Maybe she wished it was him that had died, and not Mingan. The gate squeaked as he pushed it open. He went out onto the road and read the painted writing, which was an answer to Casey's message to head to Stonehenge.

"Headed for Stonehenge. Fifty-two souls."

He could only hope Casey's adopted family, his parents, and baby sister Molly, were among the fifty-two. He moved closer, examining the script, and concluded it was his mother's style of handwriting. He connected to his mother's emotions when she had written it. Kevin slipped into a deep state, and it was like being jolted out of sleep when Casey came up behind him and gave him a fright. Casey adjusted his backpack. *It must get heavy carrying those books all the time*, Kevin thought. A glint of light bounced off Casey's chest. It was Sophia's medallion, with the twelve seals of Solomon. Kevin searched the sky for the source of light. There wasn't any. The necklace captured Kevin's attention; Casey, aware of Kevin's stare, quickly tucked it under his shirt.

"I suppose you want to know who wrote it," Casey said.

"Yes."

"I think it was my mother; if not, let's hope it's someone we know." Casey crouched by the number fifty-two. His fingers were millimeters away from the tail end of the number two, when suddenly he was repelled backwards through the air, landing hard on his back. The contact between Casey and the writing created a powerful surge of energy. "What the hell?"

"Casey! Are you okay? What happened?" Kevin pulled Casey onto his feet.

"Fuck me!"

It wasn't like Casey to swear. Kevin stared at Casey, waiting for him to reveal what had happened. "What is it?"

"There are at least a hundred emotional imprints. So many memories from one spot is crazy. But I did feel your mom. It's them…"

Blue light illuminated from the rubble of the estate as Jade, Shaun and Rachel searched amongst the debris.

The atmosphere was void of sound, but the smell was like rotting corpses. It passed him by on a phantom breeze. The earth trembled, like it had on the day the giants had destroyed the estate. "Casey. We have to go."

But Casey leaned over the letters again, slowly touching the dry paint for a split second, as if touching hot coals. "Callie, your mom, is hurt. She was bitten on the leg."

Kevin didn't want to see into Casey's eyes. They moved as if he was watching a movie. A movie about his mother being bitten.

"It was a Jackal, an inter-dimensional hellhound. There's at least three, and they're following them. The Jackal was going for Molly. Your mom was bitten while saving her. She's exhausted. Her leg is infected. Blood poisoning."

"Stop!" Kevin didn't want to hear anymore, and wondered why his father wasn't mentioned. Why wasn't he protecting Molly? What had happened to him? A dog growled in the shadows. He prayed it wasn't the Jackal.

"They're okay. All of them. Terry, Amy, and the twins. Molly and your mom and dad. But your mom was still sick when they arrived back at the estate, when she wrote this message. Jade's parents are with them. They're not alone." As Casey stood up, a dog barked in the darkness.

"Let's get out of here." Kevin turned back to the rubble of the house. Jade was standing with her arms wide apart, and her head tilted up towards the dark sky, her body illuminated by Shaun's light. Kevin followed her gaze as the stars appeared in the sky. It was night-time, after all.

Sharp dog claws clicked on the road as it headed in their direction. "Come on, Casey!" Kevin headed for the gate, wanting to shut out the image of a Jackal stalking them in the darkness.

"Wait a minute." Casey turned his body towards the sound. The shadow leaped up towards Casey.

"Lucy!" Casey pushed his face into the Labrador's neck and cuddled it. He allowed Lucy to lick him all over his face before commanding the dog. "Down, girl."

Kevin went to close the gate behind Lucy, although anything could easily hide amongst the trees inside the property's perimeter.

Jade slung her drum over her back. Whenever she used her shamanic tools, she radiated peace and strength.

"No one is here." Rachel sighed with relief.

Shaun and Kevin turned their heads towards Alex's grave.

"You got Isabella's notebook?" Kevin rubbed his hands together, getting ready to draw on the emotional energy from the pages.

Casey pulled his backpack over his shoulder and took out the stuffed notebook. "What are you looking for?"

"Open it up to the pages that reveal the secrets of Stonehenge." Isabella's family had passed the book down from generation to generation, until Casey and Sophia found it in Isabella's emporium in London.

"Wait!" Shaun ran over to Alex's grave and came back with the gemstone Shaun had left with Alex for safe-keeping. "Ready," Shaun said, tucking the stone into his pouch and shoving it back into his pocket.

Jade stood next to Rachel, and everyone knew she was angry at Kevin. Nervously, he touched the notebook, and prayed their families had made it to Stonehenge.

A vision of a woman sitting on a blue rock, surrounded by a low, chalk-white wall, entered his mind. Kevin prayed the rock was at Stonehenge. The energy in his hand tingled. He welcomed the stillness of the membrane as he entered the portal. If it wasn't for his sense of responsibility, he would open the portal in between worlds, where it was peaceful, and where he had seen pink waterfalls and rivers. He had always intended to go back to the parallel world he had discovered, and explore it with Jade and Tim.

Shaun banged into Kevin from behind. The brilliance of the light reflecting off the chalk-white mound blinded Kevin for a moment. Once his eyes adjusted, he saw people circling Stonehenge. Kevin counted seven rings of people standing, holding hands, and it looked like they were all women. The smallest circle, the one in the middle, had only six women. At the center of the circle, in the middle of Stonehenge, was a very tall woman with an elongated face and head. She had long, white, angelic hair. Different frequencies of the energy moved like waves through and around Stonehenge. It was the same hyper-dimensional energy as the portals he created, but so much more.

Jade, in a soft voice so as not to disturb the woman, but loud enough for the others to hear, whispered to Rachel, "I bet it's the mystery woman from the megalithic mound in Salisbury Plain. She's a queen or high priestess."

"Well, of course it is," Shaun smiled at Jade.

"How do you know that?" Rachel asked.

"I studied the European Neolithic period. Some of her remains are at Cambridge." Jade blushed.

The light that glowed around the woman mesmerized Kevin. He didn't know if she was an illusion, a spirit, or even a hologram standing in the middle of Stonehenge. She reached out her hand and spoke. The sound of her voice played on his bones. Every cell in his body seemed to come alive. The smell and taste of the fresh air was like nothing he had ever smelled before. It was super crazy.

"Guarded by our Sister Warriors of Light, the key and the sacred stones have returned," the glowing woman said.

Kevin studied Shaun, Jade, and Rachel, to see if they had any idea what the woman meant, and if they were feeling as he did. Their faces were peaceful and relaxed. Jade's chest glowed. They were all affected; it wasn't just him that felt the bliss. Jade's wand in her back pocket cast an aura of light around her. She reached out her hand and took his, and their energies merged. Kevin asked, "Who is she? Is she an angel?"

"Nobody really knows. She has starlight energy. I feel the connection. But there is a theory that Stonehenge is a gateway to the Pleiades." Jade squeezed his hand.

"That's why we're here, Jade. We all know that," Shaun said.

"Does this mean the gate is open?" Rachel stepped forward.

There was a group of cars and mobile homes parked away from the monument. Seeing the automobiles grounded Kevin. His mother and father were close by. He sensed their presence. He studied the women as they let go of each other's hands, breaking the circuit of light. They turned to each other and hugged. The light folded into their beings, and that's when he spotted his mother standing next to Jade's mom, Ellen, and Casey's adoptive mother, Amy.

His spine tingled as the energy disappeared inside him and Jade. Something returned to its place. He let go of Jade's hand and searched behind them for the unseen eyes in the sky, waiting for them to make a mistake so it could…

He didn't know what the presence wanted. The fallen angels and the Jinn were evil and cunning; they could be anywhere. Now wasn't the time to become complacent.

The brilliance of the illumination at the center of Stonehenge channeled into a single spark, until it was gone. Kevin watched in awe.

His mother limped over towards them and hugged Kevin and Shaun as if they were both her sons. Kevin didn't mind. Shaun now was like the older brother he had never had.

"Your leg… the jackals. What happened?"

"My leg will be fine. We believed you would come," his mom

said, pushing Kevin's hair off his face. "How did you know about the jackals?"

"It was Casey. He touched the message you wrote on the road, and he had a vision of you being bitten by a jackal."

"Mom, what did that woman mean when she spoke of the Sister Warriors of Light, and the key and the sacred stones?" Jade asked Ellen, who was hugging Rachel.

Lucy ran off after Casey. Amy ruffled his curls as she always did, only now she had to stretch up. Headlights of a camper van flashed, and Kevin knew – as joy mapped its way across his being – it was Tim's. Kevin smiled. It was good to feel Tim's optimism and joyous wonder. The door of the campervan opened. Tim met them halfway. Kevin embraced his friend. Shaun usually made a smart-ass remark to Tim. But this time he didn't. He pulled him into a bear hug.

"Shit, it's good to see you, man," Shaun said to a dumbfounded Tim.

"Good to see you too, man."

Seth stood back and waited for Tim.

"Mom, I don't think we're safe here!" Kevin said.

"Yes. I hear you. I feel it too." It was all his mother needed to say. "But hey, now you're all here, everything will be okay. No matter what."

"What's going on? Who was that woman? Why were…"

Ellen cut Jade off in mid-sentence and said, "Breathe, girl."

"Dad, Molly… everyone… are they okay?" Kevin asked, as he stopped walking.

"Yes, but Joe is gone."

"What? What happened?"

"We didn't see it. Tim said a giant ate him. Joe lured the beast away from the other cars. He sacrificed himself."

"That's so sad. We'll miss him. I bet he's with Sophia, watching over us. Does your leg hurt?"

"Just a little."

Kevin embraced Tim. "I'm so glad you're alive. I'll catch up in a minute."

Kevin walked towards the megalithic rocks. He wanted to touch the rocks of Stonehenge. It was very different. Everything had changed. When he'd first stepped out of the portal, he thought he had seen a chalk-white mound surrounding the monument. But there was no mound. Without the energy flowing through them, the place was nothing more than a bunch of old rocks.

"What are you doing, K?" Shaun asked.

"I wanted to touch the rocks."

"Me too."

Together, they placed their hands on the rock and a strange hum passed through his body. "Did you feel that?"

"It's like touching a speaker full of bass," Shaun said.

"Yes. It's vibrating at a very low, dense frequency. What do you think it means?"

"It's sleeping? How should I know?" Shaun said.

He took his hand from the rock and wiped it on the side of his cargo pants, accidentally touching the leather sheaf that held his bowie knife. Kevin swiveled around. No one was there. He hoped the sky would reveal to him the unseen forces that watched.

"What is it, K?"

"I got a bad feeling. Something is there." He pointed into the sky. It shimmered just enough for him to notice a difference.

"I see it. It's like vapors from a jet plane. Why doesn't it attack?"

"It's waiting for something."

"She's mad at you. You know that, right?"

"I know. But I don't know why."

* * *

"WHERE DID YOU TWO GO?" Rachel asked, gathering some plates from the cupboard above the sink in Tim and Seth's campervan. She had made soup. It was green.

"We went to touch the rocks. What soup is this?" Shaun asked.

Where did she get fresh broccoli from? Kevin wondered.

"Broccoli. It's all there is, and some bread."

"You can keep the soup, but I'll take the bread."

The campervan tilted to the right as Tim and Seth stepped up and entered. "It's so good to see you, man," Kevin wrapped his arms around his friend again. He didn't dare let anyone see his tears. Tim was everything they had lost. He represented freedom, fun, adventure, immaturity, and no responsibilities. But as he pulled away, Tim's eyes had only a glimpse of the boy he had been. He was now a young man loaded with responsibility. His smile was still big and his optimism vibrant, and that made everything feel okay.

"It's good to see you, too." Tim gave him a half smile. Death had touched him too many times. It touched them all, and they were all tired of it.

Jade stood outside the van and leaned against the outer wall with Casey. He was showing her a drawing. Casey sometimes drew things his conscious mind didn't want to know. He saw so much and felt too much. His subconscious mind tried to protect him, so he wouldn't break.

"What is it? Come inside," Kevin said.

Casey glanced up, but Jade fixed her eyes off into the distance as if he hadn't spoken. She walked off.

"I think we need to gather everyone together, so I only have to say it once. It makes me sick to my stomach as it slithers around inside me. I need to purge, so let's make this quick. But I think you need to talk to her first." Casey closed his sketchbook.

"Why isn't Metatron protecting you anymore? Did you do something wrong?"

"He does. But he can't enter the dark realm. None of the angels of light can enter the dark realm. Not even Uriel."

"I don't know the names of all the angels. I know Michael," Kevin said as Jade wandered off. *Not a smart thing to do*, he thought. Whatever he felt was watching them, it wasn't a benevolent being.

He hurried across the dew-covered grass to catch up with Jade. "Wait up, Jade. We need to talk."

Jade stopped and turned around. "Yes. I just want to say I'm sorry. I'm sorry for ignoring you, and latching onto Mingan. I was confused, the energy drew me to him, and it triggered my chakras, like when... But it never changed how I feel for you."

He thought it would be easy to hear her apologize, but it wasn't. There were so many things that he loved about her that mixed into one giant, overwhelming feeling. He couldn't speak.

"That's all I wanted to say. I hope you can forgive me." Jade turned back in the direction she had come from, and headed over to Ellen, who was talking to his mom, Callie.

"Wait!"

"What, K?"

She was calling him K. She always called him K, and he could feel the love and passion as she spoke It was a wonderful feeling. "I'm sorry."

"For what?"

He didn't know what to say. He had tried to think of all the reasons why she would be angry at him, and there were too many answers.

"Not saving Mingan?"

"Is that a question or an answer? Why are you apologizing?"

She wasn't going to make it easy for him.

"I left you. I left without even saying goodbye. You needed me, and I wasn't there for you."

"I'm naked without you. The absence of your aura, and the absence of your love, was devastating. Why you left was my fault?"

Every word she spoke made him realize how stupid his thoughts of jealousy had been. Shame kept his lips tight, but he had to answer. "I thought you wanted Mingan, not me." It sounds so juvenile to his ears. Childish and petty. "I'm sorry. I fucked up."

"No, I did." Jade took his hands in hers, and the energy coursed through him.

From the first time they had met in the woods, their combined energy was like exploding stars. "I may be only sixteen, but the past year has made me into an old man, and I believe I know love. The love of my family, the unconditional love of God and all things. And then there's a special love I feel for you that expands like the universe with every breath I take," Kevin told her.

Her fingers entwined with his. She pulled him close, until their lips touched, and their spirits entwined. Free from gravity, their spiritual bodies floated into the astral realm as one.

"Earth to K, come in K." Tim waited for them to separate.

Kevin heard Tim as if he was on the other side of the world.

"If you two would like to bring yourselves back to earth, that would be marvelous. Casey has called a meeting." Tim cleared his throat. "Hello!"

Swimming in each other's souls, allowing themselves a moment to bathe in bliss, Kevin and Jade didn't want to stop, and they ignored Tim.

"Kevin!" Tim lightly touched him on the shoulder and the energy sent Tim flying as it grounded the pair, bringing them back to earth. Kevin pulled away, biting his bottom lip, savoring the taste of Jade. He waited for a moment before breathing.

"We should help him up," Jade smiled.

21

DELIVERY US FROM EVIL: SHAUN.
STONEHENGE.

As Shaun pushed the tarp flaps of the tent aside, he heard Callie speaking. She was talking to Casey.

"I really think we need to talk to everyone," she said.

In the middle of the tent, there was a table. Shaun imagined their families had used it for meals. Callie was having a hard time convincing Casey to share the vision he'd drawn. The sketch was at the center of everyone's attention. Daniel, Kevin's dad, nodded at him as he entered. He took a step sideways, making a space for Shaun to join them. Terry, Casey's adopted father, had a hand towel dangling out of his pocket. He wiped his hands before lifting a plate of cut vegetables. He passed the plate and Shaun's polity declined. Chomping on a carrot, he wouldn't be able to hear anything anyone said.

"We have to show the others," Amy said from the fold-up camp bed where she sat.

Amy nursed a twin, while the other played with its own toes beside her. She pushed the baby's hair away from its eye.

"Casey. Look at me, Casey. You must trust these women. They've been expecting you. They know all about Sophia. We must show them the picture." Amy took a sip of water.

It was good to see everyone together, but Shaun wished it was under better circumstances. Shaun hated these get-togethers. The last one hadn't ended so well.

Kevin's cheeks were red, and he didn't imagine it was from the sharp, cold air outside. It didn't seem to make much difference what season it was in Salisbury, it was much too cold for Shaun. He liked the sun, warm ocean water, and the feeling of sand between his toes. The thought of sand reminded him of the sandstorm at the Sphinx that was rough as sandpaper. He shivered. At that moment, Casey's eyes met his, searching for his guidance. Shaun nodded, as if answering a silent request.

"Okay." Casey picked up the sketch.

"Come with me," Callie said.

One by one, they all left the tent, and he waited outside for Rachel. Kevin and Jade waited with him until Rachel emerged. She was the last one, and was carrying Amy's baby. It was a shame they'd never get a chance to have a baby of their own. He took the baby's diaper bag from her and carried it. Up ahead was a massive tent with hundreds of women inside, that could have been used once for big weddings. He wondered where the men were. Callie searched above their heads until she found who she was looking for. Shaun nudged Kevin. "You sorted things out with Jade, yeah?"

Kevin blushed. "Yeah, all good."

Shaun leaned into him, giving him a friendly nudge.

"Did you see the haze in the sky again?" Kevin whispered.

"Yeah, have you seen Casey's sketch?"

"Shh."

Shaun didn't know who was hushing him up, but the woman

Callie was looking for signaled them to make their way toward her, at the back of the tent, and between the women sitting on the floor. Each woman seemed earthy to him; women that made daisy chains, and chased butterflies. Rachel smiled at him. She was nothing like these women.

"What are you getting all mushy about? I know that look," Rachel said.

"Nothing. Just admiring your radiant beauty, and undeniable intestinal fortitude."

"My what?"

"Inner strength; guts," Jade said in a not-so-whispered voice.

"Who are these women?" Shaun asked Jade.

"Long ago, women used to worship the moon here at Stonehenge. I don't remember what they called themselves, but these women may be descendants."

"There's actually something in this world you don't know?" Shaun got an elbow in the side from Rachel. She liked Jade, and every time he playfully took a jab at her, Rachel would have a go at him. Jade was awfully smart, and he actually expected her to know everything. Tim always called her a walking Wikipedia. Shaun enjoyed the nudge. He enjoyed the simplicity of everything he could see. They had decorated the place with handmade craft items. Pieces of stones, shells, and plants. Very earthy.

"Sorry to interrupt," Callie said.

The woman put down the radish she was eating. She sat in the middle of seven others. The one on her right picked up a plate of radishes, offering them around. Everyone took one; it was as if it was mandatory to have a radish. Boy, the radish was hot inside his mouth. His eyes wept, his sinuses cleared, and he tried not to cough as he swallowed.

"Make room so our sisters and brothers may join us." The

woman gestured with her hand, flicking her fingers back and forward for them to scoot on back.

Jade slipped her drum off her back, nearly hitting him in the face. "Sorry."

Casey kept his backpack on but shifted his dagger towards the back. A woman stood up and approached. "I believe you have something that belongs to me?"

"Isabella Sumer?" Smiling, Casey reached around for his backpack and took out her overstuffed family notebook of supernatural, mythological creatures and potions.

"My grandfather told this day would come. It's an honor," Isabella said, taking possession of the books.

Casey nodded, returned his backpack onto his back, and knelt before the leader. He placed the drawing in front of his knees, pushing it with both hands towards her. She studied the image before picking it up for a closer look. She went over every detail on the page, then passed it to the woman on her left, then Isabella on her right. The women put the sketch back on the ground in front of Casey's knees. Shaun wanted to get a closer look, to see what all the fuss was about.

The women sat silent. Not even a child moved or made a sound. Shaun scanned over all the women behind him. It was unnerving. In Jade's lap, partly hidden by her drum, her wand glowed, and so did her heart. Somehow, she connected with these women, and Kevin was no different, except he was male. Rachel glanced down. He followed her gaze to his hands. The icosahedron pulsed with light. Even Rachel's heart radiated light, and then his whole being glowed with the light of the stones.

"Reveal more of the light from the sacred stones," the woman instructed.

"First, tell us what you see in Casey's drawing."

"My name is Ceridwen. Your friend has drawn the end of an ancient battle for the key to the heavens. Where there is light, there is always darkness. Through our dreams, we have awoken, and are ready for the new beginning that is coming. But first, the old ways must die. Like the fire that burns the tree; from the seed, they will be reborn. We also must transform. Our ancestors left a code, a key, that would activate when humanity must ascend and return to the Pleiadeans, where our creator and loved ones dwell."

Casey passed the sketch to Shaun. *What the hell?* Tall, muscular men that resembled reptiles, circled Stonehenge. Thousands of red eyes glowed in the dark sky. A few feet off the ground, the fallen angels battled angels of light. Jade stood with her arms opened wide. Kevin was at the center of Stonehenge. Shaun stopped and handed the piece of paper back to Casey, as if it was poisonous, then his eyes fell on the images of lifeless bodies. He didn't want to know anymore.

"Who are the geeks dressed up for the event, like creatures from some swamp land?" Shaun tried to keep his voice calm and light.

"They're from another planet, and have searched for the key to the heavens. They have even tried to recreate the harmonics of Stonehenge on the North Pole of Saturn, endeavoring to create a hyper-dimensional portal of their own. But they have failed time and time again. The others, in battle with angels of light, are the Watchers."

"Hang on a minute. If there was a Stonehenge on Saturn, don't you think NASA would know about it? This is all just mumbo-jumbo," Shaun said, interrupting. He was feeling confident that Ceridwen was just reciting folklore, until Jade smiled at him.

"They do, Shaun. NASA had images from the Cassini Mission. There was and is a six-sided shape, a hexagon, with a dominant center. The polygon covers Saturn's North Pole." Jade pursed her lips and raised her eyebrows, as if to say sorry.

"Okay, fair enough. But if they're aliens, why can't they just fly their spacecraft to the Pleiades? I've seen an alien spaceship."

"Why are you so resistant? Our creator has foretold this day time and time again."

"Just answer the questions." Shaun felt anxious.

"The Pleiades are the gateway to other dimensions, guarded by the hunter in the sky. If they get access to the gateway, they can enter our heaven, or go anywhere within the myriad of galaxies. Stonehenge encompasses every facet of sacred geometry that can create portals to many galaxies. You possess the same abilities. And you, young man – you and your friends are the key to humanity's survival."

"The Watchers are the fallen angels," Casey said.

"Yes, and that's why they want the sacred stones that are obviously in your possession. They want the same as the Reptilians, the creatures in your friend's drawing. Where there is brilliant light, there is also great darkness."

"So you keep saying," Shaun said, standing up. Rachel tried to tug at his black pants, to pull him back down. He slipped from her grasp and hurried out before he exploded with an emotional outburst.

"Wait up!" Kevin said, running out into the night after him.

Shaun bent over and put his hands on his knees. "Fuck me!" The tears welled in his eyes. "Why the hell is this happening? Fuck! Fuck! Fuck you, son of a bitch! Show yourselves. Cowards!" He screamed into the dark sky. Kevin stood beside him, feeling his pain, letting Shaun release his anger and frustration. "I finally have everything that I ever wanted, and now it's all going to be taken away. Just my fucking luck." He rubbed his eyes and turned to

Kevin. "I don't deserve your friendship. I don't want this world to end. I don't want to die. I don't want any of you to die."

"It will be all right. Have faith. We've got this. I won't let you die. Come on, let's show Ceridwen your little gems."

"My life is in your hands." Shaun stood outside and took a deep breath, then entered the big white tent. No one had moved. He handed over the leather pouch with the sacred stones that had once been embedded in the chest plate of Thoth; the ones that activated the Emerald Tablet. He had carried them with him for twelve years. Ceridwen selected five of the gems, leaving the four spheres aside. She favored the tetrahedrons' star and grouped the other four together.

"This is the Merkabah. It is the flower of life. It contains these polyhedrons, including the one lodged in the palm of your hand."

Casey reached for Sophia's necklace at the mention of the flower of life. Jade nodded at Shaun, as if to confirm that what Ceridwen said was true. Casey took out the necklace, and showed it to Ceridwen.

"The seals of Solomon. Welcome. These once belonged to one of our sisters. If these were gifted to you, I'm sorry for the burden placed upon you. But you must be strong to endure the pain, otherwise you would not have been appointed," Ceridwen said.

"Why must we endure the pain you see in Casey's sketch if we can leave now?" Kevin asked, leaning forward.

"What do you propose?"

"We activate the portal now. I have opened them across the world. Already, thousands have ascended."

"That is what we were just doing. That is why we summoned the goddess. But we couldn't complete the code. The key was incomplete. Your mother's and sister's DNA was missing part of the code."

"Well I've opened ancient portals before, and I can do it again. Let's not wait for those things to appear. We don't need to fight. We just need to go." Kevin pointed at the drawing Casey had made. "Burn it!"

Ceridwen sat in silence. She closed her eyes. Shaun glanced behind, and all the women had their eyes closed too. A full minute passed. Whatever was happening, he could swear they were all connected. Kevin slightly bowed his head. *Not you too,* Shaun thought. Patience was not his forte.

"Thank you," said Ceridwen.

Shaun's eyes darted from left to right, wondering who she was thanking. He caught Tim's eye. Tim shrugged.

"You are the key." Ceridwen projected her voice for everyone to hear. "Sisters. Reform the seven circles. We're going home."

The women didn't contain their excitement. The silence in the room turned to a surge of cheers.

"Wait!" Kevin yelled.

A hush rolled over the women.

"What do you mean, the key?" Kevin's heard was pounding, he was feeling anxious and nauseous.

"You," she said, first looking at Kevin, then Jade, Shaun, Rachel, finally lingering on Casey. "It is written in your DNA. Combined you are, the light, the door, the warriors, and the key. And you will pass your gifts to your children, and one day, one of your descendants becomes all that you are combined, the key to the survival of the universe."

"That's bullshit! How can we have any descendants when the world is about to end? Fuck this!" Shaun said, pushing his way past a few women, leaving. He needed some air, and time to think.

Rachel caught up with him before he could make it halfway

across the room to the exit. She took hold of his arm. "Wait. Come on, just hear her out?"

Shaun allowed Rachel to lead him back Ceridwen.

"There is nothing more I can say to you. It's up to you; what will be will be," Ceridwen said.

"No, it's not up to us, at all!" Shaun yelled. "God has already decided our fate, he has already begun to tear the earth apart. He has allowed the dark realm and the Jinn to rise up."

"We can't presume to know the mind of God. Hasn't she looked after us? Hasn't she looked after you, and guided you along YOUR, chosen path?" Ceridwen said looking at the sisters for agreement.

"What about all the people that are dead? My mother, Kevin's brother, Sophia, our friends, billions of people have died. Why? Why didn't God look after them?" Shaun said, furious, stepping closer to Ceridwen.

"How do you know they are not with the creator? Just because you can't see them doesn't mean they don't exist. Life of your soul, your spiritual body, is eternal. Our bodies are no more than mere garments." Ceridwen adjusted her white robe at the neck, as if she was suddenly cold.

Deep in his heart, Shaun believed his mother, Sophia, and Alex existed in a dimension he was unable to fully see or understand. *There is a form of existence after earthy life; there's no denying it.* The anger, frustration and defiance left his body; he could keep up the argument no longer because he simply couldn't understand when he couldn't see. He had to have faith, and focus on what he wanted, not what he didn't want. He was ready to let go of the fear of being out of control and dying, but was the fear ready to let go of him?

Kevin passed through the women. Shaun followed, along with

his friends and family. Shaun was sure Kevin would make them go through first.

* * *

SHAUN HAD NEVER APPRECIATED the stars as much as he had in the past few hours. Kevin wasted no time, and stood in the middle of Stonehenge, waving his arms around, pulling the energy from the stones and the atmosphere. Sparks of lightning struck the megalithic stones as a channel of light surrounded everyone within the perimeter. The doorway opened, and the women made sounds and gasps of wonder. Everyone stood in awe as the spectacle of light illuminated everything around them, thanks to one magnificent person.

Kevin reached out his hand to Rachel. "It has to be you that leads them into Heaven."

"Follow Rachel!"

Rachel kept eye contact with Shaun. There was no time to embrace, or to tell her how much he loved her. In a flash of light, she was gone. Then Callie, Daniel, Hugh, Bo, Amy, the twins, Terry, Seth and his family; everyone Shaun had come to know and care about, disappeared in the blink of an eye. The women followed behind in groups. They passed into the circles of light of the portal while Casey, Jade and Shaun readied themselves to support Kevin if his energies faltered.

Casey ignited the piece of paper he had sketched. An ending Shaun prayed they had all narrowly escaped.

"Come, people!" Kevin yelled. There were only a few women left to pass through the portal, including Ceridwen.

Wondering if Rachel could see him from above, or wherever she was, Shaun took a step forward. His body turned to jelly seconds before the icosahedron burst into life, shielding him from the hundreds of glaring red eyes in the sky, which grew as they came closer and closer, until he could see the leathery wings of the army of the fallen angels. They smothered the channel of light that had penetrated the sky. The light and the portal closed as Ceridwen stepped into the membrane. Before she disappeared, she bowed, as if she had known this was their destiny, to stay behind.

Casey was by Kevin's side, ready to protect him. The dark realm opened and released hell. Jinn flew down from the skies. Like ghosts, they passed through his body, stealing energy. Jade, Casey, Tim and Kevin were also under attack by the supernatural, ghostly Jinn. The jackals ran out of the darkness.

It all happened so fast. The light from the sapphire in Shaun's hand glowed and he expanded a shield of blue light to encompass the others. Jade jumped out and raised her hands up to the sky of the dark and created a tornado. The clouds of the dark realm moved aside, only to close in again, but she kept summoning the four winds, scattering the dark realm. Casey blasted the Jinn, pushed them away with his telekinesis, but it was pointless. In their natural form, the Jinn were nothing more than smoke. They were unde-featable.

Shaun screamed at the others to get inside the hermetic shield, but no one listened. Casey ran and flew into the air, slicing throats and stabbing fallen angels in their hearts. He was so fast, Shaun had lost sight of him when a half-circle of Reptilians materialized beyond the megalithic structure. They grew in numbers, holding their ground as more creatures materialized, until they completely circled Stonehenge. Kevin couldn't open a portal in the dark realm. Jade would need to push the dark realm aside if they were going to get out of there.

The ground trembled, and a haze covered his view of Kevin. Suddenly, Tim was there, jumping on the back of a Reptilian. Shaun raced over and blasted the Reptilians until he had Tim and Kevin safely within the hermetic shield.

Kevin coughed. "Where's Jade?"

High in the air, the streak of light that had been Casey stopped. A demonic fallen angel had Jade by the hair.

"Give me the sacred stones!" The voice boomed like thunder and the ground shook, as if God himself had spoken. Even within the safety of the sphere, Shaun was afraid.

"Give him the stones!" Kevin yelled at Shaun.

"No. We can't do that, K. You know we can't," Tim said. He walked out beyond the shield. "Take me!"

"Stop wasting my time! Do you know who I am?"

Jade screamed and clawed at the fallen angel.

"Why doesn't Casey call Metatron? What good is it to have an angel for a guardian, if it can't protect you or your friends from the fallen angels?" Kevin shouted.

"It can't enter the dark realm. We're on our own. That's why it's taken Jade. Only she can push back the dark realm. Let's make some noise and piss it off before we die." Shaun said.

"Who are you? Do you know who I am? I'm your worst night-mare!" Tim said.

"When did he grow a pair?" Shaun said to Kevin as he reduced the shield.

Casey disappeared from the sky and landed with a thud by his side. "Ready?"

"Ready."

"I am Samyazah, ruler chief of the Watchers, appointed by God."

"I'm Tim. An embodiment of the Light. Which means you answer to me, motherfucker!"

"What the hell are you doing, Tim? Get the hell back!" Shaun tugged Tim back behind him.

"What do we do, K?" Tim asked.

Kevin and Tim had been friends for over a decade, and they communicated in half-sentences. Shaun was getting used to it.

"Okay. Shaun, blast this motherfucker's hand off, and Casey, I want you to catch Jade when he does. Tim, do nothing!"

Before they could execute Kevin's plan, Jade fell from the sky. She had her wand, and she stabbed Samyazah. The Jinn dove to catch her. The army of fallen angels stayed vigilant around their leader. Casey, quick off the mark, was ready to snatch her from the air when she turned suddenly into a raven. She skimmed the earth, transforming back into herself. Shaun couldn't believe what he had just seen, and Tim was just as dumbfounded.

"Shaun! You've been hanging around Tim and Kevin too much. Shaun, you need to distract the demons, and the reptilian creatures. Let's hope they stay outside Stonehenge while I clear the skies, so we can get out of here. Hopefully should give Kevin enough time to open a portal to get us out of here," Jade said.

No matter what the Jinn did, they couldn't catch Casey, as long as he stayed out of the dark realm. With a single thought, Casey pushed the demonic angels back. His telekinesis was stronger than before, and nothing could stop him. Each time a fallen angel or a group of Jinn corralled Casey, he prevented them from advancing. Sophia's medallion glowed beneath his shirt. The seal of Solomon surrounded Casey, protecting him. It was the first time Shaun had seen Casey's aura, and it had all the shapes of the sacred stones. He was unbreakable.

Jade raised her arms up. The Reptilians didn't move.

"Hurry, Jade!"

The clouds shifted. Shaun touched Kevin, lighting him up with energy from the sacred gemstones. Kevin touched Jade, and the Reptilian advanced forward. "Now, K!"

In a calm voice, Tim said, "You've got this, K."

Against Shaun's and Kevin's wishes, Tim rushed towards the Reptilians. It was worse than David and Goliath. He had guts. Shaun couldn't leave him. Casey, like a classic hero, landed next to Tim, picked him up, and rocketed straight up, before the charging Reptilians could trample him as they sprinted for the opened portal.

Shit, that's what they're waiting for; Kevin opening the portal, Shaun thought.

Jade pulled at his arm to move into the portal, but he pulled away and reached into his pocket. "I can't leave." Jade disappeared as the portal closed, depriving the charging Reptilians of access to the upper world of Heaven.

With a thump, Casey landed behind him, sandwiching Tim between them. "Don't you move," he said over his shoulder.

"You want these? Come and get them!" Shaun yelled, holding up the stones to the fallen angels. The light from every gemstone exploded into life. Suddenly, the air was like a vacuum. There was no running, and there was no way he was going to open a portal with the power of the stones. He put the stones on the ground for all to see. Energy generated from the icosahedron and channeled through every cell of Shaun's body.

"No! Get him. Get me those stones!" Samyazah yelled, and all its followers swooped down from the skies.

Shaun aimed his hand at the stones, and a blue laser of light turned white as he blasted the stones to dust, sealing the fate of the fallen angels, the Jinn, and the Reptilians – the enemies of God. Suddenly, he was yanked away from Tim and Casey. He felt the rush of air and heard his friends scream as he was raised into the sky. Darkness surrounded him.

Hot, stinking air covered his face as Samyazah roared with anger. "Forever, you will be my slave."

No longer of any value, Samyazah chucked Shaun to the ground and his back broke on impact. Shaun glimpsed a spark of light from Casey's chest. Casey lay motionless next to Tim. In his hand was his dagger, the blade embedded in Tim's heart.

Pain radiated through Shaun's upper body. He felt nothing below his waist as he lay beside Tim. He could still feel the warmth from Tim's body. Shaun's eyes closed, shutting out the world that had become hell on earth.

Shaun, free of fear and pain, thought, *It's up to you now, God.*

Light penetrated his eyelids. He just had to look. The dark realm was pushed back, revealing a divine, starry sky. It was glorious. The sky filled with light. Angelic Angels descended. Metatron picked up Casey and Tim – one under each arm. No room for him. *That's okay.* Just as the Reptilians had arrived, they flashed out of existence. He kept his eyes open to witness the battle between the Angelic Angels and fallen angels in the sky until the light blinded him.

Just one more dream of Rachel, he thought, drifting away from consciousness.

22

___

THE PROMISE: KEVIN.

"Let me go! I must go back for him!"

The elders never moved their mouths or restrained his body, but he couldn't step onto the on celestial gateway. "What's happening to me? Why can't I make a portal?"

They ignored his words and pleas. Kevin tried to convince himself he didn't understand why he couldn't go back for his friends. But he knew the battle on Earth, between good and evil, was about to end, and there was no way the gatekeepers to the galaxies were going to allow him to open a portal.

"The crystal walls are polygons. Each one a doorway to another world, another galaxy. You have a choice. You can stay here and migrate into Heaven now, or you can choose to pass through a gateway into another universe and live your life to the fullest, until you're old and ready for reincarnation. But when your body dies, you will reincarnate into the galaxy that you now choose. Or the last option God is offering is to return to the Earth Realm after the cleansing and be a part of the new Earth and the new dawn of humanity. Every generation of your descendants will carry the code to the stars in their DNA and, like you, they will be guardians. You have an hour of Earth time to decide."

Kevin didn't know what to choose. He wanted to see Shaun. He wanted to see everyone together one last time, to say goodbye. To hug them and know they were all happy. He just had to let go, and as always have faith.

"I've seen another world in which we could live," Kevin said to Jade "It's beautiful, with two suns. There is no war. It's governed and judged by the weight of your heart. To a new place, light years in the future, that we can call home?"

"Yes. But first maybe we could say a real goodbye to our families, then explore the parallel universe? And maybe we could ask the others if they want to join us?"

Kevin smiled at Jade and felt buoyant with the possibilities; exploring the parallel universe and to do it with his best friends would be marvelous. He knew in his heart it was the right choice.

Rachel and Sophia were standing by the shimmering gateway, waiting for Shaun and Casey. Jade shared their idea with them. Kevin was surprised to see them both agree. Rachel and Sophia folded their arms over their chests, nervously waiting for Shaun and Casey to arrive. Kevin was scared for them. Something was wrong.

Soon there were sparks of light that grew bigger, turning into a swirling vortex of energy until it was almost blinding, covering the gateway as Metatron appeared and delivered Casey and Tim into Heaven. The Heavenly elders greeted them.

Sophia ran into Casey's arms. They wanted nothing but each other. It was beautiful. Seth moved forward from the ascended crowd, who were waiting for their new beginnings to start, and embraced Tim, lifting his feet up off the crystal floor.

Rachel walked closer to the edge of the gateway and turned back to look at Kevin. "Where is he?"

Rachel turned away, not waiting for an answer.

"Before we explore the parallel universe, I would also like to see the crystal city – Heaven. If that's okay?" Tim asked Kevin, putting his hand on his shoulder.

"Where's Shaun, Tim?"

"I don't know. He was right next to me. I died. I don't know what happened after that," he said, rubbing his chest where blood had soaked through his clothes.

"Is that Shaun's blood?"

"No, it's mine."

"Metatron healed us," Casey said.

"But what about Shaun?" Kevin asked.

Rachel stood vigilantly at the end of the gateway, waiting for Shaun. Everyone else had arrived. Jade and Kevin moved up beside her. Kevin put his hand on Rachel's shoulder. "We'll wait with you."

But Kevin had a bad feeling. He had to go back. He must go back for Shaun. He had to believe in himself. He must believe he could create another portal while on the gateway. Quickly, he pecked Jade on the cheek. "I'll be right back," Kevin said, running to the end of the celestial gateway and jumping off. As he fell into the nothingness, the desire to save Shaun became overwhelming, enabling him to open a portal within a fraction of a second, which must've looked to the others as if he dove headfirst into the ocean of the cosmos and dissolved into the nothingness.

He connected into Shaun's energy and flew out from the portal, landing on top of Shaun's still body. Kevin didn't know if he was alive or dead, but he did feel Shaun's spirit was still connected to his body. The skies were filled with warring angels. A handful of

Reptilians remained. They were disappearing, returning to wherever they had come from. One reached out towards Kevin, but he opened a portal under Shaun's body, and they both fell through the earth and into the heavens, leaving the creature behind.

EPILOGUE

It was the most wonderful dream, the best dream he had ever had of Rachel. She was meeting his mom, and they were in a room filled with glittering light. They were together.

The pain left his body, and the visions of the battling angels disappeared and as if bathing in warm love, like a newborn, he began to feel his arms and legs. He opened his eyes and Rachel stared back at him, Kevin stood beside her smiling from ear to ear.

Shaun got to his feet, embraced Kevin and whispered in his ear. "Thanks, K. I love you man."

-The End-

Rise of the Dark Realm:

Chronicles of the Supernatural, Book Six

EPUB: 978-0-6450396-7-2

Print ISBN: 978-0-6450396-8-9

ACKNOWLEDGMENTS

I would like to thank my supportive family and friends for their encouragements. A big thank you to structural editor Susan Bischoff, copy editor Katharine Smith from Heddon Publishing, and cover designer from Creativindi, as well as the ARC team who have been a tremendous support throughout the process for each book in the series and even more so in Rise of the Dark Realm, the final book in the series. No book is complete without the vital service of editors, proofreaders, great book cover designers, and most of all you, the reader.

AUTHOR'S NOTE

Enjoy this book? You can make a big difference.

Reviews are the most powerful tools in my arsenal when it comes to getting attention for my books. Much as I'd like to, I don't have the financial muscle of a New York publisher. I can't take out full-page ads in the newspaper or put posters on the subway. (Not yet, anyway.)

But I do have something much more powerful and effective than that, and it's something that those publishers would kill to get their hands on: a committed and loyal bunch of readers.

Honest reviews of my books help bring them to the attention of other readers.

If you've enjoyed this book I would be very grateful if you could spend just five minutes leaving a review (it can be as short as you like) on your favorite online bookstore, or on Goodreads, which you can access through my website as well as my other books.

https://jmhartwriter.com/buy-now/

Thank you very much.

ABOUT THE AUTHOR

Now semi-retired, JM (Jeanette) moved to a sea side town south of Sydney, to focus on her grandchildren and writing.

JM Hart is the author of six books in *The Chronicles of the Supernatural Series*. She makes her online home at http://jmhartwriter.com

You can also connect with Jeanette on social media. Click the links below.

If the mood strikes you, you can send her an email at author@jmhartwriter.com